# HONEY BEE MINE

*A Novel*

## SARAH T. DUBB

**GALLERY BOOKS**

NEW YORK   AMSTERDAM/ANTWERP   LONDON
TORONTO   SYDNEY/MELBOURNE   NEW DELHI

G

Gallery Books
An Imprint of Simon & Schuster, LLC
1230 Avenue of the Americas
New York, NY 10020



This book is a work of fiction. Any references to historical events, real people, or real places are used fictitiously. Other names, characters, places, and events are products of the author's imagination, and any resemblance to actual events or places or persons, living or dead, is entirely coincidental.

Let's stay in touch! Scan here to get book recommendations, exclusive offers, and more delivered to your inbox.

# PRAISE FOR SARAH T. DUBB AND *BIRDING WITH BENEFITS*

"This book is unqualified joy! . . . Readers will absolutely relish watching the love between John and Celeste take flight!"

—Christina Lauren, *New York Times* bestselling author of *The Paradise Problem*

"Pensive and playful, tender and steamy . . . This one is a gem."

—Kate Clayborn, *USA Today* bestselling author of *Georgie, All Along*

"Once you're immersed in Sarah T. Dubb's gorgeously drawn world, you'll never want to leave. . . . This will stay at the top of my all-time favorite list forever."

—Jessica Joyce, *USA Today* bestselling author of *You, with a View*

"*Birding with Benefits* takes its time, will make you blush, will make you want to go BIRDING (I have never been so hot for birds in my whole life). My heart is about to explode after reading this beautiful book."

—Alicia Thompson, *USA Today* bestselling author of *Love in the Time of Serial Killers*

"The slowly simmering romance that blossoms between plucky heroine and heart-of-gold hero results in some love scenes that are as hot as the desert sun in July."

—*Booklist*, starred review

"Dubb is a writer to watch."

—*Publishers Weekly*

**ALSO BY SARAH T. DUBB**

*Birding with Benefits*

*For my therapist, Michelle.*
*Much of our work together is present in these pages.*

♥

# AUTHOR'S NOTE

Following my debut novel, *Birding with Benefits*, I created a story for one of the book's beloved side characters, doing my best to weave him his own happily-ever-after. Despite my best efforts, and many rewrites, the book never shone as you, my reader, deserved.

*Honey Bee Mine* was my second chance at my second book, and it's very fitting. The story is all about second chances—second chances at coming home, second chances to shed assumptions and expectations, and second chances at creating the joyful and safe lives for our kids that we deserved for ourselves.

This is a sunshine-y romantic comedy, but it does have some more serious themes of which you may want to be aware. The following pages contain memories of difficult childhoods, including emotional neglect, substance use disorder in a parent, undiagnosed mental health disorders, transphobia, and parental abandonment. Please read with care, and be comforted that the characters you meet here will be treated with love by one another.

*Honey Bee Mine* also contains joyful, consensual, and graphic sex scenes, so don't say I didn't warn you.

Now, pour yourself a glass of iced tea and enjoy!

# CHAPTER 1

For Penny Becker, nothing beat standing in gauzy late spring sunlight with bees in her hands.

"All right, ladies. Let's see how everybody's doing, shall we?"

Birdsong trilled from the thin forest bordering the bee yard as broad leaves of nearby sugar maples rattled in the wind, flashing pale undersides like butterfly wings.

She held the frame at eye level to watch hundreds of honeybees teem across the wax comb, earning their reputation as some of nature's busiest creatures. Wax-capped cells of honey bulged at the edges, so full that Penny's thumb, clumsy in thick gloves, dented a small section in the corner and smeared honey and wax along the wood. Four workers hurried to the scene of the crime, cleaning up the honey to move to new cells.

Penny scanned the frame before flipping it to inspect the other side, where more bees scurried across stores of rich honey glowing in the streaks of sunlight. Her gaze slowed, picking out the various jobs at play on the comb at once—some workers drew out more wax as foragers deposited nectar into waiting cells as their sisters fanned open deposits of nectar, working the muscles of their tiny wings to evaporate the liquid's moisture.

Penny was eight years old when she first joined her grandmother for hive inspections in the orchard, and fourteen when she claimed this spot in the woods at the edge of their property as her very own. Now, all these years later, it took just a glance at each frame to make sure that the queen was laying eggs as her daughters kept up with their tasks, to see the health of the colony alive between her hands.

But Penny still always lingered, watching honey glow under the sun as the busy movement of bees settled something inside her. Like Penny, the bees knew the most useful ways to be of service to the creatures around them. They knew, too, that slowing down too much led to waste—or, worse, destruction.

And even though she played her own role for the hive—protecting the bees from predators, checking them for disease and other risks—they didn't *need* her. If Penny never came back to this bee yard again, they'd still collect nectar as everything bloomed, then slow themselves down and let their numbers drop before closing in for the long New York winter, when they would take turns vibrating their tiny bodies to keep the hive warm as they ate through their honey stores until the cycle started again.

Penny worked in the bee yard to create scenarios that would result in extra honey for her to sell. The bees themselves would be just fine without her.

And they didn't care if she broke even that month or if she worked overtime to fit more farmer's markets into each week. They didn't shower her with new ideas when she struggled with the basics, didn't tell her to relax when there were endless chores to be done. They just went on with their perfectly ordered lives, and let Penny do her best to do the same.

"I haven't seen you all suited up for inspections in ages. Bees giving you trouble?"

Ruth Becker, in her daily uniform of worn jeans and a Becker Farms T-shirt, stood watching at the edge of the clearing. Her mom reminded Penny of the trees in their orchard—beautiful in their usefulness, coming into their truest form over time. Penny shared most of her features with her mother and grandmother: they all had stout, strong bodies, pudgy noses dusted with freckles in the summer, and wide smiles that dug laugh lines into their faces. They'd also shared the same hair, the gold of midsummer apple blossom honey, though Penny was the only one still holding on to that color now.

Only Penny's eyes set her apart: a shining blue that everyone noticed.

Blue, she assumed, like her father's.

The Beckers: three generations of women with dirt under their nails, famous in their tiny corner of the world for living off the land, talking to bees, and scaring off every man within a hundred miles.

First, Penny's grandfather, who'd come to the area talking big about starting a new life, only to panic and flee the first hard winter, leaving his wife with a growing belly and a life to recover.

Then Penny's father, who left just after hearing the news of Penny's conception.

And finally Henry, who'd stayed long enough to help Penny build her cottage at the edge of the Becker property, who'd been all in on Penny's dream of running Becker Farms side by side. Until it was obvious he'd never stick around long enough to see any of it come to pass.

It wasn't for everyone, but Penny loved living in Sullivan's Glen, nestled amid the wooded rolling hills of upstate New York. Her small town had everything a person could need branching off its two-lane road, and they were close enough to the tourist-rich

Finger Lakes to keep Penny's market tables busy, but far enough that the town wasn't overrun in the summer.

And she knew her role there, just like each worker bee scurrying over the comb knew theirs.

She lowered the frame carefully back into the hive, nestling it among the others as she shrugged under the weight of her full bee suit.

"Pe-nny!" her mom singsonged. "You with me? What has you all dressed up today?"

"Just in a weird mood." Penny replaced the lid on the hive. Her bees had docile genetics, and on a usual day she'd inspect the frames with only a veil. But she'd been on edge this morning so she'd suited up.

Penny's mom ran a hand through her gray pixie cut as she stepped fully into Penny's bee yard, where two dozen hive boxes dotted the clearing. Behind her, a trail formed by Penny's own feet over the years wound through the trees to their family home. Between the hives, bunches of baneberry and wild garlic bloomed in white bursts, all covered in the buzz of bees.

Ruth chuckled, shaking her head. "You and your mimi, so superstitious."

Penny's grandmother believed the bees could sense her moods. Ruth called the assertion "pure bullshit."

"Anything specific causing the mood?"

Penny shrugged. "PMS probably."

The fib came easily enough. Penny had a lifetime of practice.

Her mom had tons of love to give but wasn't one to often indulge bad moods or pessimistic thoughts. Ruth Becker preferred shiny new ideas, trusting the universe, and stockpiling gossip. And when Penny was a girl, she'd seen how running an orchard, managing a business, and raising a child strained her mom and grandma, who had no one around to help but themselves. So early on, she'd learned an important lesson from the bees: be useful and take care of yourself.

And for years, that's exactly what she did. Until Henry had a big idea, and Penny went all in. And now a letter was spread on the table back in her small cabin at the edge of their property—a letter giving Penny two more months before her loan was in default.

The loan that held Becker Farms as collateral.

Her problem was way bigger than PMS.

The groundwork was laid five years before, just before Penny's thirtieth birthday. After losing a close friend to a stroke, Mimi'd become obsessed with planning for her own passing.

"What if I die tomorrow?" she'd asked one morning in the kitchen. "Or if I decide to run off and join the circus before it's too late? I want everything to be in order."

Part of getting things in order was deeding ownership of Becker Farms to Penny.

It was just a formality, until Henry had an idea that required a lot of capital. Capital Penny accessed as the sole owner of Becker Farms, without telling her family.

Capital she couldn't pay back now.

She cleared her throat and threw a weak smile at her mom. "What are you doing out here?"

"Just felt like coming out for a walk," her mother answered. "Realized I haven't come over here for a while, thought I'd check up on you. Lord knows I need a break from your mimi talking my ear off at home. And also, Pen, I was thinking—"

"Mom, I can't right now." Penny busied herself at the hive box. Her mom was always *thinking*. Thinking about the next project that sounded like fun, thinking about chasing the next new trend, like the thousands of Becker Farms stickers in the warehouse, cute little things with bees buzzing around—but not even a URL or phone number on them to bring in sales. When Penny was younger and eager to please, she followed each of her mom's ideas like a puppy dog. Now, they were just more red lines on the budget Penny had to manage.

When Ruth's eyes narrowed, Penny adjusted her tone. "Sorry, not feeling great today. But the frames are heavy. This week I'll pull some out and spin them."

"Can you handle it on your own?" Her mom plucked a bloom from the wild garlic. "Mimi has a pinochle date and I thought I might join."

"Of course." Penny preferred working alone so she wasn't stuck cleaning up someone's mess later. Even bringing on RJ as orchard manager had taken some convincing, despite the fact that he'd grown up carousing with Penny in the orchard rows and knew the place as well as she did.

Ruth nodded to the stand of oaks blocking the view to the neighboring property. "I may have something to distract you from the PMS. Word is somebody's staying at the Bouras house."

"What?" Penny's narrowed gaze shot to the trees. She couldn't see the old farmhouse from here, but it was just beyond the copse of elms and sugar maples, its blue siding faded by the sun. The place had been empty since Mr. Bouras passed away a year before, though the grass had grown long around the house years before that.

The fate of the Bouras house was a common topic for the town gossips. Mr. Bouras had a daughter, but she'd been noto-riously absent since leaving Sullivan's Glen young and pregnant before Penny was born. Who owned the house now was anyone's guess—and people were definitely guessing.

For the last year, Penny'd held her breath over the property's fate. What if it landed in the hands of a developer who parceled the land, or a farmer intent on putting in yet another twenty acres of corn that would come with gallons of chemicals?

Because as sure as she could always count on her bees to be busy, Penny had no hope of determining where they went every day. Whatever happened on the Bouras land would end up back in her hives with her bees, and a heavy dose of pesticides could mean an end to entire colonies.

As if she wasn't already balanced on a thin enough tightrope.

"Debbie has a theory about who it is," her mother teased, yanking Penny from her thoughts.

"Of course she does." As the owner of the hair salon that boasted Sullivan's oldest—and therefore nosiest—clientele, Debbie was a regular font of gossip.

Ruth lowered her voice, like the bees might carry away her prime intel. "Debbie said that Felicia told her that when Gary was coming home from his hike yesterday, he went past the mailbox at the end of the drive and saw a man checking the mailbox. He was tall, with big shoulders, and dark hair."

Penny's mind filled in the rest: and an annoying smirk like he was the hottest shit within five hundred miles, like everything and everyone in Sullivan's Glen was beneath him.

Impossible.

"He wouldn't be back. He hated this place." And had made sure everyone within hearing distance knew it.

"Sometimes places call us back." Ruth sighed and looked meaningfully at the hives, where forager bees crowded the bottom boards of each box, all called home by the pheromones of their queen.

"Zander Bouras is not a bee, Mom. And this will never be

home for him." Even saying his name made Penny want to roll her eyes.

Ruth sighed. "I suppose we'll see. Could make for an interesting summer."

Which would be great for the town gossip mill. But the last thing Penny needed was an interesting summer. She needed a profitable summer, a farm-saving summer. It would require an abundant honey harvest, a great U-pick season in their small but mighty vegetable patch, and some better-than-average sales at every farmer's market stand Penny could manage.

But most of all, Penny needed her Hail Mary, the Honey Festival. The event was a mainstay for Sullivan's Glen, a daylong event that Penny poured her heart, and finances, into each year. Becker Farms nearly always broke even, but that wouldn't do this year. This year, she needed *more*. Enough to get the lender off her back and forestall foreclosure.

It had to be the biggest festival yet. Which meant Penny had no time to speculate over some brooding bad boy who used to spend summers next door.

"Let me know when you've got more reliable intel." Penny turned to the next hive box. "Until then, I've got work to do."

Ruth chuckled and turned on her heels to leave the clearing. "You always do, Penny. You always do."

# CHAPTER 2

Zander Bouras, thirty-five years old and the father of a preteen, felt like a kid again.

Just not in a good way.

He'd dwarfed this bed at fifteen. But now, with his full height over six feet and plenty of meat on his bones, it was a miracle he hadn't rolled off during the night.

He groaned into a stretch and groped for the phone vibrating its way to the edge of the cheap nightstand.

If this was some eager chef calling after getting Zander's number from a friend of a friend, he'd do the kid a favor and tell them to fuck off and take their dreams elsewhere. Because Zander was taking a break.

He'd overseen the opening of a family-run Italian joint before leaving Boston, sublet his small apartment to a couple of line cooks, and put the word out that he'd be back in action in late August.

The only project until then was the old house creaking around him.

Zander blinked at the name on the screen and bolted upright. "Mal? Everything all right?"

"Good morning!"

Zander stared at the phone. His ex sounded suspiciously cheerful. She was *not* a morning person. It had been years since they'd woken up side by side, but some things never changed. "Everything is totally fine," Mal soothed. "Winter is still sleeping, actually."

Zander took two long breaths to steady his heartbeat. Six years living apart from his kid part-time, and he still panicked when Mallory called instead of texting. "That must be nice for him."

"Was that mattress as miserable on night two?"

"Worse." He tucked the phone into his shoulder as he leaned forward in an aching stretch. "I can't believe I used to sleep on this piece of shit."

"It wasn't always so bad," Mal quipped.

Zander chuckled through his groggy throat. The few times he'd managed to sneak Mal upstairs that last summer, they *had* given the mattress a run for its money. Two horny eighteen-year-olds didn't give a shit about a poky spring.

"And I told you," she said more seriously. "You're welcome to stay here. My parents said it's fine."

Zander's eyes adjusted to the light diffusing through the room. Shit, it was midmorning.

His bare feet hit the wooden floor with a creak. "Right, because staying with my former in-laws, my ex-wife, and her girlfriend sounds like a barrel of laughs."

"You know you're way more than my ex-husband to them, Zander. And to me. And Quinn would love having you here."

This at least drew a laugh. "Yeah, to be a buffer between her and your parents? No thanks. She agreed to come along, she can handle that scene on her own."

"That doesn't mean you should be ignoring her."

"I'm not—" he started, but then looked to the notifications

on his phone, showing five missed calls from Quinn. They'd all come in the night before as Zander sat in the dark kitchen, daring the ghost of his grandfather to make an appearance. By the time he'd finally gone upstairs and thrown his sleeping bag on the bed, he was too exhausted to call her back.

And his best friend did not like being ignored.

He made his way to the window, toying with the frayed beige curtain. "She put you up to calling me?"

"You ignored all her calls, Z. She's worried about you. *I'm* worried about you."

"And she knew I had to answer if it was you, since you're my coparent."

"I mean . . ." Zander sensed Mallory's shrug from across Sullivan's Glen. "It worked, right?"

"Christ." He rubbed at his sleepy face. Two days' growth was rapidly turning into a short beard, a sign he needed to pull himself together. Which Quinn probably knew, hence the five calls. "I should never have given you her number that day. Just put her on, would you?"

"She's about to snatch the phone out of my hand anyway. Love you!"

"Love you, too."

It was a funny thing to say to your ex-wife, but their relationship was a little funny.

They'd gone from young loves to newlyweds to parents, all in just a few years. Then came divorce, the awkward years, and eventually a slide into a comfortable coparenting friendship. Mal was a bigger thread in the fabric of Zander's life than anyone else. Anyone but their eleven-year-old son, Winter.

"Hey, loser." Quinn's wry voice took over the line. "Look who remembers how to answer his fucking phone."

"You know"—Zander pushed back the curtain, filling the room with light—"when you look up 'pain in the ass' in the dictionary, I'm pretty sure it's a picture of your face."

"But such a pretty face, isn't it?"

Zander's gaze traveled over the hillside behind his grandfather's property. No, *his* property. *Fucking hell.* "If I call you pretty, your girlfriend might want to have words with me."

"You know I love it when you two fight over me. Makes me feel special."

"Believe me, I know. But I knew you first, and that's got to count for something."

He'd met Quinn years ago when she was pitching some too-modern-for-Zander tech solution to reservation booking. She'd clearly hated the job, and something about that pissed-off gleam in her eye told Zander he'd found a kindred spirit. They went out for a beer and Quinn had been a staple in his life ever since.

Last year she was hanging with Zander and Winter when Mallory arrived for the biweekly kid transfer. His ex had taken one look at Quinn—tall and toned, with black hair that hung over her pale, angular face and enough rings in her eyebrow to set off a metal detector—and Zander knew he was in trouble.

So now his best friend was his ex-wife's live-in girlfriend, and his kid spent his time between all of them. Not quite a Hallmark movie, but it worked.

And their big, happy, kind of strange family was back in the three-road town his mom had shipped him off to each summer, the place he'd avoided ever since he'd whisked Mallory out of here seventeen years ago.

He fiddled with the window latch, pushing it hard until it finally unlocked. "How's Candace doing?"

"How's *Candace* doing?" Quinn mocked. "You're going to send me to voicemail all night and then ask how Candace is doing?"

"Sorry, isn't she the one who was just in the hospital?"

Mal's mom's surgery had prompted the return to Sullivan's Glen. After spending the past few years repairing her relationship with her parents, Mallory wanted to help out as Candace recovered from a hip replacement.

Quinn groaned, surely noticing Zander's deflection from talking about how *he* was feeling.

"She's fine. It's obviously hard for her to accept help. And she's kind of uptight, but not nearly as much as you made her sound. I see her trying. With Mal and Winter, and with me, too. You know I had a million nightmare scenarios about how they'd react to the trans girl showing up with their daughter, but they've been surprisingly normal."

Zander knew there was no way Mallory would have asked Quinn along if she'd anticipated anything other than open arms, but it was still good to hear. "I'm glad it's going well over there."

He tugged at the window, managing to wrench it open a few inches. "How's the kid doing?"

"Oh, you know."

"Ah." Zander chuckled as fresh air swirled in through the window, smelling of pine. "That good, huh?"

Winter was, as Mallory liked to say, *going through a phase*. The kid who used to be all goofy smiles and knock-knock jokes was now withdrawn and sullen, swinging into moods without warning.

Zander had been ready for the teen years. Hell, he'd written the book on the teen years. But he wasn't ready for his son icing him out before he was even twelve. It felt like any minute the universe might yank Winter away and laugh at Zander, wondering how he thought he'd earned such a precious gift.

Which was why being separated from his kid for the entire summer was a nonstarter. Because Mallory hadn't just wanted to come to Sullivan's Glen to help her mom—she'd wanted to bring Winter with her. When Zander had objected to being separated from his son for so long, it had been Quinn who'd suggested he come along, too.

*You can't go that long without your kid? Then come with us. Deal with that old house he left you, face your demons, all that.*

A real softie, his best friend.

On the phone, Quinn cleared her throat pointedly. "Should I take your silent treatment yesterday to mean everything at the house is just fine and dandy?"

"Ah, yes." He scanned the old beige walls of the room, the closed door he'd tried to stare a hole through the first night he spent here, twenty years ago. "Fine and dandy indeed. Remind me why I'm here again?"

"Because your grandfather left you his house and all the land around it, and even if that pisses you off, you can't ignore it forever."

"Couldn't I, though?"

He hadn't talked to his grandfather since walking out of this house the final time when he was barely an adult. What reason could the old man possibly have had for leaving Zander this place? It was nothing more than some power play from beyond the grave.

Outside, the tree-covered hillside fanned out in an array of greens as grass and flowers waved in the breeze. He'd spent three and a half long-ass summers staring out this window, thinking it was the worst place he'd ever seen, like the wildflowers had bloomed just to spite him with their easy beauty.

"Zander, you've got to get off your ass and stop brooding. I know this is a lot." Quinn's tone softened, just barely. "I don't know what the fuck I'd do if I was back at home right now."

Estrangement from their parents was an early bonding theme for Zander and Quinn. Her parents were in Missouri, prepping for the apocalypse and feeding on a steady diet of barbecue and bigotry.

As for Zander's childhood, his mom was a perpetual mess, his dad a lifelong mystery, and Zander himself often *nothing but trouble*, *too much to handle*, or some combination thereof. He was fifteen the first time his mom sent him to Sullivan's Glen for the summer, starting off an annual tradition that consisted of Zander arriving at the nearest bus station with his worn duffel in June, disappointing his grumpy Greek grandfather until August, then boarding the bus back to Detroit for the school year.

"You also came here to spend time with Winter," Quinn said. "So pull yourself together and make it happen."

He pressed his forehead to the wobbly glass of the window. "I hate it when you're right."

"Then you must be miserable most of the time," she quipped. "What's the plan?"

Zander returned to the bed to sit on the drooping mattress, taking in the peeling paint and sagging windowsills.

"I need to survey the house and make a list of the most desperate problems."

"Okay. Have you started looking through any of his stuff?"

Zander'd planned to approach the house like one of his restaurant projects: he'd take control of it, step by step, room by room. Look for problems that needed solving, and solve them.

Then he'd walked inside two nights ago to find an old bill on the kitchen counter, a small spiral pad with Papou's indecipherable scrawl slashed across the pages, and an old coat hanging on a hook next to the front door.

"I gathered all evidence of him, stashed it in his room, and shut the door."

"*Zander*."

"I know! I'll get to it. But it's not the priority, okay? I'm going to figure out what needs fixing and clean the whole place up so Winter can spend time here."

There was a weighted pause on the end of the line. "Okay. What then?"

"Go for a walk, touch some grass, then go to the store and hope no one recognizes me so I can get some food."

Quinn laughed gleefully. "You *will* be recognized. I'm new in town and I can already tell you're a living legend around here. Mal said everyone is on tenterhooks to see you again."

He ran a hand across his face. "Jesus."

"We drove downtown for coffee today—they actually have a decent place, by the way, made a killer Americano—and Mallory was reminiscing with some old-timer about that time you got an old tractor working in your grandfather's barn and got pulled over trying to drive it out of town."

He should pack up and leave. Now.

"You're not packing up," Quinn warned.

"I didn't even—"

"You didn't need to. I know your sighs. I know *you*." She paused. "And I love you, Zander. I'm proud of you for coming, and I know you can do this. Now go touch some fucking grass, and that's an order."

Twenty minutes and a cup of coffee later, Zander was following Quinn's orders, pulling the golden blades between his fingers as he crouched outside the kitchen's side door.

Knee-high grass swayed in golds and yellow and even shimmers of blue across the field around the house. On two sides, the grass gave way to the rise of hills and dense forest. Close to the house, the field stopped at a thick group of trees that signaled the border of the Bouras property with the place next door.

He'd walked that way only once. It was his third day in Sullivan's Glen, the summer after his first year of high school. By then he'd had one failed runaway attempt, two failed calls to his mom, and a thorough understanding that his grandfather—a hulking man with Zander's dark features—wasn't like the grandpas in the movies who spoil their grandkids with hard candies. Nikolai Bouras made clear from the start that his job was to put Zander back on the straight and narrow so he wouldn't turn out like his mother.

And on that day, after trying again to get his mom on the phone and being told by Papou that he didn't know the right way to wash dishes—and why wouldn't a boy his age know how to do it *right*—Zander walked into the trees. It was a day just like this one—the easy warmth between spring and summer, bright green leaves obscuring every view.

He'd been winding his way between the trunks, no clue where he was headed, when he heard laughter.

Stopping behind a tree, he'd watched the scene. There was a girl, maybe his age, smiling next to a strange white wooden box that sat in a small clearing. She had corn-colored braids and a face full of freckles. Two women were close by, one of them telling some sort of story, talking enthusiastically with her hands. It was clear they were related—all three had the same curved cheeks and strong frames, and even the older of the two women still had hints of golden corn in her hair.

A daughter, her mother, and her grandmother. All laughing in the sunshine.

He fled back to his room at the top of the stairs, where he'd spent the next day cursing that freckled girl and her perfect life. The family who wanted her, who made her laugh in the forest like it was so damn easy.

He never went into those trees again, but the freckle-faced girl was everywhere each summer. Beaming at the farmer's market beside her grandmother, nodding kindly as she helped someone across the street, always so *perfect*. The kind of kid everyone wanted around.

And it wasn't just his imagination. His papou had said it aloud, more than once.

"That Penny Becker, she's a good one." The shadows of his Greek accent rolled the words around. "You could stand to be a little more like her."

Now, Zander plunked his coffee mug on the back stoop and stood, flexing and unflexing his hands as he stared into the trees. Before he knew it, his feet were taking him there, crushing grass as he weaved past trunks. It was embarrassing, and juvenile, and far below him, but Zander walked with purpose, hoping to find an empty clearing, an old pile of white wood, some evidence that beautiful things around here couldn't last.

But when he came around the last tree, he saw it: the wooden box, just where it had been those years before.

But now there were more. Groups of them, scattered across the clearing.

A person in all white stood in the center of it all. Zander's first thoughts were of government agents shrouded in hazmat suits, villains in the movies he'd watched as a kid waiting for his mom to return home.

The figure turned, movements smooth even in the bulky suit, white netting over the face. Gloved hands rose up, grabbing at something along the loose neck of the suit. In one long movement, the top of the suit detached and came off.

First, all Zander saw was the glint of gold in the sun. Then with a shake of the head, the gold furled out, falling over the still-suited shoulders. A gloved hand swept the waterfall of hair away to reveal round, freckled cheeks and sharp blue eyes.

And Zander knew the world wasn't fair. Because little miss perfect Penny Becker was still right here. And worse, she was fucking beautiful.

# CHAPTER 3

Penny hated when her mother was right.

Especially when it meant that Zander Bouras, the guy who'd waved his middle finger at Sullivan's Glen for four summers—and who'd left his grandfather alone and never looked back—was standing in her bee yard like some bear, all broad shoulders and dark mussed hair.

She'd never known Zander well. He had made sure of that, never showing an interest in socializing with the locals beyond tussling with the Brads or shooting a cocky smile at a group of girls as they dissolved into giggles. Anytime she did spot him, he'd give her the stink eye, like somehow her sheer presence offended his too-cool sensibilities.

But she still recognized him easily. He had the same wide, imposing body she'd watched him grow into summer by summer from a distance, and the same way of standing with his body slightly turned in, like he was bracing for something.

Back then his near-black hair was always obscuring his face, but it was cut shorter now, messy on top and leaving room for the late morning sun to hit his thick, dark brows and cheeks dusted with dark stubble.

The sharp, long angles of his body were filled in, and he looked strong but soft, like he'd give a little under her fingers. A curl of black ink peeked from under the collar of his long-sleeved shirt, hinting at more art beneath.

Penny cleared her throat and shifted her gaze to his face to find him watching her with narrowed eyes. "I guess the rumors are true. You really are back."

His brows rose, framing eyes that carried the richness of the forest, all dark browns and coppers. "If it isn't Penny Becker, Sullivan's Glen's golden girl," he said in a rumble.

His searing attention on her didn't waver, so Penny straightened as a line of sweat dripped between her shoulder blades. "What are you doing here?"

He shrugged, a haughty grin playing on his lips. "Everybody comes back to Sullivan's Glen. Isn't that what the locals always say?"

She crossed her arms over her chest. "Pretty sure that graffiti you gifted us when you left made it clear you weren't interested in coming back."

Zander's chest puffed out enough to tug the fabric of his shirt tight. "Graffiti? I don't know what you're talking about."

"Yeah." Penny pushed out a strained laugh. "I'm sure. Maybe you finally came back to apologize?"

His amused expression closed off as his smile flattened. "No. I actually came to claim my inheritance."

"Your *what*?"

"The house next door is mine now," he answered, nodding to where the Bouras property began less than thirty yards away.

Penny pulled her gloves off and shoved them in her pocket as her brain reeled. She'd disregarded her mom's gossip, sure that Zander would never step foot in this place again. But not only was he here, he was her *neighbor*.

And while they'd known of each other—in a place the size of Sullivan's Glen, it was impossible not to—Penny's busy path hadn't crossed his for more than glances in town, when he'd always mustered up a scowl to send her way.

"I came to invite you to my housewarming party." He interrupted her thoughts. "It'll be potluck style, and it'd be great if you could bring the potato salad."

"*What?*"

Zander's laugh bellowed. "You should see your face. It would really be *that* bad, huh?" When Penny only stuttered, Zander shook his head. "Don't have a heart attack on me here. I'm kidding."

"Kidding?" Penny's long exhale emptied her lungs. "Right, obviously. You wouldn't—" *Possibly deem this place worth your presence.* "The house isn't really—" *Yours. Why would he have left it to you?*

"Well, half kidding. I know you'd never come to my potluck. But the house is mine. Fancy lawyers confirmed it and everything."

"But *why?*" Mr. Bouras kept to himself, but a couple of years ago word filtered down that the older man was getting treatment for cancer, with all his home care provided by hired nurses. People wondered, often and loudly, if his daughter or Zander would make an appearance, but they never did. "Why would he leave it to *you?*"

Zander laughed again, but this time it was darker, edged with gravel that scraped on Penny's skin.

"Good question." He stepped farther into the clearing, walking slowly around the edge of the bee yard as he looked up at the trees. "I bet there's more you want to ask, too, right? Like, *Why did that man leave his property to his no-good grandson when he let him die alone, when he didn't even come back to bury him?"* His gaze dropped to Penny with a challenge. "How about, *Why didn't this place go to someone who deserves it?"*

Penny blinked at him as she pushed down a dry swallow. She was thinking all those questions, along with some others, like, What would happen to the property now? And how would it impact Becker Farms?

"Zander!" another voice called from in the trees. "Are you out here?"

Mallory Robinson stepped into the bee yard, yanking a twig out of one of her black space buns. Her dark brown skin glowed in the morning sun, as did the collection of silver rings and studs that decorated the sides of both ears like shimmering vines.

Mallory and Penny had gone to school together, where they'd shared some honors classes early on. But as high school progressed, Mallory started ditching classes and getting into minor trouble until finally running off with Zander after graduation. She'd started coming back a couple of years ago, always bringing her son, Winter, whom Penny had met a few times at the farmer's market. But she had no clue Zander and Mallory were still in touch.

Zander blinked once at Penny before exhaling loudly. "Mal? What the hell?"

Mallory smiled, gazing around at the scattering of goldenrod, eyes not yet landing on Penny. "Good morning to you, too, Zander. Upon a second cup of coffee, I was sent by my delightful partner to ensure you actually did get out of bed. And here you are! So proud." With a chuckle, she looked back to where she'd emerged from the trees. "Luckily for us, you walk through grass like the bear you are and left us a trail to follow."

Zander pinched the bridge of his nose. "Us?"

Mallory stuck two fingers in her mouth and whistled. "Winter! I found him! This way!"

After a few more crashing steps, Mallory's son appeared through the trees. He was taller than when Penny had seen him last summer, with curly black hair cut short to his head and skin a few shades lighter than his mom's.

Penny knew Zander was his father. Mallory had stayed in touch with enough friends that news traveled when she'd become pregnant, then actually married Zander. But a few years later when she heard they'd split up, Penny assumed things had gone the way they always had in her own life. Father gone, Mom on her own.

But now Zander's body was relaxed, his fighting stance abandoned for something loose, almost goofy. He jogged the few feet to Winter and mussed his hair as the kid rolled his eyes. When he turned back to the clearing, the ashen look he'd had a minute ago was washed away by an easy smile.

This was even more unexpected than the town's former bad boy appearing in Penny's bee yard. Because she realized that Zander might not just be Winter's father, but his *dad* as well.

Mallory laid a gentle hand on Zander's forearm. "Quinn had to reply to some work emails, but we thought it'd be good to say hi. Don't be pissed. And anyway, what are you doing out— Oh my god! Penny! I didn't even see you there. I'm so sorry!"

Penny raised one hand weakly, feeling awkward and frumpy in the bee suit. "Morning."

"You remember Winter, right?" Mallory urged the boy forward with a hand on his back.

"Yeah, of course." She looked to Winter, who was surveying the spread of hives. "You're a lot taller than last year." Penny winced. "Sorry, you probably hear that from every adult."

Winter shrugged. "Yeah, but it's okay." He was clad in skinny jeans, beat-up Nikes, and a T-shirt from a science fair, and looked on track to inherit Zander's height. He glanced from hive to hive. "Is this where you keep all the bees?"

Winter stepped close to a hive box but was halted by Zander's hand on his shoulder. "Watch out, buddy. They're all over the place."

"Dad. It's *fine*."

Penny couldn't look away from Zander's hand, curled protectively over Winter. It was so at odds with the man she'd encountered a few minutes ago, the one poised at the border between fight and flight.

Her gaze traveled up Zander's thick arm, over the smooth bulge of his bicep, then caught again on the tattoo peeking just above his collar. It could be anything—the tail of a small snake, or the edge of a leaf, branches spreading across his chest.

Damn, it was too hot outside for this bee suit.

Penny cleared her throat and smiled back at Winter. "This is where we keep some of the bees. We have more on the other side of our house, in the orchards."

"This is *so* cool." Winter stepped closer to the hive, Zander an oversize shadow behind him. "We did a unit on honeybees in science this year and watched a bunch of videos, but I haven't seen this stuff up close. Can I see them closer up?"

Normally, Penny loved showing off the bees and revealing the magic of the colony.

But this—Zander, appearing out of nowhere with a chip still on his shoulder, as her neighbor and a *dad*, looking fairly stressed at the thought of his kid dabbling with venomous insects—was too much. Superstition or not, she wasn't opening up a hive feeling like *this*.

But she couldn't deny the kid's excitement. She knew exactly how he felt.

"I would love to but can't just now." Winter's smile dropped, and Penny went on. "But you're welcome to come back another time. We could probably squeeze that in while you're here. How long will you guys be in town?"

Winter huffed, shooting a glare full of daggers at his mom. "We're here all summer because *Mom* is making us."

Mallory sighed. "I'm so glad we all have beautiful attitudes this morning." She directed her attention to Penny. "My mom just had surgery, so I wanted to be here for longer to help out. Which means we have plenty of time. Hey—do you still do the market? Maybe we can stop by Saturday and figure out a time for Winter to come back over?"

Penny smiled and nodded as her brain went fuzzy again. "Yeah. Yeah, sounds good." She dared a look to Zander. "You'll be here all summer, too?"

He cracked a wide smile, like he knew just how frazzled she was, and *liked* it. "Where my kid goes, I go. And like I said, I've got a whole house to deal with right over there."

Zander Bouras next door. All summer. As if Penny didn't already have enough to worry about.

# CHAPTER 4

"Careful with the knife, little man. It's sharper than it looks."

"I know, Dad. I'm *fine*."

The blade landed hard on the cutting board as Winter made his point. He'd been *fine* all morning. *Fine* when Zander picked him up, *fine* when he suggested they cook one of their favorite dinners, *fine* when Zander had asked how his day had been.

In the past six months, Winter's once-impressive vocabulary had narrowed down to *fine*, *I guess*, and an occasional shrug.

Once, this kid had talked Zander's ear off about everything from velociraptors to Pokémon, giggling and pulling every bowl out of the cabinet to brew up disgusting concoctions. Zander knew the change was normal early puberty stuff, and he and Mal had agreed to keep an eye on whether Winter might need more support, but he missed having greater access to what his kid was thinking.

But at least he'd agreed to cook, and he was smashing the garlic clove with the flat of the knife like Zander taught him last year. Even if he was a little more forceful than needed.

Souvlaki pitas with homemade tzatziki was one of Winter's favorites. He'd been making the sauce since he was just a tiny kid standing on a chair in their apartment kitchen.

But today they weren't in their little apartment in Boston, but here—in Papou's old house. Zander himself had never cooked in this kitchen beyond turkey sandwiches and packs of ramen. His papou had been no better, subsisting on frozen meals and overcooked oatmeal. Any Greek recipes, like the one he was making now with Winter, Zander had learned on his own later when a chef he was cooking under had scolded him: *With a name like Bouras you sure as hell better know how to do a souvlaki.*

He slid the container of yogurt across the counter to Winter, holding back another warning about the knife. Instead, he skewered the marinated chicken as Winter dumped the garlic in the bowl.

"I'll work on getting another bedroom ready for you here, okay, bud? I just need to move things around and clean some more up there."

The upstairs boasted three rooms—Zander's room, then and now; his grandfather's room; and a small spare room full of furniture Papou had insisted on keeping forever due to its perceived value. Back then, Zander tried to convince the old man that something being *really fucking old* didn't make it valuable, but his grandfather never cared about Zander's opinions.

"That is," Zander hedged, "if you want to stay here sometimes. I get that this place is old and musty and—" Hiding unpleasant memories around each corner. Like the time Papou had told him he would *amount to nothing* just like his mother, spurring Zander to slam the screen door so hard it fell halfway off its hinges.

"It's fine," Winter piped up, beginning a coarse chop of the dill. "This house isn't so bad."

Zander couldn't help his double take. "You think so?"

"Yeah." Winter shrugged. "It's kinda creepy, but in a cool way." His fingers flexed around the knife as he scowled. "I mean, if I *have* to be here all summer, I may as well have a room at both places, I guess."

When told of the plan to spend the summer in Sullivan's Glen, Winter had thrown a mega fit, slamming every door in Mal and Quinn's house between declarations that he'd just stay in Boston, even if it meant he *had* to stay full-time with his dad.

But Zander couldn't keep Winter full-time with his work obligations, and he couldn't pay his Boston rent without work. And as much as he hated having to be back in this house, Zander understood Mallory's hope—that their kid would have the kind of close, loving family Zander never had—and that those relationships could be strengthened with a whole summer in town.

So he'd formed a united front with Mal, door slamming be damned.

Zander put the last skewer in the pan and washed his hands before wiping them on his jeans. "I know this wasn't how you imagined spending your summer, but we can make the best of it, okay? You get to spend tons of time with Granny and Pops, and I don't even have to really work while we're here. It'll be fun."

Winter didn't look up from the green threads of dill on the cutting board. "Yeah, *fun*."

"You know," Zander ventured, "I saw that there's a skate park just one town over. We could go there tomorrow, maybe, see what it's like?"

But Winter just rolled his eyes. "I don't skate anymore, Dad."

Zander pinched his nose. "O-kaay. I've heard there are some awesome waterfalls we could hike to. That could be fun."

Winter slammed the knife on the cutting board, sending

dill flying. "Why are you pretending this is all fine when Mom dragged us here?"

"Whoa, dude, I thought the house was cool?"

"That doesn't mean I want to be here. And I know *you* hate it here."

"Hey—" Zander slid an arm in front of Winter, lifting the knife and scooching it away. "Your mom didn't drag me." Not *exactly*. "And I don't hate it here."

Winter glared at him, hitting Zander with the upside-down feeling of seeing his own brown eyes, flashing with anger, in his little boy. "If you don't hate it, how come you've never come back with us, not *once*? Or on your own? How come you didn't even come when your grandpa died?"

"Hey—"

"How come when we got here you didn't answer Quinn's calls? How come I keep hearing Mom and Granny and Pops whispering about how you're *doing*?"

Zander dragged a hand across his face. "Those other times you've come, I had to work." He repeated his old excuse. "I had to stay back and—"

"*Every time?*" His son's eyebrows shot up. "You had to work every single time? Why is *everybody* always lying to me like I'm some dumb kid who doesn't understand what's going on? *God.*"

Winter pushed through the door leading to the side yard, leaving the screen door to slap shut behind him.

Zander slumped against the counter, thoughts whirling between present and past. His papou had probably stood right here, watching that same door slam.

Back then his grandfather seemed old as hell, but he'd only been in his mid-fifties that first summer. He was a big man, hefty like Zander was now, with a thick head of black hair seasoned with gray, and wide shoulders always curling in.

"Do you know why you're here?" he'd asked Zander that first night, cold spaghetti on the table between them.

"Because my mom doesn't want me?"

The man hadn't denied it, just sighed and looked at Zander with hard eyes. "She's afraid you'll mess up your own life the way she messed up hers. You're here to stay out of trouble."

Staring now at the screen door, Zander wondered what the fuck he thought he was doing coming back.

Then he heard a short, muffled sob from outside, and pulled his head out of his own ass.

His kid was sitting on the small concrete landing just outside the door, tossing pebbles into the tall grass. Zander squished himself next to him, knocking Winter's knee with his until his son got the hint and gave him a little more room, swiping quickly at his cheeks.

"Listen, buddy." Zander leaned forward onto his knees, knowing that his old BS wouldn't fly anymore. That shit he'd never hoped to tell Winter had to be aired out, at least a little. "It's never been my intention to lie to you. I've just tried to protect you from my stuff. When I was a kid, my mom had a hard time. She had a lot going on, mentally and emotionally, and parenting me was . . ." Zander cleared his throat. "Difficult for her. So for the summers when I was in high school, she'd send me here to stay with her dad."

He glanced up at the house, remembering the long evening shadows it cast on the grass the night he'd arrived. "The problem was, he had a hard time with me, too, so the summers weren't great. I was a pain in the ass, and he was a mean old man, and we didn't like each other much."

Winter shot Zander a short, worried look. "Did he—"

"It was never physical," Zander clarified. But for a few stern grips of his shoulder, his grandfather hadn't touched him at all in all those months they shared a house. "But he was determined to make me act a certain way and I was determined to fight him at every turn, and it was really, really hard. So I've avoided coming back here. But I didn't mean to ever spread that feeling to you."

Winter blinked at him a few times, worrying his lip with his teeth. "Is that why you don't talk to your mom? Because she sent you here?"

Going no contact with his mom had been one of the best and worst decisions he'd ever made. The guilt of cutting off someone clearly impacted by depression and addiction was a heavy blanket—he didn't want to blame his mom for an illness beyond her control, but Zander needed space for his own healing. To be better for Winter.

"No. I was mad about that for a while, but things between her and me weren't always terrible. Just . . . really complicated." Like the way she'd ghost for months and then contact Zander when she needed to be dug out of a problem, or how'd she get vicious with him when he expressed concern about her health and safety. "And that's not for you to worry about, bud." He laid a hand on Winter's back, relieved to feel his son lean into him instead of away, at least this once. "But the point is, I'm here now, and so are you. And we might have complicated feelings about it, but we're going to make the best of it, you and me, all right?"

Winter tossed another rock. "Do we have to?"

"Yes," Zander said, resolved. This was more important than any to-do list for the house. If Zander was going to help Winter grow up, he needed to do some growing up himself. Hiding away for the summer wasn't going to cut it. "We do. How about you and I make an agreement?"

He angled toward Winter, waiting till his son peered up at him to continue. "We'll both make the best of this summer and try to have a good time here, okay? Even if it's hard sometimes. We'll commit together."

Winter's brows went even higher. "You're going to do that? Have a *good time*?"

"Yeah, I am!" Zander pushed his shoulder into Winter's. "I promise to try if you do. What should we do first to give this town a chance?"

Winter cracked a smile now, the kind reserved for when he knew he was about to get his way. "It would be cool to see the bees again."

Zander's fist clenched against his thigh. Of all the requests, it had to be this one. "The bees. Right. Penny's bees."

"She said she'd be at the farmer's market. Will you go talk to her about it, figure out a time she can show me everything?"

He'd been in town only a matter of days and this woman already haunted him like when he was a teenager, when his papou went out of his way to tell Zander all about the perfect Penny Becker, the girl who made her family proud.

Now she was next door, freckles and all, and Winter—the kid Zander had come here to connect with, the kid he'd do anything for—was already infatuated with her.

Would Zander willingly encounter Penny again, this time asking for a favor? Would he give her another chance to hit him with that haughty, judgmental stare, just to keep his kid happy?

Damn right he would.

# CHAPTER 5

"Um, Pen? Those people look like they might eat us alive." RJ scooted closer to Penny, lowering his voice to a conspiratorial whisper. "Do you remember last year when we had that heat wave and a fight broke out in the line at the ice cream truck and Karen dumped her iced coffee over Sarina's head? I think we're in the danger zone. Like, we might want to consider arming ourselves with lemonade or something."

It *was* a long line. A really long line. And the market didn't officially start for another twenty minutes.

But her table was ready, decked out with jars of honey and beeswax candles, plus bundles of flowers, herbs, and fresh vegetables from their garden. And she'd made space for their latest best-seller: RJ's mini fruit pies, made with love by hand.

"It's because May was so rainy," she mused. This market, like the others she visited around the county, had been dead for weeks as the whole area got record rainfall. "Too many customers is better than no customers at all. I just hope it's like this in Morrowville and Seneca this week, too. We need it."

"True, but . . . Wait. Morrowville *and* Seneca?" Her best

friend stared down at her, hazel eyes narrowing as he raised one thin black eyebrow.

RJ had a six-foot-three frame from his Norwegian mom, light brown skin from his Venezuelan dad, and a body bulky from a lifetime of ice hockey. He'd recently cropped his black hair close to his head after a failed experiment with a man bun.

She and RJ had been connected at the hip since toddlerhood while their mothers—best friends in their own right—chatted in lawn chairs and watched their kids play. In a small town like Sullivan's Glen, everybody had family around, so Penny and RJ stuck together like glue, agreeing to be cousins in name and spirit. Each summer that he went to Atlanta to stay with his dad, and later, when they'd parted ways for college and life beyond, Penny was left with a little hole in her heart.

*Everybody comes back to Sullivan's Glen at some point.*

Zander'd said it as a joke. But for a lot of them, it was true. When his mom got her MS diagnosis, RJ accepted that his career in ice hockey wouldn't go beyond the farm leagues and decided being close by was more important. Now he split his time between caregiving, coaching youth hockey, and managing the orchards at the farm. He'd taken classes and connected with other operations to make sure he was taking great care of their apple trees, and Penny couldn't be more grateful.

But that also meant one more person she loved was tied into the fate of Becker Farms.

"Pen. You told me you weren't doing Morrowville and Seneca. We agreed you'd slow down to make more room for festival planning."

Penny broke their staring contest as she adjusted jars on the table. "You suggested that and I didn't respond. Technically I didn't agree to anything."

"You're going to make yourself sick."

"You know I don't have a choice."

"Penny—"

"I should never have told you." Penny crouched to check the supply of jars on hand under the table. "I'm going to figure it out."

For months, she'd kept the loan disaster a secret, even from RJ. But one day while they'd been bottling honey, he'd said they should take a trip together, really enjoy some time off, and she'd burst into tears and explained the whole situation.

RJ crouched beside her. "I'm *glad* you told me, Pen. But I really wish you'd tell your family. And I wish you'd call Henry and tell him this is his mess to clean up."

"I'm the one who signed the papers. It's my mess. I'm the one who didn't really think—"

"But you trusted him, Penny. You thought he'd be around to help. This isn't fair."

She sighed, circling her finger along a golden jar lid. "It doesn't change the facts."

And the facts were that at Henry's urging almost three years ago, she'd gotten a loan to build out a microbrewery facility for hard cider after months of hearing *It's all the rage, babe, it can take this place to the next level*. Penny didn't tell her mom and Mimi about the plan—once everything was set and building ready to begin, she'd announce the project with a flourish, demonstrating her expertise at running things, her usefulness in guaranteeing them all a more secure future.

Except that the "contractor"—a friend of Henry's friend who vouched for him, who did deals by handshakes and not contracts—disappeared with her money, and everything fell apart from there.

And when it did, Henry focused on the next big idea rather than acknowledging the disaster, and, to her continued embarrassment, Penny let him. Months later he was gone for the last time, leaving a heap of debt for Penny to remember him by. For a while, she'd been able to manage the payments. But then the interest rate ballooned, just as the apple harvest was hit by a scourge of codling moths, and months later she lost a dozen hives to varroa mites. Profit margins were already diminishing each year as shoppers wanted to pay grocery store prices for Penny's premium honey and produce, and the setbacks ate their savings, forcing Penny to stop paying the loan to keep Becker Farms going day-to-day.

She just needed a great summer to get to the other side. Which meant going to as many markets as she could squeeze in and staying up late to plan the festival.

"Stop worrying about it, RJ," she said firmly. "I've got it handled."

RJ stood, tugging Penny up with him before wrapping an arm around her shoulders. "I'm only dropping this for now because we're about to have a literal honey riot on our hands." He shuddered as he looked over the top of her head, then lowered his voice. "Don't look, but Marjorie Grey is in the line. That woman terrifies me."

Penny laughed as she pulled out of the hug. "That's because she wants to get her claws in you."

"I swear she looks at me like I'm a piece of meat. She's my mother's age!"

Penny covered her grin with a hand as she got ready to start helping customers. "I'll make sure you're the one to help her."

RJ groaned. "You're evil, Pen. You've got this town wrapped around your little finger, but I know the real you."

And then the market was open, and everything was a whirl. She and RJ had done countless farmer's markets together, but even their practiced ways were challenged by the crush of the crowd.

"Actually, I was in this spot of the line already and—"

That was Maurice Simon. He ran the records office and started every sentence with "actually."

"Do you have the cherry pies, dear? I only see blueberry here, and blueberries just don't agree with my stomach. Every time I eat them, I—"

Jasmine Hollister. She always had tummy troubles.

"If you could just hold on a second!" Penny called to someone waiting at the side. She'd promised them more chard, but it was in the back of her truck and there were people asking for honey, and—

"Pen. Oh, shit, Penny." RJ tugged on her sleeve as he stared at his phone. "It's Terry. She was hanging with my mom this morning, but her grandkid just got taken to the hospital after a soccer accident, and—shit."

Penny blinked up at the market crowd, then back to RJ, who was typing something into his phone. She grabbed it, pulled out his card reader, and pressed the phone back into his hands. "Go."

"This is too much on your own."

"I said go!" She glanced to the line and gave her bravest smile. "I've got this."

RJ's shoulders dropped in relief. "I'm just going to check on her. I'll come back as soon as I can get somebody else over there."

"Go!" Penny turned him toward the parking lot. "I'll be fine."

Just five minutes later, Penny wasn't fine. People were clamoring for RJ's pies, near-wrestling over honey samples, and asking her questions about colony collapse like she was hosting a beekeeping workshop instead of trying to run her damn business, all as she ran back and forth from the table to resupply. Things really couldn't get worse.

Then she looked up to help the next person in line, only to peer straight into the dark brown eyes of Zander Bouras. His short beard was gone, revealing a sharp jaw with a small nick on the soft skin of his throat.

She swayed slightly before snapping her attention back to his face. "What do *you* want?"

"And a very good morning to you, too, Penny." His mouth held a smirk, but his eyes were shifty. He darted a look over one shoulder, then the other, adjusting his Red Sox cap like he hoped to pull it over his entire face.

"What are you—" She followed his gaze to two women in the next line over, watching him unabashedly as they talked behind their hands. Zander's shoulders curled in further. "Are you in *disguise*?"

"No." He shook his head. "Just trying to stay low-profile. Listen, I thought we could talk about Winter and—"

"Not right now, okay?" She motioned to the line behind him. Next to Zander, Mr. Zigler griped about *moving things along*.

"But Winter is really excited, and I promised him I'd figure it out with you today."

"Look around. I'm swamped and the person helping me had to go, so I'm doing this all on my own. Come back in a few hours."

"Come on, Becker, it will just take a few minutes. The world's not going to end."

Penny's hands slapped down on the table. "I don't have a few minutes!" Who was this guy, to waltz up and expect her to give him her attention when she had work to do? *So* much work to do. "Maybe you think I can blow this off because it's just some little farmer's market in some stupid town, but this is my business. This is my *life*. Come. Back. Later."

Zander's eyes narrowed just before he nodded and stepped out of the line.

Penny sucked in a deep breath, grateful he hadn't caused an even bigger scene.

But as she turned to the next customer, a booming voice soared over her market table.

"All right, everybody, listen up! If we could form two orderly lines, everything will go much faster for all of us. We'll have one line form in front of the lovely Ms. Becker, and the other one right here with me."

Penny's gaze shot to Zander standing beside her, directing the crowd like a symphony as people split into two lines.

"What," she spat, "are you doing?"

He pulled off his hat and tossed it to the ground before running his fingers through his hair. Somewhere in line, a woman sighed.

"If I need to talk to you about my kid, and you can't talk until you manage your customers, then there seems to be only one solution."

"Oh, *no*."

"Oh, *yes*. Penny Becker, I'm here to help."

# CHAPTER 6

Zander always did have problems with impulse control.

Whether he was stealing his grandfather's tractor or clearing the Sullivan's Glen rose garden of its blooms in a romantic gesture to a teenage Mallory, his tendency to act before he thought about the consequences had, well, caused some consequences for him over the years. But adulthood, good ADHD meds, and a lot of therapy meant that it was mostly under control.

So *why* was he standing behind Penny Becker's farmer's market stand, shouting at a bunch of unruly townspeople to get in line if they wanted their damn honey?

"What are you *doing*?"

A pissed-off Penny was clearly wondering the same thing.

"I told you." He shot a smile at a white-haired woman observing them closely. "I'll help until you have a minute to talk about Winter and the bees. No offense, Penny, but your crowd management could use a little work, and you're not expediting for shit."

The flare of her nostrils made it clear she did not appreciate his feedback, but he wasn't about to be scared off. His alternative was to wait around for hours to catch her, and he was ready to get started on the house. The sooner he made some basic improvements, the sooner he could get it on the market.

And he had to admit, while he should have enjoyed seeing the perfect Penny Becker treading water at her market stand, he'd had the ridiculous urge to throw her a life raft.

The chaos at Penny's booth had him nostalgic for the kitchens where he'd cut his teeth as a line cook. He started in the back of a crowded greasy spoon, where his booming voice, big stature, and determination to get home in time to catch a few hours of sleep before waking with his son had established Zander as a keeper of order. Turned out he had a knack for finding efficiencies in a kitchen, and his bosses were happy to put him on task. After an adolescence where no one ever listened to him, it was pretty great to boss people around sometimes.

"I see the prices on the table, how do we process payment?"

Penny looked at him like a gasping fish for a moment, then groaned. She glanced again at the waiting customers—now arranged in two orderly lines, thank you very much—and grabbed her phone.

"Here." She shoved it at him. "My phone is already hooked up for card payment. Just use that since you don't have the account set up. I'll process cash."

Zander shot her a big smile, the one Quinn promised him would *clean up* at bars if he ever went out, which he didn't. "I think we'll make a great team."

Penny just rolled her eyes.

Before he got down to business, Zander allowed himself one look at the woman next to him. She'd been enveloped in her bee suit for their last encounter, and now she was . . . decidedly not. Instead she was in light denim overalls, which should have looked ridiculous given her freckles and honest-to-God pigtail braids. But the tight red V-neck underneath hugged her curves and stopped just short enough to show a peek of skin along her waist, making her look less country bumpkin and more sexy farm girl next door.

Shit. She *was* the sexy farm girl next door.

"Hey." Fingers snapped in front of his face, blocking his view of the line of Penny's collarbone exposed by the neckline of her shirt. "Are we working or not? Because if you're just here to sabotage me—"

"Yes." He swallowed and looked away from the freckles on her throat. Far away. "I mean, no. Not sabotaging. Working, yes."

So he worked, easing into the rhythm of handing over honey, or candles, or small pies with perfectly flaky crusts. He knew his way around the garden produce and resupplied his part of the table from crates by his feet when needed. When people had cash, he smoothly transitioned them to Penny and cut off extra conversation before it got started. An efficient line didn't leave room for socializing.

It wasn't as fast-paced as some kitchens he'd worked in—not even close—but it was a nice change from the duties of his job lately, which involved a lot of arguing on the phone and adjusting budgeting spreadsheets. His body thrilled at the movement of the work.

Each time he passed over a jar of honey, he noticed the weight of it in his palm, the way it glowed in the sunshine. It was a fitting product for Penny, all golden and glowing in her own right. Now that she had some help, she was taking more time with each person at the table, smiling and making easy conversation, sometimes pointing to the pictures she had up on an easel that showed close-ups of bees on a honeycomb.

"We've got about thirty-eight acres total, most of it given to our apple orchards." She handed off a bag of goods to a couple with two young kids. "We have five varietals of heirloom apples and a great U-pick season in the fall if you ever come back our way."

From the entranced looks on their faces, this family would definitely be back for some apples.

Papou had loved talking about the perfect girl next door—*your age, you understand?*—who helped out at her family farm and still got straight A's. Penny was the model by which Zander was intended to measure himself and his slew of failures.

By the time he was eighteen, the words *Penny Becker* made him cringe.

But here she was, managing thirty-eight acres, smiling at tourists and inviting them to come pick her heirloom apples. Perfect as could fucking be.

He shook his head and passed a bundle of radishes to a waiting customer, but his rhythm had faltered, and when he glanced again at their shortened line and the people mulling around the larger market, it hit Zander in the gut: he'd voluntarily put himself front and center in downtown Sullivan's Glen. Some people were watching him closely, not as subtly as they thought. Whether they were confused about the stranger behind the honey stand or remembering the time he'd been caught climbing into the county pool with boxes full of food dye in his backpack was anyone's guess.

Something warm and soft pressed against his shoulder. "Can I, sorry, just—" Penny leaned across the table, cutting across Zander's body so her blond braids were just under his nose, filling his head with the coconut scent of her shampoo.

She snapped up a pie from his side of the table and evacuated his space, leaving him a little dizzy.

"You could ask," he said, sounding angrier than he intended.

But he did not appreciate the way his body responded to the softness of hers, and he wanted his brain clear of that coconut. "Just ask me to pass something to you."

"I can reach just fine."

"Yeah, but I'm right here—"

"Zander. I didn't ask for your help, and now you're just—"

"We-ll," a smarmy voice interrupted. "If it isn't Zander Bouras. Everybody lock up your daughters, am I right?"

The owner of the voice was a medium-size puffy white guy, the kind Zander knew well. He was the diner who complained that his lettuce was too wilted and demanded a full refund after clearing his plate, or the investor who thought putting in seed money for a restaurant meant free dinners for life.

His white polo was stained on the shoulder, his cheeks a splotchy red because he probably thought he was too good for sunscreen. And he was staring at Zander like they knew each other, but for the life of him, Zander couldn't—

"Brad." Penny's voice was flat. "Do you need something?"

The memory unfurled like the flick of a tablecloth. Brad Preston. Daddy's boy, dipshit, high-and-mighty Brad Preston.

"I just wanted to see for myself that the rumors were true." Brad's eyes lingered on Penny's V-neck as he leaned his pasty hands onto the table. After a beat too long, his attention swung back to Zander. "Finally come slinking back this way, huh? Hope your right hook has gotten better with time."

Zander white-knuckled a jar of honey. "I don't know, *Brad.* I recall it was pretty effective back then."

Zander wasn't a violent person, except that one time. He'd been seventeen, walking down Main Street in Sullivan's Glen with his head down when he ran into Brad Preston. Brad bumped his shoulder and said something seriously shitty about Zander's mom.

Yeah, his mom was a total mess. But she was *his* mess.

So he'd left Brad with a bloody nose, a black eye, and—most dangerously—a wounded ego. After that run-in, Brad tried to rile Zander up every time they crossed paths.

Wow, how great to be back in Sullivan's Glen.

"You know," Brad continued, his voice slimy like oil slicks on a parking lot, "I heard the funniest thing. I heard that ex-wife of yours showed up to town with a girlfriend. What, did you turn her gay?"

Activity at the table slowed like molasses as people either watched openly or from poorly concealed sideways glances.

"Brad." Zander put the honey down gently and flexed his fingers a few times to get his blood flowing again. He didn't miss Brad's gaze watching the movement of his fist. "I'm glad to see you, actually. Gives me a chance to apologize."

"Apolo—what?"

"For when I punched you when we were kids. It was so long ago, maybe you don't even remember. I had some anger management issues back then, stuff I've addressed in therapy over the years. Do you do therapy?"

"Do I—" Brad shook his head. A drop of sweat trailed down his forehead. "No, I don't do fucking therapy."

"I can't recommend it enough." Zander pulled a twig of rosemary from a bundle of herbs and rubbed the thick leaves between his thumb and forefinger. "Especially for men. Very healing to examine toxic masculinity. I think it could help you sort out why you were always so desperate for your daddy's approval."

Somehow, Brad's face went even redder. "What the fu—"

"But the point is"—Zander rubbed his thumb just above his upper lip, taking in the sweet, earthy aroma from the plant—"I realized how wrong it was of me to punch you that day, when you were obviously so much smaller and weaker than I was. I imagine that was very scary for you, and I'm sorry." He kept his gaze on Brad's narrowed eyes. "Do you accept my apology?"

"Do I accept—" Brad choked on his words. "What the hell do you think—"

"That's a no, then? I understand." Zander leaned forward, just an inch, but close enough to watch the drop of sweat land on Brad's stained polo. "Then I'll have to ask you to move along. We have a lot of people here waiting to buy some honey, and Penny and I are very busy."

Zander held his breath and waited to see if the gamble would pay off. Only when Brad shook his head, mumbling, "Whatever," and a few choice words not suitable for mixed company as he stormed off, did Zander exhale.

"All right, folks." He let his voice boom again as he wiped his sweaty palms on his jeans. "Show's over. Next in line, please?"

Like someone had flipped a switch, activity restarted at the table. But even as Zander worked to slow his heartbeat by re-arranging the jars of honey, he felt the weight of Penny's scrutiny. She probably never had ugly confrontations rear up from her past, never had to cycle through therapists before finding someone she could be vulnerable with. She didn't have to fight between past and present versions of herself, or look at other families and swallow down ugly envy. When he finally got to ask her about showing her bees to Winter, she'd probably tell him to fuck off.

"Hey, Zander."

He jumped at the sound of her voice, knocking a jar and sending it rolling. It tipped off the table and landed in Zander's upturned palm.

"Pass me a blueberry pie, will you?"

When he did, Penny's chin tipped up so her blue eyes looked right at him.

"Put your number in my phone. I'll text you later about finding a time to bring Winter over."

# CHAPTER 7

"And believe me, dear, I understand that everyone has busy schedules these days. But if we let people get used to putting their trash bins out a day early, what's to stop them from putting them out two days early? Or even *three*? And from there it's just anarchy, isn't it?"

Penny glanced up from her laptop, smiling just enough to be friendly but not encouraging. Or so she hoped. "I wouldn't say anarchy necessarily, Ms. Splicer."

Lee Splicer, who'd been Penny's former kindergarten teacher, now spent her retirement looking for violations of Sullivan's Glen town ordinances. "I don't think you understand the consequences of allowing—"

What Penny hadn't considered the consequences of was trying to do her festival planning in Brewtopia, the small coffee shop nestled in the strip of stores and restaurants in downtown Sullivan's Glen.

She'd been awake since early light to squeeze every extra minute from the day. With only eight weeks until the festival, Penny's brain buzzed with the last details she needed to hammer down. Between morning chores, a meeting with RJ, and a trip to Mystic Mayhem to deliver a restock of beeswax candles, she still had the vendor tables to finalize, supplier contracts to sign, and permits to sort out with the township. If it were up to Penny, she'd have settled this all months ago, but any attempts at early planning had been met with grumbles. The residents of Sullivan's Glen moved at their own pace.

Brewtopia seemed like as good a place as any to concentrate, away from the distraction of chores at the farm, and she'd gotten down to business making her *Best Honey Festival Ever Checklist!*—the exclamation point added in an effort to feel optimistic.

But now Ms. Splicer, one table over, would not stop talking about the trash bin crisis. And she hadn't been the only one eager to chat. Since ordering her tea and muffin, Penny was interrupted by no fewer than four people eager to pass on their juiciest piece of gossip. For better or worse, she now knew that Lorraine Langston was going to prom with her best friend's brother, that Sun Lee's nephew would be home from Marines basic training in August, and that Nancy Watkins was on a mission, again, to convince the Mason County volunteer firefighters to pose for a racy calendar.

But the people hadn't just wanted to dish out info. They'd also asked a lot of questions.

Each interview began innocently enough, asking after her mother or grandmother, wondering how things were at the farm. But they all circled around eventually to one topic: Zander Bouras.

One would think the man had shown up in Sullivan's Glen and walked straight across the lake, given how interested people were in his return. And now, after he'd stepped in to help her at the farmer's market—without being asked, when Penny was doing just *fine*—she was also a matter of public interest.

"I just want people to show some self-respect regarding their own property, Penny, you understand. And speaking of property, I heard a little rumor that someone is here to take care of Nikolai's place. . . ."

Penny took a long sip of her tea to keep from screaming. Even Ms. Splicer was infected with the Zander Bouras virus.

"I really don't know anything about that." Penny threw out the line she'd been using all morning. "I'm actually just trying to—"

"Penny!" A blur of navy slumped into the seat across Penny's small table. Natasha Wrenfield, dressed head to toe in blue coveralls and holding a cup of coffee in each hand, beamed at Penny. "So fun seeing you out—you're never here!"

Natasha was a local like Penny, and now ran her family's mechanic's shop with her younger brother.

Resolved that her morning was already lost, Penny closed her laptop. "I thought I might get some work done."

"Ha!" Natasha put down the cups and gathered her curly black hair into a ponytail. "My sweet summer child. Tourists can sit here and work because no one will interrupt them. Locals, on the other hand, come here to gossip."

Penny cast a sideways glance at Ms. Splicer, who'd now spotted someone new in line to warn about the impending anarchy in Sullivan's Glen. "I figured that out the hard way."

"And I'm sure everyone else tried to be subtle and beat around the bush. But I'm on limited time, so tell me." Natasha leaned in. "What is the deal with Zander Bouras?"

Penny blinked innocently. "I really wouldn't know. We don't know each other."

Natasha only raised an eyebrow.

"What?" Penny said. "We don't."

"Oka-ay, except he's living right next door, and I heard you guys were buddy-buddy at the market."

"We were not—" Penny lowered her voice. "No one is buddy-

buddy. He inserted himself into my business because I had a little bit of a line and he was too impatient to wait to talk to me."

Natasha's eyes narrowed as she spun one of the cups in her hand. "So . . . he saw you were swamped and stepped in to help? That's sweet."

"It's not sweet," Penny said, reminding herself at the same time. It was not sweet, or generous. He'd helped only for his own purposes. "He wasn't doing it out of the goodness of his heart."

"Was he helpful, though?"

*Yes, very.* That was the worst part.

"Mildly."

Zander had worked wonders with that line, and clearly had a knack for customer service. She'd even heard him encouraging someone to grab an extra bundle of herbs, giving them advice on how to best use the rosemary with the chicken they were making that night.

How did Zander Bouras know how to use rosemary?

And when had he acquired all those tattoos?

And what was it about his knowing smirk that sent her stomach rioting?

Penny swallowed a groan and tugged at the end of her braid. She was sick of questions about Zander, especially the ones spiraling in her own head.

Natasha was still talking. ". . . don't tell me you didn't notice."

"Sorry." Penny shook her head. "What?"

Natasha grinned. "Don't tell me you didn't notice that that man is *hot*. I saw him as he was leaving the market, walking like a bull with his head down trying to get out of there. I mean, his tattoos?"

Penny shrugged. "I didn't notice."

Except for the snake twisting around his forearm, and an

intricate snowflake on the soft underside of his wrist. His short-sleeved shirt had left more room for examination than when she'd seen him in the bee yard.

"I don't know what he's been doing all these years," Natasha continued. "But the guy looks like he could toss a girl around the bedroom, that's all I'm saying."

"*Natasha*." Penny's face flamed.

"Jorge's new boy toy, Finn, was in line during the whole Brad thing. I heard Zander handled him like a pro, sent him off with his preppy tail between his legs. Tell me *everything*."

"It was . . ." Penny sighed, knowing she couldn't shrug her way out of this one. "It was impressive, okay? I'll give him that."

When Brad started in on Zander about Mallory, Penny braced herself for the worst. Her mind shot five steps ahead, when she'd be screaming at Zander for losing his temper and scaring away her customers.

But he'd stayed calm, and he'd been *smart*, handling Brad with mastery. It was unexpected, just like the wave of heat it sent through Penny's body.

For a flash, some boundary between them had cracked, revealing a glimpse of this grown-up Zander against the one who'd glared at her each summer years ago. So she'd told him to give her his number to follow up about bringing Winter over to see the bees.

But every time Penny opened to his contact, where he was entered as "Zander B," she froze.

Natasha groaned as she checked her phone. "Shit. Little bro wants to know where his coffee is, I gotta run." She pinned Penny with a knowing look. "But we *will* continue this conversation later, Penny Becker."

As the door jingled behind Natasha, Penny dared to reach

for her computer. Maybe she could still review last year's invoices to look for places she could cut corners. Trying to squeeze a significant profit from the Honey Festival meant looking for efficiencies wherever she could.

But before she could get started, someone else took Natasha's recently emptied chair. Penny prepped herself to smile and nod through another round of gossip, but the woman across from her definitely wasn't local.

She was stunning, with sharp cheekbones and black hair cutting across her face. Silver rings decorated her left eyebrow.

"I'm sorry, I am being so weird." The words spilled from her mouth. "But I heard that person call you Penny Becker. Are you Penny Becker?"

"Um." Penny closed the laptop again. "Yeah, that's me."

"Awesome. I'm Quinn. I'm Mallory Robinson's girlfriend. But also Zander's friend. I was Zander's friend before I was Mal's girlfriend, actually. It's a whole thing."

Wow, Natasha would be devastated she was missing this.

Quinn's hand thrust over the table, the word *T-R-U-T-H* tattooed along her fingers. Penny met the hand in a quick shake. "Um, good to meet you?"

"I just wanted to say hi because I heard about you through Winter. He was telling me about the bee stuff. And I don't know anyone here, beside Mal and Z of course, so—"

Quinn looked down at her own fingers, twisted together on the table. Penny realized she was nervous, which was sweet, considering she looked like she'd blend in fine at a biker bar.

"I'm glad you said hi," Penny offered warmly. "And welcome to Sullivan's Glen."

Quinn brightened as she smiled back at Penny. "Thanks! It's beautiful here. From what I've heard about this place from

Zander, you'd think you had to pass through the gates of hell to enter. But it mostly seems to be a normal place."

"Yeah," Penny answered. "No demons in sight." Despite his polite smiles at the farmer's market, Zander clearly hadn't been forgiving about the town in his stories to Quinn. "I guess he's always hated this place."

Quinn rubbed at her jaw. "He *thinks* he hates it, for sure. But Zander is . . ." She let a full breath draw in and out. "You know how when you come back to a place from a different time in your life, and it's like you're traveling through all the same places and interactions, but now there are these potholes all over?" Quinn's painted nails tapped the table. "Like all your old habits of who you were then wore everything down, and it's easy to trip and drop into one and kind of fall into being that person you used to be."

Penny opened her mouth to say she didn't know. Even when she left for college, she came home frequently, and had never truly had an experience of coming back after a long time away.

But she did have her own potholes—cycle of conversations with her mom that were as regular and reliable as the seasons that set the rhythm of Penny's life. Maybe it was a spontaneous idea from Ruth that Penny quickly shot down with a dose of reality, or another promise that if Penny just worked less *everything would turn out just fine*. Each time those holes were worn a little deeper. And over and over, each time Penny fell into one, she smiled and kept the peace, making sure everything ran smoothly.

"Look at me." Quinn shook her head. "I sat down to say hi and try to make a local friend, and I made it dark right away. I would tell you I'm not normally like this, but it would be a lie."

Penny laughed quietly. "No, it's fine."

Refreshing, actually, after a morning of gossip and surface-level conversations.

"And it's not my place to say, but I'll say it anyway. I know you haven't followed up with Zander, and if you don't want to, I would get it. He's kind of mean and prickly. But it's because he had to be, for a long time. We all have the armor we put on to survive, but most of us are soft underneath, Z especially." Quinn blushed and swiped at her hair. "Yikes, there I go again. I have this inability to do small talk, I apologize."

"I appreciate it, actually," Penny assured her, her thoughts still circling on potholes and armor, the kind she wore and that Zander might don as well.

Quinn glanced at the line. "I should get moving, but think about texting Zander, okay? It'd mean a lot to him if he got to bring Winter over for the bee stuff." She stood and shot Penny one more smile. "It was awesome to meet you, Penny, and I hope we cross paths again."

"I do, too." And she really meant it.

As Quinn hustled to the end of the line, Penny slipped her laptop back into her bag. She had to meet RJ at the warehouse soon to extract honey, so festival work would have to wait until tonight.

But before she stepped back out onto Sullivan Glen's Main Street, she pulled out her phone and typed a message to Zander B.

*I'm free Thursday at 10 to show Winter the bees. We'll meet at your place.*

# CHAPTER 8

"I was crying because it hurt so bad, and everybody was standing around me in a circle."

"Oof, I bet everyone watching didn't help."

"My dad was the worst. He started patting down my whole body looking for where I was hurt. It was *so* embarrassing."

Penny's laughter lifted to where Zander stood listening on the stairs. He'd been there for too long, listening to Winter regale Penny with the story of his first bee sting.

She had a beautiful laugh—light and airy, like the sway of the long grass outside. He'd heard snippets of it at the farmer's market as she talked with customers, but never as free and full-throated as this. He leaned against the railing, waiting to hear it again.

"Da-ad!"

Instead, his son's impatient holler broke him from his stupor.

Wait, *why* exactly was he lurking on the stairs waiting to hear Penny Becker laugh?

"Come *on*!"

"Chill, little man! Coming."

The stairs deposited Zander in the small sitting room, where an old paisley couch sat as the only survivor of Zander's morning purge. Penny perched on its edge in a full bee suit with her hood on her lap, Winter was already decked out to match Penny, and a third suit was draped over the armrest.

Penny looked his way, her blue eyes too bright for the drab room, making Zander aware of his messy wet hair and the tug of his shirt across his shoulders.

When had this shirt gotten so tight? And why was the room so hot?

And why, for the love of all things holy, did Zander like the sight of perfect Penny Becker sitting on that ugly couch?

He cleared his throat and shot a look at Winter. "For the record, I had a perfectly normal reaction to my kid yelling, and I quote, 'I'm dying! I'm dying! Oh my god, I'm dying!'"

Winter rolled his eyes, but there was a hint of a smile on his face, a lot like the one he'd flashed when Zander had shared the news about securing plans with Penny, finally.

When he hadn't heard from her after the market, Zander assumed Penny wouldn't actually follow up. Mallory offered to use the Sullivan's Glen grapevine to get her number, and if all else failed, the Becker Farms website had a contact page. But Zander wasn't about to chase Penny down again, especially after giving up a whole morning at her market table without even a thank-you. Then by some miracle she'd actually reached out, and now she was in his papou's house, brighter than the place deserved.

"When Winter had that sting," Penny asked him, "he didn't have a reaction, right? No trouble breathing or anything?"

"No, nothing like that. Why? Do you think he's at risk out there?"

"I don't see any reason to think so," Penny said evenly, maybe seeing the worst-case scenarios playing out in Zander's head.

"He didn't have an allergic reaction in the past, and we've got the suits on. I checked them all before I came over and they're in good shape. And I always have an EpiPen with me, just in case." She stood and passed the third suit to him. "What about you?"

Zander stepped awkwardly into the suit, which reminded him of the janitorial job he'd had when Mallory was pregnant. He slipped his arms through and looked back to Penny. "What *about* me?"

"Any recent bee stings?"

As he tugged at the zipper the suit got tighter, particularly across his chest. "Don't worry about me."

Penny scoffed quietly. "This isn't the time to get macho."

He peered down at her. "I'm not being macho. I'm asking you to concentrate on my kid."

Penny's jaw tensed as she glanced toward Winter and glued a clearly fake-as-hell smile to her face. "Anyone who goes out there with me is under my supervision and care. Even you, Zander. If you can't accept that, you can stay here."

His fingers fumbled with the zipper. Everything about him felt too big in this thing. "No way. If Winter is going out there to what could turn into the beepocalypse for all I know, I'm coming, too."

Penny's lips quirked like her fake smile might turn into a real one. "Fine. So, bee stings?"

"I'm not sure when it was exactly," he grumbled. "Within the last few years. There was a bee on my kitchen sponge, no serious reaction."

"Was that so hard?" Penny tilted her head, and Zander swallowed back a retort. "Now let's head out."

Out in the sunshine, Penny walked in a circle around each of them, making sure each part of the bulky suit was all zipped up, then took them through putting on the hoods and gloves. She directed all her instructions at Winter as Zander followed along, and soon they were walking through the trees, following the same path Zander had trod down that morning only a few days ago.

Feeling curious the night before, Zander had looked up Becker Farms online. Most of the property was dedicated to apple orchards, and the website mentioned U-pick days, produce sales, and honey, along with bee removal and pollination services.

It also featured an unfairly adorable picture of Penny Becker at six years old with a giant beekeeping veil draped over her tiny blond head.

The trees opened into the clearing, and Zander was back among Penny's bees. He knew from his research that each box constituted its own bee colony, and each colony could have tens of thousands of bees. So right now, his kid was surrounded by at least a hundred thousand bees.

Cool, cool, cool.

With quick and easy movements, Penny picked up a silver smoker from the ground, another item he recognized from his Google crash course. She pulled a lighter from her bulky pocket and lit the brush in the smoker, then blew on the contents until they smoldered.

"This makes everything a little easier," she told Winter. "Bees do almost all their communicating through smell, so the smoke blocks them from raising too much alarm when a giant monster starts messing around with their home. It also tricks them a little into thinking there might be a forest fire coming, and they get busy gathering up honey just in case."

"We're scaring them?" Winter's voice cracked.

Winter had loved animals since the day he could point his

chubby baby hands at his board books. He was the kid collecting ants and saving baby birds, doing every school report about an endangered animal somewhere across the globe. The glimpse of that kid still in there hit Zander with a swell of parenting warm fuzzies.

"Think about it like this." Penny lifted the flat wooden top from a hive and worked the smoker, sending a small poof into the box from above. "Bees always want something to do. When I smoke them a little, they're going to keep themselves busy gathering up honey in case they have to relocate. But a few minutes later they'll put it all back and move on. We aren't harming them, just keeping them busy while we poke around."

"How do they gather it?" Winter asked.

"They actually have special pouches inside their bodies." Penny spoke as she reached into the hive, all her movements calm and practiced, like she'd done this a million times. Considering that picture of little Penny, she probably had.

"That's also how they collect nectar or water and bring it back to the hive," she continued. "So right now they'll use them to store some honey until they're sure it's safe to put it back in."

"All right," Winter replied cautiously. "As long as they're okay."

Penny lifted her arms, pulling out a wooden frame about ten inches by seven inches, maybe two inches thick, and completely covered with a carpet of bees.

"Whoa," Winter exhaled. "Awesome."

Winter stepped forward to look, and Zander leaned over his son to see for himself, as much of his tension about the bees melted away. Penny clearly knew what she was doing, and as much as they'd butted heads, she wouldn't put Zander's kid in danger. Somehow he just knew that she took care of the things around her.

"This is a frame, and I have eight of these in each box," Penny said. "There's a lot happening in a hive at any given minute, but we're going to simplify it into a few basics. When you're inspecting a colony, like we're doing right now, you're paying attention to three main things." She lowered the frame and turned it so one side was facing up. "You want to see honey, you want to see pollen, and you want to see brood."

"Brood?" Winter curled over the frame. "What's that?"

"That's where the baby bees come from."

"No way! Where?"

Penny flipped the frame over, revealing another side of bees and honeycomb, where more bees teemed along the surface. "Look up at the top right corner. See where it's a little darker?"

Zander squinted at a section of cells covered by a layer of dark copper wax.

"Inside there," Penny said, "are baby bees, transforming from larva."

"They make a cocoon, right? Like butterflies?" Winter asked.

"They do!" Penny's smile was clear through her netted hood. "Nobody warned me you were already an insect expert."

And shit, now his kid was *beaming*, and Zander was smiling, too.

She was great at this. Clearly an expert at what she was doing, and a gifted teacher on top of it. As Penny rested the frame on the hive, beckoning Winter closer, Zander suspected the family farm rested largely on Penny's obviously competent shoulders, and she was probably damn good at managing it.

And worse, he was having trouble holding it against her.

"These cells look empty," Penny continued. "But if you look closely, you'll see something inside about the size of a grain of rice. That's an egg. Once it hatches, it's a slimy white larva, like . . . this."

Winter gasped as Penny located a cell holding a white, slimy larva. "That is *so* gross."

Which, in Winter-speak, meant it was the coolest thing ever.

"When it's time for to the larva to pupate, the cell will be capped like those ones up there. Through all the stages, other bees are taking care of the brood. They're cleaning everything up and feeding everyone."

Winter watched the frame for a moment before turning back to Penny. "But only the queen lays the eggs, right?"

"Oh, come on." Penny tsked playfully. "I thought I was the one giving the lesson here."

She returned the frame they'd been inspecting and took out another, turning it around in her hands. Zander and Winter watched as Penny examined each side before returning it to the box and repeating the process.

One night back in Boston, Quinn had been over for her usual hangout, as Zander cooked them dinner, when she'd said, "You're the most *you* when you're working in the kitchen. It's like I can see your burdens drift away. You look lighter."

Quinn was so rarely sincere that Zander had just laughed it off and thrown a piece of onion her way. But now, watching Penny's lips move silently as she scanned the frame of bees, he understood. He didn't know Penny well, but it didn't take a genius to see that she was in her element.

How many people got to stand here with her to see her like this?

She hummed and smiled, then held the frame up high. "There she is."

Winter bounced on his heels. "The queen?"

"Yep. Like you said, the queen is the only one who lays eggs. When there's a nectar flow, and the colony is growing, she might lay up to two thousand eggs every day. She is mother to all the bees in the colony."

"Wow," Zander muttered. "Props to her. I thought having one kid was hard."

Something suspiciously close to a laugh bubbled from Penny before she cleared her throat. "She might have fifty thousand kids at a time, but they all take care of each other, and of her. They clean her and bring her food and do everything in the colony so that she can just lay eggs."

"Okay, *that* doesn't sound so bad. I'm still trying to get some-one to wash his own dishes."

"*Dad.*"

Winter grumbled, but Zander couldn't seem to mind as Penny smiled at him, her eyes bright even through the suit's netting. Since the farmer's market, Penny's body—the curve of her hip peeking from the gap in her overalls, the pale swirl of her ear against her golden braid—had risen up vibrantly in his mind more than he liked, especially late at night. He'd hoped a morning with Penny hidden in the bee suit might help douse his inconvenient and unwanted attraction.

Unfortunately, her confidence and competence were only making matters worse.

Penny blinked away their eye contact, turning to Winter.

"You want to see the queen? Come see if you can spot the bee that's different."

This outing had been for his kid, but there was no denying Zander's own eagerness as he scanned the frame. At first, he couldn't decipher anything different in the clusters of fuzzy bees, but then he spotted her. The queen's body was longer than the others', and she had a little green dot just below her head.

Winter's inhale told him his son had found her, too. "What's the dot on her?"

"That green is paint," Penny answered. "Queens are often marked like this, to make them easy to spot in inspections."

As Winter leaned in closer, watching the queen, Penny pressed the frame toward him. "Here, hold on to it and take a look around."

"Wait, for real?"

"For real."

Knowing this was a time when Winter might actually be enthusiastic for a picture, Zander went for the phone in his pocket, only to realize he wouldn't be able to operate it with the gloves on. He started to tug one off, but Penny stopped him with a hand on his arm.

"Gloves stay on."

Penny's gloved fingers folded over his suited forearm, starting a domino effect of reactions in Zander's body—a tightening in his chest and throat, his breath gone shallow—that was hardly warranted by a touch through two layers of thick fabric. Maybe his years of celibacy were coming back to bite him in the ass, his touch-starved body hungry for anything.

No matter that he hadn't had this problem until he rolled up in Sullivan's Glen and saw Penny Becker.

Zander struggled for focus. "I need to get a picture of this. Winter's going to go back and tell Mal every detail, and I'm going to be the shitty co-parent if I don't have pictures for her. I'll be fast, scout's honor."

The netting didn't hide Penny's eye roll. "Something tells me you were never a scout. I'll take pictures for you. I'd rather have my gloves off than yours. I usually do the inspections without the suit anyway."

She lifted her hand from his arm and brought it up, then bit the fabric of the middle finger and gave it a tug that Zander felt along his spine.

A trickle of sweat dripped from his temple. "You were in the suit the other day, when I stumbled on your bee kingdom."

Penny stuffed the glove in one pocket and pulled her phone from the other. "That was just an off day. I was in a bad mood."

"Why would that matter? And what was wrong?"

And why did he care?

Penny cast him a sideways glance as she turned. "Maybe I knew *you* were about to show up."

Zander had to laugh. "Touché."

She proceeded to lead Winter in a photo session, taking breaks to help him return one frame and pull out another. Each time, Zander eavesdropped as Penny shared knowledge about capped honey cells, drones, and something about pollen protein.

When a passing bee landed on Zander's netted hood, he studied the insect with rapt interest, an odd excitement in his bones. He stared at the bee's oversize eyes, just inches from his own, shocked by how safe he felt, how happy to be in this moment.

The best he'd felt since pulling back into Sullivan's Glen.

"Dad! Dad! Come look!"

Winter and Penny bent over a frame resting on top of the hive box, watching intently.

"A baby bee, Dad! It's coming out!" He pointed to a copper-colored cell, where antennae poked from a small break in the cell cap.

"No way," Zander whispered.

"It'll eat its way out." Penny's voice was calm and light. "Just wait."

At first only the antennae were visible, but as Zander watched, the bee worked the hole wider, until the shine of her eyes and tiny head of yellow and black appeared. After a few minutes, the bee began wiggling its way out.

"How many times have you seen this?" he asked Penny in a whisper.

"So many," she answered just as quietly. "And it never gets old."

The bee crawled out entirely, taking its first slow steps on the surface of the comb.

"She'll walk around for a few minutes to dry off and strengthen her wing muscles," Penny told them. "Then she'll get to work."

"Always working," a deep voice called from the trees. "Just like someone else I know."

A guy—a big guy, which was a lot coming from Zander—came into the bee yard with a smile. He had light brown skin, a buzzed head, and a blue T-shirt that said *Hockey Is So Pucking Fun!* in rainbow lettering, with gloves hanging from the back pocket of his Carhartts.

"RJ?" Penny straightened from her spot at the hive. "What are you doing here?"

"What do you think, Pen?" He shot Zander a hundred-watt smile. "I came to meet Zander Bouras."

# CHAPTER 9

Watching RJ shake hands with Zander was very, very strange.

And not just because Zander was still in the full bee suit, meeting RJ through the netting of the veil.

Seeing her best friend greeting her—neighbor? Nemesis? Guy who meant nothing to her so why was she coming up with a label?—only added to the sense of disorientation spinning Penny all around.

Being around Zander threw her off. Was he the brooding bad boy who hated being back in Sullivan's Glen? Or the fawning dad who beamed when his kid found the queen bee?

Whoever he was, he filled out the bee suit more than Henry ever had, and listened more intently than most people managed when Penny talked about her work. She'd watched him stare rapt at the emerging bee, unable to find a jaded excuse for the awe on his face, or the gentleness in his expression as the bee took its first unsteady steps.

Who was this guy, and why did he make her feel like this— squirrelly and out of sorts?

"I was always down at my dad's in Atlanta when you were

here for the summers," RJ was saying. "So we never met. I sure heard a lot about you, though."

Zander laughed. "I hope you don't believe everything you heard . . . only most of it."

And for that, RJ patted him on the shoulder like they were old buds. Traitor.

"Hey." Penny interrupted the budding bromance. "I didn't think you were around today."

"Actually, Ruth came over to hang with Mom, so I thought I'd check out the wax worm situation in the orchard hives. And I happened to remember you guys had plans out here, so I figured . . ." He shrugged.

Since hearing of Penny's first encounter with Zander, RJ was unsatisfied with her limited sharing of details, scoffing each time Penny redirected the conversation to the Honey Festival.

"Hey man," RJ said. "I heard how you stepped in at the market the other day, and I owe you big. I got pulled away and I know Penny really appreciated the help."

Zander cut a look toward Penny with a small grin. "I'm not sure she did, but I was happy to pitch in regardless."

"Whatever magic you worked, I appreciate it. Pen said we sold out of all my pies, and I made twice as many as last month."

"Those were yours?" Zander whistled. "I didn't get to try one, but the pastry looked perfect."

RJ's jaw dropped. "Did you hear that, Penny? Zander called my pastry perfect. And he was in *Bon Appétit*!"

He was in *what*?

"Oh gosh," Zander said with a laugh. "How'd you see that?"

"I googled you as soon as Penny told me you'd come back. Duh. Pen, did you see that article about a restaurant Zander started?"

Penny shook her head vehemently. "I didn't google him. That's not actually a normal thing to do."

"You should. This guy is, like, a big deal." He grinned at Zander. "What do they call you, a restaurateur?"

Zander's laugh was deep and resonant. "I avoid that word because it sounds too fancy, but technically, yes. All it means is that I help start restaurants."

"And you've started a bunch, right?"

If Penny had a clear view through his veil, she would swear Zander was blushing.

"Um, yeah. Over a dozen in the last few years."

"That's so cool," RJ proclaimed. "What's that like? Like, what do you actually do?"

Penny turned quickly and moved to dampen the smoker. She had nothing to gain by learning more about Zander, which was why she'd resolutely *not* hit enter after typing his name into a search engine the night before.

"I help start restaurants, but I'm not the chef or anything," Zander said from behind her. "I help pull together all the pieces. I work with chefs but also investors, contractors, and marketers. I got into it because I'd worked a long time in kitchens and wanted to keep more human hours for my days with Winter."

"That's *so* awesome," RJ replied enthusiastically, as if Zander had told him he'd solved climate change. "I've just started gravitating to baking in the last few years. You saw those pies I've been doing, and I have a few other ideas if I can find the time."

"Always here to taste test, man."

"What?" RJ sounded like he'd won the lottery. "That would be awesome. I'll bring you guys some samples for sure! Speaking of you guys—hey, Winter!"

From her crouch, Penny looked over a shoulder to see Winter

kicking the dirt. The smile he'd had for the bees was long gone. Hadn't taken him long to return to the brooding kid she'd seen the other day. "Hey."

"I remember spotting you last June, but word is you all are here for the whole summer, right?"

"Yeah." He shrugged. "Mom and Dad are making me stay the whole time."

Zander clapped a gloved hand over his shoulder. "And we're going to make the best of it, aren't we, bud?"

Winter only rolled his eyes, but RJ wasn't dampened.

"It won't be half bad, I promise. I teach a basic skating skills class for kids your age if you ever want to get out on the ice while you're here. And we have a pretty cool Fourth of July celebration with fireworks over the lake, and then . . ." He glanced at Penny as the easy smile on his face morphed to something else. Something calculating. "The Honey Festival." RJ smiled back at Zander. "You guys will be here for the Honey Festival."

"That sounds cool," Zander offered. "Right, Winter?"

"I guess. Honey's cool."

"It's a great event," RJ went on. "It was really small years ago, started by Penny's grandma, but now it's a whole thing. Downtown closed off, vendors all over, music, food, the whole shebang. And it's all planned by this little lady right here."

Penny stood quickly. "I doubt they're very interested in hearing about it."

"And you know what? This year it's even bigger than before, but Pen is still doing all the work. I can't do more because of my family stuff, and Ruth isn't the best co-planner."

Penny cleared her throat. "RJ." They'd known each other forever, so RJ had to recognize her *cut it the fuck out* tone.

"But Zander," RJ bowled ahead. He knew her tone all right,

and was blatantly ignoring it. "You've got this great skill set from your work. Juggling all those balls, right? You probably manage invoices in your sleep. I mean, setting up a restaurant sounds a lot like planning a big event."

Zander shifted on his feet, his big bee suit rustling. "Um, maybe?"

"Dude! It's fate that you're here for the summer, just as the hardest parts of the festival are coming together."

"I'm not sure I know what you're—"

But RJ interrupted Zander with a happy clap. "You can help Penny with the festival!"

As soon as Penny stopped this conversation, she'd sneak into RJ's house and break all his hockey sticks.

"Oh, I don't know—" Zander started.

"I bet you could be so helpful," RJ rushed. "You have the perfect experience for this! Think about how you could show off your new life to the whole town."

But Penny had had enough. "No, RJ." She threw the rest of her hive tools into a bucket and stomped to her friend's side. "I don't need Zander for this."

Zander glared at her as his jaw went tense. "While I have no doubt that I could prove to be extremely useful, my priority this summer is to spend time with Winter—"

"But the Honey Festival sounds cool," Winter chimed in. "If Penny needs help, you should help her. We made a deal."

At the mention of a mysterious deal, Zander's face softened. "Hey now, I said I'd try to make the best of it. Not that I'd start planning local festivals."

"Whatever," Winter huffed. "Knew you'd back out."

"Really. It's not necessary." Penny unzipped her hood and yanked it off. "I don't need any help."

RJ stepped toward her, tipping his face down and lowering

his volume. "You know that's not true, Pen. Not with everything riding on this."

Behind them, Zander and Winter engaged in their own whispering battle.

"RJ," she warned quietly. "*Enough*. This isn't happening."

"Penny, you are being so—"

"I wish you'd just stay out of my—"

"It's because I care about—"

Zander interrupted their go-around. "Actually"—he nodded to Winter, then focused on Penny—"I'd love to help out."

No fucking way. "Did you fail to notice I didn't ask for your help? If you think you can waltz into town and act like you—" Winter's widened eyes stopped Penny's words in her throat. She shouldn't ruin his time with the bees by unleashing on his dad, even if Zander was asking for it.

RJ stepped in, smiling broadly. "Tell you what, Winter? Sounds like your dad and Penny need to work out some details like mature, reasonable adults. Why don't we do some of that pie taste testing right now? I happen to know Penny's mom has some in her kitchen."

"There's not anything to work out—" Penny blurted.

RJ flung an arm around Winter's shoulders. "I'll get his suit back in the trunk, and Zander can come grab him at the house." He passed Penny, bumping her shoulder with his as he whispered, "I know you're pissed at me right now, but try to consider this. I think it could be really good."

"RJ. I swear to god, if you actually leave right now—"

But they were already gone, headed down the path as RJ asked Winter if he ever watched hockey. Penny tossed her veil on the ground before stomping to the hive and replacing the lid, all too aware of Zander behind her, watching.

"You can take your suit off," she called behind her. "The bees are docile; we were mostly suited up for Winter's sake. Just leave it on the ground and I'll take it back."

The zipper scraped open as he cleared his throat. "You don't want to talk about—"

"No." Penny turned as Zander stepped out of his suit, his hair ruffled and wild. She would absolutely not think about how it would feel in her fingers, just like she wouldn't imagine the sandpaper of his cheek beneath her palm. The steady order of her day—the order she needed to get everything done—was disturbed, but not beyond repair. She just had to get away from this guy. "RJ was overstepping. I don't need any help."

Zander shook out his suit and folded it carefully. "Between this and the way you tried to bite my head off when I stepped in at the market, I get the feeling you don't like letting people help you, Penny."

"Wow, so observant."

Penny knew that most so-called help was rarely useful. For her mom, help usually meant chiming in with extra ideas or flighty plans that didn't materialize while Penny did the grunt work. And Penny was paying the price, literally, of Henry's "help" in expanding Becker Farms. Accepting help meant accepting more messes to clean up.

Messes she couldn't afford when her whole way of life was on the line. And if Zander promised anything, it was mess.

She reached for the suit in Zander's hands. But when she tugged, he didn't let go.

"You don't think I can do it." He glared at her, dark eyes sharp. "This place doesn't let a kid just grow up, does it? It doesn't matter to you that I'm actually successful, that I have people blowing up my phone to get me to take on their projects.

It doesn't matter that this weekend I actually *was* helpful, even if you're determined not to admit it. I'll never be more to you than that kid who ran away."

"Is that what this is about, Zander? Your ego? You're upset I'm not begging you for your expertise? Does it hurt your feelings to think that I could put together the festival without your know-how?"

"I don't give a shit about your festival, Penny. But I'm tired of you thinking I'm some kind of fuckup."

Penny clasped her hands on her hips and stepped closer. "Why do you care what I think?"

Zander laughed but didn't look happy. He just stared at her, shaking his head. "I wish I knew. I really do."

He paced away from her, then spun back. "Just do whatever you want. Forget I offered to help. Do everything perfectly all on your own."

"I will." Penny yanked off her remaining glove and reached for her zipper. She would do it on her own, just like she always did. Even if it meant a lot of sleepless nights for the next few weeks. Because someone like Zander, for all the magazines he might be in, couldn't ever understand what this festival meant to her. "And I'm not *perfect*," she added. "But I am reliable, and I know what I'm doing because it's always come down to me to do it."

The clearing was quiet but for the buzz of the bees and the grating of Penny's zipper. She shrugged the suit off her shoulders, leaving it to hang off her hips as the breeze cooled her arms, left bare in her ribbed white tank. Penny raised her eyes back to Zander, ready for his cutting glare.

But he didn't look angry anymore. He was focused and intent, his blue T-shirt straining over his chest as his gaze moved over her body. Slowly. Thoroughly, like he was committing something to memory.

In their short interactions, Penny had seen Zander sarcastic and closed-off that first day, then soft and charming with his son and the farmer's market customers. She'd seen him curious and cautious with the hive, then tinged with wonder as they watched the bee emerge. But she hadn't seen him like this, studying her without pretense. It made her dizzy, and angry, but also warm and liquid, like the heated honey she poured into her tidy-jars.

She resisted the urge to tug at her braid, planting her hands firmly on her hips instead. If this was some intimidation tactic, he'd be sorely disappointed, because Penny never backed down. "*What?*"

Zander chuckled softly, shaking his head. "I don't know."

"What do you mean you don't—" Penny stopped as Zander stepped toward her. "What are you *doing*?"

"I told you." Leaves crunched under his feet as Zander came closer still. "I don't have a clue."

"If you're trying to play some kind of mental game to get me to back down, you're out of luck. I'm tougher than that."

"I know." His grin widened. "I bet you're tougher than most people realize. Those pretty braids don't have me fooled."

Penny grew traitorously warm, her brain tripping between his throwaway comment about her toughness and the remark about her pretty braids.

Zander's hand lifted slowly between them, hovering in the air as his gaze trailed up the braid draped over her shoulder. She should step back, put space between them, but she didn't. Whatever game Zander was playing, she'd be there toe-to-toe. So when his fingers stretched toward her, she only watched as he stopped just before touching her hair, then stood steady as his index finger and thumb rubbed together slowly inches from her. She sucked in a breath and let it burn her lungs as his eyes raked over her face.

"Penny Becker." His voice was rough like the tree trunks around them. The kind of rough that felt good on her skin. "You really fuck me up."

Her breath released, carrying with it an awkward, stilted laugh. His eyes dipped to her mouth, narrowing as she reflexively licked her lips.

"Zander Bouras." It was barely a whisper. "Likewise."

And even with the bees buzzing inside her head now, Penny knew it was the first true thing they'd said to each other.

With a sharp inhale, Zander stepped back and cleared his throat. "I better find my kid."

Penny swallowed and nodded, wondering what in the hell had just happened. "Just follow that path where RJ went. It passes my cabin, then the vegetable garden, then you'll see the house."

Zander started his way there, giving Penny a wide berth as he passed. His footfalls stopped for a moment, but she didn't turn around.

"And Becker." His voice was smoother now, back to normal. Missing something. "Good luck with your honey festival."

# CHAPTER 10

It was just Zander's luck that the day after walking away from Penny in the bee yard and vowing to avoid her at all costs, he'd find a goddamn beehive in his grandfather's house.

He was chipping old paint from the windowsill in Winter's room when he noticed bees, a lot of bees, moving in and out of a small opening under the eave.

Winter inspecting a beehive with a full bee suit on was one thing; thousands of those stingers outside his son's window was another. So Zander'd searched online, sure he could find someone *else* to come remove the hive.

Someone he wasn't always fighting with. Someone who didn't look at him like she was just waiting for his next mistake. Someone who didn't make his blood boil and his hands restless and his brain revert to some sort of adolescent stage of dirty thoughts, like wrapping his fist around that pretty braid and tugging her toward him.

But everyone he called told him the same thing: if you're in Sullivan's Glen, Penny Becker is the one to call.

Which was why, the day after Zander's brain was rearranged just from watching her unzip that bee suit, Penny Becker was climbing a ladder leaning against the house.

She'd arrived just a few minutes ago without fanfare, simply slamming her truck door and grabbing her ladder. Before he could offer to carry it for her, she'd boosted it over her shoulder and followed his directions to the side of the house, then did a few trips from her truck to collect buckets and a black bag, leaving them all at the foot of the ladder.

"Um," he finally said, hands stuffed in his back pockets. "Thanks for coming."

As Penny paused with a hand on one rung, brow furrowed and lips tight against her teeth, Zander was struck again by the sensation of watching her through a pane of glass, something distorted and a little wobbly keeping them each from seeing the other clearly. But at that moment near the bees the day before—when he'd spoken a few honest words and almost touched her golden braid—he thought maybe he'd tapped a crack in their barrier.

She ascended the ladder in jeans and a loose-fitting Becker Farms shirt, her eyes blocked by a pair of red sunglasses.

"What about the bee suit?" he called up.

When she looked down, the sun behind her lit her up like some kind of shiny angel.

"I doubt I'll need it," she called back. "If you want to make yourself useful, you could bring my stuff up to this window and pass me things from there."

He fought a smile. "If I didn't know better, I'd say you were asking for my help."

"You think I don't do this by myself all the time?" she shot back. "I'm trying to give you something to do so you stop pacing down there like some mother hen, but I already regret it."

"I'm not—" But the worn ground beneath him didn't lie. Watching Penny throw a ladder against the house, secure it with rope, and climb twenty feet up might have made him a little anxious. "I don't love heights, okay? But lugging tools I can do."

He carried everything upstairs in two trips, then managed to shimmy open the window. Just outside, Penny slid her glasses off her face and inspected the area above the window. She was irritatingly vulnerable, bare arms and hands, her freckled face available to any passing bee.

"Are you *sure* you don't even need gloves on?"

Penny didn't bother looking at him. "If I get a sense that they're liable to get upset, I'll go down and suit up. But generally, if we're gentle with them, they're gentle back. Just don't kill any that fly your way. A dead bee releases pheromones that signal to the others that they're in danger."

"Oh, shit. Okay. No killing bees, got it."

Her fingers curled around the wood at her eye level. "I'm going to pull off this soffit. I think they're behind here."

"Okay." Zander nodded. "But also, what's a soffit?"

She lowered her eyes to him. "Seriously? Aren't you fixing up this house?"

"Trying." And realizing he was in a little over his head. "But what does that have to do with a—whatsitcalled?"

"A soffit." Her hair was pulled back in a bun today, and a few strands blew loose around her face. "It's the piece under the eave. It's a basic part of a house."

"I've, uh, never lived in a house, so—" Zander shrugged to hide his embarrassment. "Just apartments and shitty duplexes and stuff. Besides this place, I guess. But I didn't really care about soffits when I was sixteen."

"Right." Penny blinked at him. "That makes sense. Anyway, I'll take it off and we'll see what's back there."

Zander crouched by the window as Penny pried off a six-inch

piece of soffit, gave it a couple of shakes, and passed it through the window without taking her attention from the bees.

She pulled a small Maglite from her pocket and pointed it under the eaves. "Doesn't look like they go back too far, so that's good. Shouldn't be too hard to get them out of here. Hand me the smoker, will you? And the vacuum in that black bag."

"Vacuum? What the hell?" Maybe Zander hadn't thought this through. "Winter will never speak to me again if he finds out I had a colony of bees killed."

"Relax." She laughed, a sound lovely enough for Zander to forget why calling Penny had been a bad idea. Or maybe it was a bad idea because her laugh was so lovely. "It doesn't hurt them, just makes it easier to move them. If you'd prefer, I could climb up and down the ladder carrying handfuls of bees—"

"No. Absolutely not." His heart beat double time just thinking about it. "Vacuum it is. Then what will happen to them?"

"I'll cut out the comb so they can reuse it, and move it and the bees into an empty hive box I brought. If I can find the queen, I'll leave her in a clip in the hive for a couple of days, and it should encourage the colony to take up residence."

"The clip—"

"Doesn't hurt her. *Chill*." Penny rolled her eyes, but a smile still played on her lips. "It's basically a little plastic cage just big enough to keep her in. Her pheromones can get out, and worker bees can get to her, but she can't leave. This will give everybody time to get acquainted with the new space and prevent them from coming back up here."

Damn. She had every base covered. "You've done this a lot."

She tilted her head, maybe as surprised by this half-polite conversation as he was. "Yes. I was in high school when I did my first removal."

"Your parents let you climb ladders like this when you were a *kid*?"

Penny's face went blank for a second. "Um, yeah. My mom was busy with other stuff; I think she was happy to hand this part over."

"What about your dad? Is he a beekeeper, too?"

"My *dad*?" Her blue eyes narrowed. "Why would you ask that?"

"He's not on the website, but I kind of figured this was a family thing. Or maybe he has a boring office job."

Penny's dad was probably a mild-mannered guy with graying blond hair and an ugly tie. He'd loved coming home to his little freckled daughter every night, and now he brags to all his buddies about his golden girl.

Penny gaped at him. "You actually don't know."

Zander leaned forward, angling his head to see her better. "Don't know what?"

Penny glanced to the bees as her hands twisted at her waist. "My dad left. When my mom was pregnant with me. He's never been around."

"Shit, Penny, I'm sorry. I didn't realize. I just assumed—"

"It didn't occur to me you wouldn't know." She finally looked back at him, her cheeks a bright pink. "It's public knowledge: my dad left us just like my mom's dad left before that. It's sort of a joke in town, how we scare men away."

Two dipshit men had walked away from the Beckers, and the town *joked* about it?

"That's a bad fucking joke," he said gruffly. "Like a man walking away from his kid is anyone's fault but his own."

She just blinked at him. From his position below her, Zander had the perfect view of Penny's pale throat as she swallowed. "No one's ever put it quite that way."

He rested his forearms on the window. "You probably already know my dad was a deadbeat, too. My mom says she doesn't know who he is, but she's slipped up enough here and there that I know it's BS. And maybe you don't need to hear it, but my therapist once said, 'A man who'd leave like that would have been a shitty father, so it's probably best he's gone.'"

Penny's eyes narrowed as she chewed on her lower lip, watching him. He'd probably made it too personal, but Zander knew all too well that jokes about someone's absent parent were actually the least fucking funny thing in the world, and it pissed him off that Penny'd been subjected to it.

After a moment, she climbed down a few rungs, bringing them eye to eye. "I thought you'd left."

"Left what?"

"When people started talking about you and Mallory splitting up, I just assumed—"

Zander's chest tightened. "You assumed I'd *left* them?" His family? His *kid*? The thought of it made him dizzy. And angry. "Because that's the kind of guy you think I am."

"No. I mean, yes. But no." She wiped a hand across her face, and even though Zander was pissed, because Winter was the center of his whole world, he would really prefer Penny keep both damn hands on the ladder.

"I didn't know what kind of guy you were," she continued, urgency in her voice. "I realize that now. I thought I knew, but really—"

She sighed, seeming resigned. "I never knew you back then. I mean, obviously, we never even talked. I just went off gossip and stories." Her gaze drifted past him, into the house. "I never thought about what it was really like here for you."

"It sucked," he told her flatly. "If you're wondering. My mom needed a break from me every summer, presumably so she could get as fucked-up as she wanted. So she sent me here, to a cold man I was constantly disappointing and a town full of people who were always just waiting for me to fuck up."

And the look on her face—stricken, sad—almost made him regret his honesty. But Zander found he wanted to keep cracking that glass between them, to see what might happen if he kept tapping. "But whoever I was then, Penny, I worked like hell to grow up, to be something different for Winter."

"I know." Penny let out a long, slow breath. "I know. And I'm sorry for assuming you hadn't. I should have let you grow up, even just in my head."

She lifted a hand again, sweeping hair out of her face, and all Zander could see was the sky behind her, all the air high above the ground. He shot a hand out to cover the one Penny still had on the ladder, wrapping his fingers around hers to keep her attached. "It would be much easier to accept your apology if you would please keep both your hands on the ladder."

Penny looked to where his hand draped over hers, then raised her brows at him. "I can't do my work with both hands on the ladder."

"Lucky for me you aren't doing your work right now. So please put your other hand back so I can apologize, too."

The corner of her mouth tipped up. "You're going to apologize?"

"Your other hand, Becker."

Penny sighed dramatically and returned her other hand to the ladder. It was time to let her go. But this wasn't a touch through the bee suit, this was the real thing—Zander's skin on hers. Penny's hand was soft and warm, flexing beneath his palm. He wasn't ready to give it up just yet.

If she noticed, it didn't wipe the smile off her face. "I hope this isn't going to be like the apology you gave Brad Preston."

Zander laughed. "That was pretty good, huh?"

She shrugged. "It was all right."

"Oh, come on—"

Penny's eyebrows arched. "Don't change the subject."

"Okay." Zander cleared his throat. "I don't know a delicate way to say this," he started tentatively. "But I kind of hated you."

Penny's pretty mouth dipped in a frown. "We didn't even know each other."

"I didn't say it was reasonable. But one of my first days here, I walked through those trees between our houses, and I saw you laughing with your family, and I just—" He swiped a thumb across her hand, grounded by the contact even as she was twenty feet up. "I hated you for having the things I wanted."

Her smile fell. "Zander—"

"And then my papou." Zander shook out a gravelly laugh. "You don't even know, Penny. You were this model child in his mind. He was always telling me about everything you did to help your family, how well you did at school, how much everyone loved you. You were everything I'd never be. You were so perfect, and I hated you for it."

Penny swallowed and blinked, her eyes shining. "I'm not perfect. I've never been perfect. And I hate that anything I did was used against you."

"So do I. But it was *my* problem that I held on to it for so long." Zander finally lifted his hand from Penny's and presented it to her, palm open. "Fresh start?"

She eyed his offer. "You know I'll have to let go of the ladder to shake your hand?"

He lifted his brows. "But you'll be holding on to me, so you'll still be safe."

Her eyes, lighter than the deep blue of afternoon behind her, stayed on him as she pressed her palm to his. "Fresh start."

But Zander didn't let go, because he wasn't done. There was one more thing he wanted.

"Let me help with the Honey Festival."

Her smile vanished. "I thought that was settled."

"That was before our fresh start." Zander lowered Penny's hand back to the ladder, making sure she was holding on before he threaded his fingers together on the windowsill. "What you said before, about how you didn't let me grow up in your mind. About how you assumed I was just like those old stories . . ."

"I said I was sorry."

"That's how everyone here is looking at me. You saw that at the market with Brad. With everybody watching, waiting for me to react like an angry teenager. Like that destructive kid who was always looking for trouble." He shook his head, remembering that afternoon with Winter, the slam of the screen door, and a promise. "I promised Winter I would try to make this summer work. And I can't do that if no one sees me as more than that kid I was. This is something I can do—something real and concrete and actually helpful—to show this place that I'm worthwhile. To show Winter that *I'm* worthwhile."

"The festival." Penny spoke slowly, like every word was chosen with care. "This year especially, it's . . ." She sighed. "It's really important. It might seem silly, because it's just some small-town event, but it's really, *really* important to me. And I can't afford to have you jump in to make yourself a hero and leave me hanging."

Zander was set to argue his case, but then he remembered all the times, even in the short period he'd known her this summer, that she'd steadfastly refused help. Maybe it hadn't been because she was perfect, but because she hadn't found the people who were good at helping her.

"Let me start with a small job to prove my mettle. If I screw it up, you can fire me, no hard feelings."

She scrutinized him with narrowed eyes. "One small job."

"One small job."

She grinned, just barely. "And if you want this badly to prove yourself, I want something else out of the deal."

"Anything."

Penny's gaze dropped to his mouth as Zander gripped the windowsill so hard that old paint chipped beneath his fingers. If there wasn't a window frame between them, if she wasn't dangerously high off the ground . . .

"I want you to help RJ."

Zander coughed, righting his overactive brain. "RJ? How?"

"He won't shut up about you since you said his pastry looked perfect. He holds a lot—stuff at the farm, stuff for his mom—and baking has made him happy. I want you to use your fancy business skills to see if you can help him take it further, maybe make a business out of it."

Penny might not want his help, but she did see some value in him for RJ, and it satisfied Zander more than it should have. "You think I have fancy business skills, huh?"

"Come on," she groaned. "Is it a deal or not?"

Never in Zander's life would he have predicted that he'd be bargaining with a woman on a ladder to win himself a spot planning a honey festival, but here he was. Back in Sullivan's

Glen, fighting to keep his promise to his kid. And, if he was being honest with himself, looking forward to spending a little more time with Penny Becker.

"Deal."

"Okay." Penny stepped higher on the ladder. "Then open up the black bag and hand me the vacuum. It's time to collect some bees."

# CHAPTER 11

"I love this color on you, it's very springtime."

RJ blew on Penny's newly painted Lovely Lavender toes. They reminded her of the lavender patch in her mom's garden, the blooms a muted purple.

"Why, thank you. Your color is very . . ." Penny scanned RJ's legs where they stretched out beside her. His fluffy blue robe split open to reveal his pajamas, a blue background covered in heart-eyed emojis, and, farther down, toes that were very . . . "Bright?"

He gasped. "You don't like my Mango Bango?"

"I love it," she assured him. "As long as it's on your toes, not mine."

"You don't have to embrace my color choices," RJ assured her. "I'm just glad you showed up for Spa Night. I know how busy you are."

Penny nudged a foot against RJ's leg. "How could you doubt me? Spa Nights are sacred."

With the exception of a week she'd been knocked out by the flu, Penny'd made every Spa Night with RJ since he instituted the tradition just after her breakup with Henry. RJ hadn't made her talk about her feelings—he knew Penny preferred action—but he *had* insisted that they spend time together outside of work, and the Spa Night tradition was born. This week RJ had gone all out, surprising Penny with fresh pajamas and luxurious robes for both of them. Penny's pajamas were pink with red cardinals on pine branches, the robe a red to match the birds. He'd even whipped up an avocado-honey mask, which they'd smeared on their faces before starting on their toes.

"Soooo . . ." RJ let the word drag, and Penny knew just what it meant. She'd gone a whopping thirty-six minutes without talking about a certain someone, and that time was at an end. "I got an interesting text from Zander today."

"Did you?"

RJ scooted across the old wood floor until his hips were lined up with Penny's. He looked fairly ridiculous covered in avocado, only his brown eyes and lips exposed.

"Zander said he'd love to help me scale up my baking business. I wonder where he got that idea. Or, better yet, how he got my number?"

Trusting that her nails were dry, Penny stood up and stretched, working out the kinks from sitting on the floor and retying her robe. It was silly to change into pajamas when she'd be going home to sleep, but RJ insisted they model their new looks. And she was super comfy.

Penny put the kettle on and riffled through the cabinet for the jar of dried chamomile flowers she'd gathered from Becker Farms gardens the summer before. "Couldn't say."

Still on the floor, RJ stretched to touch his toes. "This is your doing, I assume?"

"I may have suggested he check in with you about it. You seemed so excited about his restaurant prowess, after all."

"Interesting." RJ stood and shook out each leg. "Last I heard, you'd turned down his generous offer of help with the festival and were refusing to talk to me about anything pertaining to, and I quote, *that annoying man*. Should I take it that something has changed?"

Penny pulled out a pinch of chamomile and held it under her nose. The dried flowers evoked long evenings of summer. "I'm not sure." She dropped the chamomile into the tea strainer. "I went over to his grandfather's house yesterday to remove a swarm. We ended up talking more."

RJ pulled a mug for her from his cabinet. "And?"

"And . . ." How could she put it into words when she was still searching her mind for a landing place after the last few days? "I guess he's not as bad as I thought. We both admitted that we'd maybe made some assumptions about each other, and we agreed to start fresh, whatever that means."

"And . . . ?" RJ slid a mug to her as his brows raised.

"And." Penny sighed, knowing an *I told you so* wasn't far away. "I told him he could help with the festival, on a trial basis."

RJ's grin was smug as hell. "Because you realized it was actually a great idea, huh?"

"Because he gave me a line about wanting to prove to everyone that he's grown up, showing people how he's more than the person they remember."

Although comparisons between their childhoods were slim, Penny understood Zander's urge. Growing up under the noses of everyone in town meant everyone knew her, but she sometimes wondered which version of her they knew. When they talked to Penny at the market, did they still see the little girl with perpetually skinned knees? Or the quiet teenager who stood at the edge of school dances? Did they see her now—running the market stand, keeping Becker Farms just barely above water—and assume she didn't have a problem in the world, the way Zander had?

"And maybe I realized he had some skills that could be useful," she added. "And because he agreed to help you, too."

RJ bumped his shoulder into hers. "Aw, Pen, you're the best friend a guy could ask for. What job did you give him?"

"I'm gathering up all the invoices from last year. I figure he can look through everything for places to cut costs, and it'll keep him from messing up anything already in process this year." A twinge of guilt twisted in her gut, recalling his defensiveness about being seen as a fuckup. "Not that I think he'd mess something up, it's just—"

"Hard for you to relinquish any control?" RJ smirked. "Gosh, I hadn't ever realized that about you."

"You're hilarious." Steam curled into the air as Penny poured water over the tea. "He said that when we were teenagers, when he was here in the summers, he hated me because he thought I was perfect."

RJ frowned, pulling a jar of Becker Farms honey from a cabinet. "You two never even talked, right?"

"No, we didn't. He always just glared at me, and I never understood why. He told me his grandfather used to say he should be more like me."

She'd judged Zander for never coming back to see his grandfather, but this tiny insight into their relationship shed new light on why he'd stayed away.

RJ whistled as he pulled a quart of goat milk from the fridge and slid it across the counter to Penny. "That's messed up."

"I know. And yesterday he kept saying things about how

much I knew about the bees, how much I must do to keep the farm going."

When Penny'd continued with the hive removal, vacuuming up the majority of the bees before cutting down sections of comb, Zander peppered her with questions about what she was doing, marveling at each new detail.

"You *do* know a lot about the bees," RJ said. "And you *do* do a lot to keep the farm running. What's wrong with him noticing that?"

Penny stirred in the milk and honey, giving herself a moment to let the aroma envelop her. "I feel like a fraud. He's over there thinking, what? That I'm some kind of superwoman? Meanwhile, he doesn't know how much I have riding on this festival, how much I've royally screwed up."

"You are not a fraud." RJ took the mug from her hand and set it on the counter. "You made some decisions that are blowing up now, yes. And, in the opinion of one very wise friend, you're compounding those problems by keeping them to yourself. But you get to be a competent beekeeper *and* a person with some problems at the same time." He held Penny's shoulders and gave them a squeeze. "That's called being human. You've just been an overachiever for so long you don't have much practice."

RJ paced across the kitchen, finally stopping in front of their leftover takeout, which Penny knew he'd finish before the night was out. Her best friend consumed a mind-boggling number of calories.

He pulled out a clean fork and pointed it at her. "Now that I think about it, you and Zander have that in common. You were overlooked at home, so you compensated by working so hard and being so perfect that people couldn't ignore you. Zander felt overlooked and misunderstood, and he compensated by committing mischief and getting in trouble."

"I'm not sure I like you since you started therapy."

"And now, you just both need people who really see you."

"Enough. We're not *seeing* each other."

"You could, though."

"Could what?"

"Could see each other. I was only around you both for a few minutes, but that was enough time for me to pick up on it. Not being into sex myself doesn't mean I can't sense sexual tension. Especially when it's *thick*. He was checking you out while you were in the bee suit, Pen. That thing is practically a burlap sack. And now you've got this fresh start . . ."

Penny clutched her tea and went to the couch. "We aren't talking about this."

RJ sat beside her with a huff. "I know you haven't been with anyone since Henry, and that's been . . . what? Two years?"

Had it really been that long? Penny lived her life by the seasons, always managing one set of tasks while preparing for the next set around the bend. Sometimes she'd look up and realize a whole half year had gone by in the snap of a finger.

Things slowed in the winter months, when deep snow blanketed the ground and the whole farm went into a quiet dormancy. Winter was when she rested and read, when she laid plans for the spring and spent time with her mother and Mimi.

And time went by like that. Sometimes it was lonely, but mostly it was busy and beautiful.

"I haven't really missed it," she told RJ truthfully. "After Henry, I kind of resigned myself to doing things on my own." When RJ grinned behind his hand, she rolled her eyes. "Not just the sex stuff. *Everything*."

"Just tell me this," RJ said. "Do you like Zander?"

"I tried not to like him," she admitted. "It was easy to think of Zander as some jerk who hates this town, just another guy who's left and didn't want to come back."

"But he's more than that."

She remembered his hand over hers on the ladder, the way he'd thought of her safety even after she'd accused him of abandoning his family. "Yeah."

RJ crossed his arms over his chest with a satisfied smile. "Because we're all more than what people see."

Penny laughed. "When did this turn into an after-school special?"

"So you wouldn't be opposed to seeing him again?"

If her body's reaction—going a little warm and fizzy all over, especially when she remembered his smile in the sunshine as he examined the queen bee in her cage the day before, talking to her quietly about her new hive—was any indication, Penny was not opposed to seeing Zander again. But that fizziness wasn't something to indulge, not when she had so much to do. So she'd leave the envelope of invoices on his front porch and go about her business. Unless Zander found another colony of bees somewhere in his house, they didn't have a reason to see each other again. When a light knock rapped on the front door, RJ rushed to answer.

Penny watched with confusion. They'd already had their food delivered, and RJ always kept Spa Nights clear of interruptions. "Are you expecting someone?"

"Well." RJ pulled open the door. "As a matter of fact, I am. He's just a little early."

Zander filled the doorway in jeans and a Detroit Tigers T-shirt. He gave RJ a wide smile, and the two of them started talking, exchanging words Penny didn't catch inside her muffled brain. Then he laughed at something RJ said, and swiveled so his attention landed on Penny.

"Penny." His hands fisted over his stomach before he stuffed them into his back pockets and rocked back on his heels. "Hey."

"Hi." She tightened the neck of her robe. Oh god, her *robe*. And her *pajamas*. "I didn't realize you were coming." She did her best to shoot daggers at RJ. "No one mentioned this."

RJ ushered Zander inside. "Zander asked for some records of sales I've had so far, pricing and numbers of pies and stuff. I have all of that written down in my ledger, so I told him he should stop by for it."

*Ledger?* Penny would bet all her beehives that RJ had learned that word today.

Zander's eyes still hadn't left Penny, roaming over her face and the robe she was re-cinching tight around her waist. He cleared his throat. "Maybe I'm interrupting something?"

"No!" RJ moved to the desk across the room and opened and closed some drawers. He was such a little shit. So far, RJ's small-time baking business had been a strictly fly-by-the-seat-of-his-pants operation, which was exactly why Penny had asked Zander to help him out. "Penny and I just have these spa nights from time to time. You know we grew up together, right? We're like family."

Zander's gaze flitted between them. "That must be nice."

"It's the best." RJ shuffled papers around. "When we were kids, our moms joked about us getting married, but that's not in the cards. On top of Penny being way too type A for me, I'm ace—" He twisted to look at Zander. "That's short for asexual, if you're not up on the rainbow alphabet. But Penny isn't. I mean, she *really* loves—"

"RJ," Penny barked. "Please stop. Just find your damn *ledger*."

Zander grinned at Penny, clearly biting back a bigger smile. "Nice toes. That's a good shade on you. The color on your face is a nice touch, too."

She felt her face—her dried, cracking, green face.

Despite her silent prayers, a swarm of bees did not choose that moment to enter RJ's house and cause an end to this encounter.

"So," Zander said slowly. "I'm waiting with bated breath for that first assignment. You're not going to renege on our agreement, are you?"

"No, I'm—" *Covered in dried avocado, totally unable to think, and your T-shirt is the perfect size.* "Planning to drop it off for you tomorrow or the next day. I'm gathering up stuff from last year, thinking maybe you could—" Penny cinched her robe again. She was not going to discuss the Honey Festival in fuzzy pink PJs. "You know what? I'll just leave a note with it explaining everything. Just drop it on your porch and be on my way."

"Sure, okay." Zander nodded. "If you tell me when you're coming by, I could—"

"No, no, don't worry. I can just drop it. I don't want to bother you."

A loud bang from the desk made them both jump. Next to RJ, a pile of cookbooks was strewn on the floor. "Oh gosh, so sorry about that," RJ declared. "Didn't meant to interrupt you. Zander, I can't find that ledger after all. I'll work on typing it all up anyway, so maybe we can go over that Tuesday?"

"What happens Tuesday?" Penny asked.

RJ beamed. "Zander and I are going to do some baking."

"Wow." She looked between them. "I'm glad to hear that."

"But wait—oh *shoot*." RJ rubbed a palm along his fuzzy head. "Pen, that reminds me. I can't do next Saturday anymore."

Next Saturday was supposed to be their trip to the Fairy Light Magic display. The place had started years ago as a romantic gesture from a local man to his husband—strings of lights draped among the trees to resemble fairies at play—and was now a local tradition, where families adopted portions of the forests and tended to trails. It was still small and kept largely a secret by locals, but to Penny the place always felt like pure magic.

"Why can't you go?"

"I forgot about a hockey thing. Got a big game."

"Isn't it your bye week? That's why we were going on Saturday in the first place."

RJ swallowed. "Oh, yeah. Well, I said I'd sub for someone else. I'm so sorry, Pen." He clapped his hands. "But you know what? Maybe Zander can go with you."

*This little fucker.*

"Zander, you've never seen it, right?" RJ barreled on. "It's this awesome place in the woods with all these lights, definitely worth seeing. You could go with Penny!"

"It's fine," Penny said. "I can just go alone."

"No way, Pen. If I'm ditching you so rudely, Zander should go."

"Zander does not want to—"

"I mean," Zander interrupted, running a hand through his hair. "It sounds cool. I wouldn't mind scoping it out to see if it's something Winter would like."

"Exactly! Incredible idea. Scoping it is," RJ exclaimed before Penny could respond, then quickly ushered Zander to the door. "Again, so sorry about the ledger. I could have sworn I had it. But glad you came by so we could decide on the Fairy Light Magic plan! How about you pick up Penny next Saturday at eight? She'll know how to get there."

Zander peeked at Penny over RJ's shoulder as he was all but pushed out the door. All before Penny could say another word.

"See you then, Penny," Zander said from the doorway. "Feel free to wear your jammies if you want. They look comfortable."

"Yeah, no, she won't do that," RJ answered. "But thanks for coming by, Zander, and I'll see you Tuesday!"

RJ shut the door and turned with a grin so big it cracked his avocado mask.

"RJ," Penny groaned. "What the hell are you doing?"

"Isn't it obvious, Pen?" He leaned against his front door and sighed. "I just got you a date with Zander Bouras."

# CHAPTER 12

"This isn't a date."

Not exactly the first words Zander expected out of Penny's mouth after she'd climbed into his truck.

"Not that you think it's a date, I just wanted you to know *I* don't think it's a date," she continued, sliding her hands beneath her legs as her knees bounced. "Because, you know, there's a date feel with the whole *pick you up at eight* thing and the Fairy Light Magic, which can be romantic. I mean, I wasn't going with RJ romantically, but a lot of people do. Go romantically. On dates. But not us. Actually, I'm not even sure why RJ suggested this."

Zander nodded and bit back a smile. "Don't worry, Penny. I know."

For a woman not on a date, Penny looked really damn cute in a red T-shirt, white denim shorts that showed a dangerous amount of skin, and white sneakers. Her eyelashes looked a little thicker than usual, and her hair was in a long blond braid down her back.

Zander tore his eyes off her thighs and dragged them back to the road as he tugged at his collar. A T-shirt would have been fine, but he'd made the mistake of mentioning the outing to Quinn, who then bombarded him with fashion tips.

*Don't shave. The scruffy thing works for you. And wear the navy blue button-down. Thank me later.*

*Not a date*, he'd replied back quickly.

To which Quinn had simply said, *and Mal says the brown belt. xoxo*

And yeah, he'd worn the button-down and the brown belt. He'd get hell from Quinn otherwise.

"So." He tapped the steering wheel as his truck rumbled down the long drive the Becker property shared with his grandfather's house. "How was your day?"

"Fine. Had the market this morning, then, you know, did bee things."

"Bee things?"

"Yep." Penny's knee was about to bounce her out of the truck.

"Hey." Zander turned onto the two-lane road. On the dash, his phone was set to direct him about fifteen miles out to the Fairy Light Magic spot. "We just established this isn't a date, so relax. We don't have to be awkward."

"I'm not being awkward."

He laughed. "*Bee things?*"

"What? That's what I did."

"Okay. How was the market? Any signs of Brad Preston?"

He caught a glimpse of Penny's grin. "Nope. Not sure he'll be back anytime soon."

"I'm sorry if I lost you a customer."

"Eh." She shrugged. "I'm not."

Zander's face warmed. "I will always remember the look on his face when I apologized."

"I remember when you hit him that summer. It was all anyone could talk about."

Zander tugged at his collar again. "I'm not a violent person. I didn't go around punching people."

"I know. I'm sure I would've heard about it if you had."

"I imagine so." He laughed as they drove through a neighboring town, its main road lined with shops and restaurants just like in Sullivan's Glen. "That day, he said something about my mom. That's why I made an exception."

"I understand, and I'm sorry that happened." After a beat of silence, Penny continued. "I've heard she was really beautiful."

He arched his brows. "I'm sure that's not all you heard."

She shifted, sliding her hands beneath her thighs again. "Will you tell me about her? So I know more than the gossip?"

They pulled up to a stoplight, giving him a chance to look at Penny fully—her inquisitive blue eyes and innocently freckled cheeks.

"My mom is a complicated person," he said finally. "She's diagnosed bipolar now, among other stuff she has going on, so I imagine that was at play back then. From what she's said, she and her dad never got along. I almost suspect she got pregnant so that he'd kick her out and she'd have a final excuse to hate him." When the light turned, he pressed on the gas with some relief. It was easier to talk about his mom while they were moving. "She could be really fun, though. Sometimes she'd pack up the car with snacks and keep me out of school to go to Lake Michigan for the day, or we'd stay up all night watching old movies while she painted her nails and re-dyed her hair."

Later, Zander would understand that these high-energy periods were part of the cycle of her illness, but as a kid he'd looked forward to them, waited for them. "She has a tendency to self-medicate with alcohol and sometimes other stuff, and the cycles became too much for me. I, uh, went no contact with her a year or so ago, but I hope that doesn't have to last forever."

Penny's hand landed on his shoulder, just briefly enough for him to feel the warmth before it was gone. "I hope so, too."

She looked out her window as the town thinned around them, speaking quietly. "It's more complicated than I thought it would be. Working with my mom and grandma all these years. Sometimes my mom especially makes me want to . . ." She sighed. "Who knew being an adult with your parent could be so crazy-making, you know?"

"Oh, come on, Becker." Zander shot her a grin. "Remember, you have the perfect happy family. Don't ruin it for me."

But really, he wanted her to do just that. To show him she was as real as he was.

"I know we're lucky to still work together and like each other after all this time," she said. "But sometimes I look at my mom and wonder if we're actually related. She's always trusting in the universe, believing things will just come together."

"Meanwhile, you're doing the work to make sure everything doesn't fall apart."

Penny was silent as they approached another red light, but Zander sensed her attention. When he looked her way, she was watching him, head slightly tilted.

"Yeah," she said. "It kind of feels like that a lot of the time." She cleared her throat. "Um. So. How was your day?"

Zander wet his dry lips, trying to keep himself from staring at the seat belt cutting across Penny's body. He'd never been so jealous of a piece of fabric. "It was fine."

Penny's brows raised. "*Fine?* Who's being awkward now?"

His grin almost hurt his cheeks. "Why would I be awkward? This isn't a—"

A horn blared behind them, making Zander jump in his seat.

"Jesus." He returned his attention to the road as they moved through the intersection. "My day was interesting. I did work in the house this morning, then experimented with the recipes RJ showed me this week—he's very good, by the way."

"Sometimes I'm afraid people are going to fight over those pies. Are you adjusting his recipes? I mean, how are you going to help him?"

"I'm going to help him one step at a time. Honestly, the baking part was more fun for me than anything, but after my attempts today, I'll leave that to him. This week his homework is to track the ingredients he's using so we can break down a realistic cost per pie instead of just guessing. And speaking of homework, I did mine."

Penny tucked her feet under her as she looked at him. "Oh, I didn't expect you to get to it so quickly."

"You dropped it off Tuesday," Zander answered, grinning at the memory of stepping onto his porch at 7 a.m. only to find an envelope from Penny waiting for him. She was certainly a busy bee.

"I finished up Thursday but figured we could talk about it in person tonight."

"Okay, yeah. What did you—I mean, do you have opinions? Thoughts?"

He sure did. And he wasn't sure she'd want to hear them.

"Penny, I'll say this as nicely as possible, but what the hell are you doing?" Another traffic light gave him the chance to look at her. "When RJ mentioned the festival, it sounded like a community project. I figured you were the main organizer, but that it was put on by some municipal entity. But it's all you. The entire festival is financed by Becker Farms."

Her cheeks went pink as her jaw tensed. "We always break even."

"Yes, I saw that. And it's impressive, seriously." This time, he was paying enough attention to see the light change. No more distracting eye contact with Penny. "But it's also a huge risk, and it's all on you. This festival clearly benefits Sullivan's Glen, so the township—or, at the very least, an LLC made up of stakeholders—should be managing part of it."

Penny swallowed. "I'm not sure what that would look like, but if it will help with the money aspect, I can try to look up—".

"It's too late this year, anyway." Zander's tone was sharper than he intended, but he was frustrated as hell that the whole town would let Penny plan an entire festival *and* take on all the risk. Someone else should have stepped up long before now. He let out a deep breath. "I'm not saying you've done anything wrong. You've done a kick-ass job of this. But you should be getting more help from the people who benefit from the festival. I'll send you some sample agreements that I've used in establishing some LLCs for restaurant ventures, okay? It could be a place to start for next year."

"Sure." Her voice rolled along a sigh. "Next year."

Zander turned and followed the GPS down a narrow road that curved between vineyard rows. As the sun dipped below the line of trees on the hill to the west, the sky deepened into a dark blue.

"But for this year, I have some ideas for some folks I can contact to cut costs. I know a guy who owns an equipment rental company who does work up here, and he owes me a favor, so I'll start there. By leveraging some connections I have, and building in some efficiencies, I think I found us some ways to save money."

Penny perked up at that, sitting up straight. "That would be amazing. But what's this *us*?"

"Us. You and me." He turned down a dirt road, the darkness closing over them as they drew closer to the twinkling lights. "The planners of the Sullivan's Glen Honey Festival."

"I said you could have one job. I never agreed to be an us."

"It was a trial job, and I killed it!" Lines of cars were parked in a clearing, and Zander pulled into a spot. When he shut off the truck and turned toward Penny, her face was barely visible as lights in the forest glowed.

"Tell me why." He took his seat belt off and leaned back against the window. "If you're going to turn me down again, tell me why. Is it because you don't trust me? Because you think I'll mess it up?"

Penny crossed her arms over her chest. "Contrary to what you might think, this isn't all about you."

"What's it about, then? Why do you hate accepting help?"

"I don't."

"Cut the crap, Penny. You seem determined to carry the world on your shoulders. What, do you get off on the martyrdom?"

She gasped. "I don't get *off* on anything."

"Then why—"

"Because most people who say they want to help get bored pretty damn quick, Zander. Because I've made plans thinking I'd have help only to end up doing everything alone, and it fucking sucked."

Seeing anger and sadness in Penny's eyes, Zander knew there were stories there. Stories about people who had let Penny down, starting with her father, who'd taken off before he ever even saw his golden-haired daughter. Stories he didn't have any right asking about, as much as he wanted to.

"This last school year," he said, "Winter started getting into math I didn't know how to do. I can do the basics, of course, and can use formulas to my advantage in a spreadsheet. But Winter was starting to do some stuff with angles and geometry and multiplying fractions, stuff I never grabbed ahold of in school. It sucked not being able to help him. He'd get frustrated and start freaking out, and I was no use. So one night I told him I'd learn it. I'd learn all the math so we could do it together."

"*All* the math?"

"Well," he hedged. "All the math I needed to know to help my fifth grader. I ordered myself some workbooks, watched videos while I was working out. It was elementary school math all the time. At the end of the year, I asked his teacher to give me an exam, and guess what?"

"You passed?"

"Passed? Please." Zander hit the steering wheel. "I got an A. When I decide to do something, I do it. I know people have let you down before, and I'm sorry that's happened. But if I tell you I'm going to help with the festival, you can trust that I'll help with the festival."

Penny's smile was unmistakable, even in the dim truck. "I've never known anyone who begged to volunteer their time."

"Well, Becker, maybe you've never known anyone like me."

"Yeah," she said slowly. "Maybe not."

Her tongue swiped her bottom lip just once, and Zander's whole body went on alert. He was in his truck in a dark forest with Penny Becker, her freckles barely visible and her lips glistening.

Zander's hands flexed in his lap, itching to wrap around her braid and pull her closer to him. To show her how determined he could be when he set his mind to it.

What the hell did this woman do to him?

"Fine," she finally sighed. "You can help. But don't make me regret it or I'll kick your ass."

# CHAPTER 13

"Then three YouTube videos in, I realized it was probably the damn gasket in the P-trap. Once I got that figured out, it was a surprisingly easy fix. Of course, at that point, I was soaking wet and lying in a lukewarm puddle, looking like I'd peed myself."

Zander's shoulder brushed Penny's again as they walked side by side on the narrow path. All around them, clusters of lights twinkled in the dark trees as a gentle breeze played music with the chimes hanging from unreachable branches. Penny was a practical person, but this place—full of magic and whimsy—was something she allowed herself every year. Since she was a girl, she'd walk through this forest and let herself believe the lights really were fairies, their lives as complex and balanced as the bees in her hives.

She'd thought Zander might laugh at the place, or that walking down the trails together would be awkward. But he'd stepped out of the truck and looked at the whole place with wonder, and now Penny's cheeks hurt from laughing at the stories he was telling her about fixing up his grandfather's old farmhouse. Whether it was scraping paint off windowsills or replacing sink parts, Zander described each task as a battle of wills. Like he even had something to prove to the walls.

"But soon I'll be able to set up Winter's room, so he can stay over with me sometimes, if he's willing." Zander's shoulders slumped a little. "I'm not his favorite person lately, but I don't think he'd mind getting some space from everybody at Mal's parents' house. Quinn said he's squirming his way through every family dinner."

"Do you guys split time with him, back in Boston?"

"Yep. I have Fridays through Tuesdays, though we'll sometimes all do things together on the weekend." Twinkly fairy lights sparkled in his eyes. "You can ask, you know."

"Ask what?"

"About Mallory and me. And Quinn. People usually have questions."

Around them, couples and families strolled along the path, eyes wide as they looked from tree to tree. This was a popular spot on a summer night, but with trees looming over them in the darkness and Zander's arm brushing hers, it felt like they were alone.

"You don't owe anyone answers about your life," she told him. "I mean, I do have questions." It would be ridiculous to pretend she didn't. Their situation was unique. "But that doesn't mean I need to ask them."

Zander laughed warmly. "How about this? You ask your questions, then spread whatever I say through the proper gossip channels. That way I don't have to answer them all again from someone else."

"I thought you hated the gossip mill here."

His smile was wry. "Just because you hate something doesn't mean it's not real." The trail turned right, snaking between trees. "First thing to let the good people of Sullivan's Glen know is that Mallory and I haven't slept together in a very long time."

"Zander!" Penny's face warmed. "I don't need to know that."

"If you don't, somebody does. I know people wonder."

Penny cleared her throat, trying to push back the tightness that came with thinking about Zander sleeping with *anyone*. "Noted."

He slowed, looking into the trees just past Penny's shoulder. "And if anyone asks." Zander tipped back onto his heels. Penny was at the perfect height to watch the bob of his throat as he swallowed. "I'm not seeing anyone back in Boston."

"Okay." Penny swayed toward him, eyes still on the thick tendons of his throat and the crisp collar of his shirt. "Good to know."

When she dragged her eyes up, Zander was watching her with a raised brow. "Anything else you're curious about?"

"Um." She stepped back, sucking in air as she started walking again.

This wasn't a date. Yes, they were strolling through a magical forest, and she'd put on mascara and a little lipstick, and Zander was in a collared shirt and a brown leather belt that looked soft enough to pet.

But he was also someone who hated the place she called home, and would be leaving again soon enough. And she'd agreed to let him give her help with the festival—and couldn't risk blowing up that working relationship by giving in to the urge to press her mouth to his neck.

Even though the urge was stronger each time he spoke, or laughed, or smiled at her with that mischievous look in his eye, like he knew just what she was thinking.

She walked on and returned her thoughts to the conversation. "So Quinn and Mallory are together, but Quinn was your friend first?"

"She was. We met through work and hit it off. We'd been friends for a while before she met Mal. I swear it was like Cupid was in the room when they finally met. I couldn't have stopped them from dating even if I'd tried."

"And was that weird for you? Like, even though I'm *way* over my ex, it would be hard seeing him with someone else, especially someone I know."

They'd managed to leave much of the crowd behind, and the forest was filled with sounds of early night, what Mimi called *cricket music*.

"With your ex—" Zander started, leaving her to fill in his name.

"Henry."

"With Henry, I'm going to guess that when you two broke up, you stopped talking altogether."

"Yeah. He, uh, left town." It wasn't the first time he'd left, but it was, finally, the last.

"The last time you saw him, or very close to that last time, you were still together. And you've never had a chance to be anything else together since then. If you saw him, everything that happened between you two would feel fresh."

Penny imagined it: Henry right here in the forest, his skinny frame and curly hair that frizzed when he brushed it, his black frame glasses and green eyes. If she saw him now, would it be like meeting him all over again, when he'd smiled at her from across the room at the apiary conference in Rochester? Or would it be like the last time, his eyes wet and shining as he stood at the edge of her bed?

"Yeah," she squeezed out. "It would feel fresh."

"But with Mal"—Zander ran a hand through his hair—"we had to keep knowing each other. Winter was our top priority, and when we realized it was time for us to separate, we both committed to making parenting work. It was awkward as fuck for a while, and we both did a lot of processing on our own time. But getting to know her that way helped me love her differently, as a friend and an important member of my family. My only family, really."

Fast footsteps thundered toward them, and Zander stepped into Penny, brushing the back of his hand with hers as a child ran past. "Then, by the time she started dating again, I was ready."

"And she started dating your friend."

"Now that did suck for a while," Zander said with a short laugh. "I was happy for them both, but sharing Quinn was hard at first. She and I have done some real trauma bonding over our shitty families, and she's my ride or die. I was worried about losing that."

"Did you?"

"No." He stopped and turned to Penny. Behind him, fairies danced in the trees. "Quinn was awesome about making sure we still spent time together on our own, and once she and Mal got serious, I had to ask myself: Would I choose anyone else to add into our parenting circle? And the answer was no." He shrugged, his eyes still on her. "So here we are."

As silence settled around them, Zander's gaze roamed Penny's face, slowing at her mouth.

She barely got out a whisper. "Here we are."

Behind her, deeper in the forest, a barred owl began a series of loud, trilling hoots. Zander's eyes widened as he searched the trees. "What the *fuck*?"

"Oh, city boy." Penny laughed. "Never heard an owl before?"

"Not like *that*, Christ. It sounds like my downstairs neighbor when he watches Patriots games." Something sparked in his eyes. "Let's go find it."

He swung a long leg easily over the rope strung up to designate the trail's edge.

"Zander!" She grabbed for him, curling her fingers around his thick forearm. "We can't. It's not allowed."

His dark eyes dropped to where Penny touched him, then

looked back to her in challenge. "Come on, Becker. Live a little. You're out here with the town bad boy, remember?"

"I thought you were reformed."

One corner of his mouth tipped up. "Some things never change. Still chasing the thrill." He slipped out of her grip and grabbed her hand as he watched her. "Please?"

The soft brush of Zander's thumb over her knuckles undid any of her remaining hesitancy. "Fine," she sighed, stepping over the rope. "I swear, if we get in trouble—"

But he was already tugging her through the trees. The owl remained silent, but Zander walked on.

He stopped beside a looming pine, finally dropping her hand. "I guess it left." His gaze focused behind her. "Wow."

She spun to look back, where the clusters of lights dotted the landscape. From back here, they looked like—

"Constellations," Penny whispered.

"Beautiful."

"I think I've come here every year of my life. But I've never seen it like this."

Incredible that something in Sullivan's Glen could feel brand-new.

Zander's palm pressed into her lower back, the tips of his fingers their own constellation heating her skin through her thin T-shirt. It was a small touch, an innocent touch, except for how it wasn't.

Like how his fingers traveled up her spine, drawing her breath tight. Or how he toyed with the hem of her shirt, like he was waiting to touch her bare skin just above.

"Excuse me!" a cracking voice called through the trees. "Excuse me, is someone out there? We can't allow guests off the path."

Penny stepped out of Zander's touch to spin on him with a glare.

"Hello!" the voice called again.

"I told you!" she whispered. "I told you we shouldn't—"

Zander's finger pressed flat against her lips. The touch stilled her whole body.

"Shhh, Becker. Don't give us away." He nodded to the side. "Just follow me, I promise I won't let you get in trouble."

An hour later, the headlights of Zander's truck lit up Penny's cabin as they pulled into her drive.

As promised, he'd snuck them through the forest until they reentered the path with no harm done, then walked silently to Zander's truck as Penny stuffed her hands in her pockets to keep from touching her lips where his finger had been.

They'd had a few minutes of thick silence on the way home before Zander finally broke their stalemate, sharing his opinion on what Penny charged vendors to participate in the Honey Festival. It was just the normal, annoying kind of conversation Penny needed to recover from the slide of his fingers on her back in the forest.

"All I'm saying is"—Zander threw the truck into park— "I looked it up, and you're charging half of what they charge vendors at the garlic thing."

"That's because that festival is in the claws of Jason Altman, and he is a real asshole. He doesn't even *grow* garlic."

Zander's laugh filled the small space, and he shook his head as he looked at Penny.

"You don't have to be Jason Altman. But when you undercharge by this much, you're not valuing your festival, or your work." He shut off the engine. "I did the math. Upping the fee by fifty percent would make you seven thousand more dollars, just like that."

"Seven thousand?" Penny squeaked. That would go a long way to helping her get into the black with the festival and bring her that much closer to making a big enough payment on the loan. "But I don't want it to be inaccessible. We have community groups there doing outreach."

"How about one rate for community organizations and another rate for businesses?"

"That could work." It was a fair compromise, one that left room for everyone while charging what the event was worth for vendors, who had one of their biggest sales days of the year. "I'd have to get the word out about the change, though. Update the paperwork and the contracts and the website . . . It has to happen fast."

"I'll handle it. I'll just need all the files and log-ins from you."

Before she could argue, Zander hopped out of his seat to jog around the front and open her door.

*Not a date, not a date, not a date.*

He rocked back on his heels. "I'll walk you to your door."

"You don't have to. This isn't a—"

"I know. But I'm going to do it anyway."

He pressed his palm to her back again, guiding her to her small front stoop. One bulb lit up the small circle where Penny swayed toward Zander. She'd worried for days about how this night would go, but now found she wasn't ready for it to end.

"I know this wasn't a date." Her words were drowned out by the wild thumping of her heart. "But if it had been, it would have been a good one."

A smile slid across his face, slow, like honey. "Yeah, it really would have. Especially the part where I got scared shitless by a bird."

Penny grinned. "Or when you almost got us arrested."

His brows arched. "Arrested? No way—that kid did not have that kind of power. You clearly need more experience getting in trouble."

"Maybe I do." When Zander's gaze on her narrowed, Penny tipped her head to search his dark eyes, glinting copper in the low light. "So if this *was* a date, what do you think would happen next?"

"Hmm." He studied her for a minute as his tongue made a slow sweep of his lower lip. Then his hand rose between them, like it had in her bee yard. But instead of stopping just shy of her like he had that day, Zander cupped her cheek, his warm fingers spanning across her jaw.

"I think if this was a date, I'd ask if I could kiss you now."

"And if this was a date"—she lifted to her tiptoes—"I'd say yes."

Zander's forehead fell against hers. "And then—"

"And then—"

And then—his mouth pressed to hers, taking each of her lips between his in turn. It was sweet, and soft, and over before she could fully register the taste of him.

They exchanged one deep breath, noses still touching.

Then Zander's finger tightened on her jaw as his other hand slid behind her head as his mouth returned. Still soft, but no longer sweet. Instead, it was intense, desperate. Possessive. He teased her with his tongue, invading and retreating until Penny threaded her fingers into his hair to hold him close.

Her back hit the door as Zander leaned into her, one knee sliding between her legs. Penny pressed herself against him there, her body eager to ease the ache building all night. When his fingers dug into her skull as he took the kiss deeper, she gasped against his lips.

He whimpered when she closed her teeth around his bottom lip, then bit her back as he lifted his thigh just enough to make her groan.

For all their talk about a non-date, this kiss was entirely real. Real in a way that rearranged Penny's cells, reminding her body how it felt to be touched, caressed, needed. Reminding her that she was more than the work she did, more than everything she kept in order all the time.

It was a dangerous reminder. One she didn't have time for. Not with so much on the line for her this summer.

She eased her fingers out of his hair, slowing the kiss and concentrating on the solid door behind her and the steadiness of the concrete stoop beneath her feet. Zander sipped at her lips a final time before stepping back to leave a few inches between them as his arms fell to his sides.

For a moment he stared at her, blinking and breathing hard; then he took another step back. "Good night, Penny."

She only nodded at his retreat, lips tingling. His gaze stayed trained on her as he walked backward, the tall shape of his body blending with the looming trees. Finally, he turned toward his truck.

"Zander," she called out, her voice as shaken up as her body. "If this had been a date, that would have been a nice ending to the night."

For a second, she didn't know if he'd heard. He just opened his door and started to move inside.

But then he looked back her way.

"If this had been a date, Penny, the night wouldn't be over yet. Not by a long shot."

# CHAPTER 14

"And all the bees in the colony are female, except for the drones, but their only job is to fly around and look for queens to mate with." Winter plucked a stem off another green bean, depositing each part in its appropriate bowl as they sat on the steps of Mal's parents' porch. "And they mate in the air, *while they're flying*, and they leave this piece of themselves in the queen, it's called the . . . the phallus or something. And it kind of rips off them and they actually *die*—"

"Okay, kiddo!" Zander cut in. "This is starting to sound a little PG-13."

Across the porch, Quinn coughed into her hand. "*Phallus* is a hilarious word."

"You should watch the video, Dad," Winter continued. "It's *so* cool."

"I will, buddy, I will."

Since his beekeeping lesson, Winter was living on a steady diet of YouTube videos about honeybees, all of which he'd been describing to Zander in excruciating detail. Zander was thrilled to see his kid excited to talk to him about something, even bee phalluses.

The problem was that talking about bees meant thinking about Penny. And thinking about Penny was . . . complicated.

As soon as she'd gone up on her toes last night, the control he'd barely grasped all night broke its leash, and he gave in to his urge to kiss her.

It was supposed to be a quiet kiss—just a soft brush of lips to satiate his curiosity and close the taunting loop in his head that yearned to touch her. And after he'd gotten that, after feeling the plush softness of her mouth against his, he was going to walk away.

He'd really meant to walk away.

But then his hands were on her and Penny's back was against the door and she—fuck, he'd never forget it—she was practically riding his thigh as her fingers scraped along his neck and through his hair.

He'd come to Sullivan's Glen hesitant, but knowing just what to expect: a summer of packing up some bad memories and throwing others away completely. He'd sell the house—something he'd never asked for, never wanted—and get this whole town out of his life once and for all.

But Zander hadn't counted on his beekeeping neighbor to fog up his brain and wake up his body.

Mal popped her head out of the door. Her face was devoid of her usually shimmering makeup, but her space buns endured. "Hey, Winter, are those beans done? Pops needs some help with the mac 'n' cheese."

Winter groaned. "But we were talking about—"

She held up a hand. "Let me guess. Bee sex. I'm sure Dad and Quinn have heard enough. Come in and help please."

He sighed but carried the beans inside. After he'd slid past Mallory, she nudged Zander's shoulder with her knee. "Thanks for blessing us with your presence, Z."

Zander had thus far declined the multiple offers to have dinner at Candace and Isaiah's house since they'd all arrived in town.

This was the place where he'd once slept in the bushes under Mallory's window because he'd rather be near her than in his sad room down the hall from his papou. The house where he'd pulled up in his old beater Toyota—the car he'd saved for a year to buy—to help Mallory skip town, blowing up her relationship with her parents for years.

And who was he to the Robinsons besides that kid? Not a son-in-law, just their daughter's ex. The father of the grandchild they were still getting to know.

So yeah, he'd always found something else to do when Mallory said he should come over for dinner. Which was fairly shitty of him.

"Sorry it took me all week to come over."

Mallory mussed his hair. "I get it. I'm just glad you're here now." She crossed to Quinn and bent to drop a kiss on her mouth. "Come inside soon, babe."

Quinn beamed up at her. "Will do, babe."

Zander groaned dramatically. "Enough of being unbearably cute. I'm trying to brood out here."

Mallory headed back inside. "I've had enough of your brooding to last a lifetime, so I'll leave that to Quinn. And babe"—she lowered her voice to a fake whisper toward Quinn—"ask him about Penny."

Zander dropped his head into his hands as the door closed behind Mallory. "Please don't."

Quinn slid down the porch to sit beside him.

"You know I have to," she said. "You're being very mysterious. What's going on?"

"I'm not mysterious."

"Zander. Every time I try to engage, you give me one-word answers. It's like communicating with a fucking caveman. You think I don't know what that means?"

"I'm sure you'll tell me."

"It means you're spiraling and afraid to talk about it because saying things out loud makes them real."

Zander ran his hands through his hair. "You're a pain in my ass."

"You just hate it when I'm right."

"I'm not—" Zander shook his head.

At this point, he knew Quinn well enough to predict their conversations. Sometimes if he needed advice, he just asked the Quinn in his mind and took their pretend conversation to its natural conclusion. Which meant he already knew that, now, if he said anything about Penny, the conversation would end with Quinn telling Zander that he'd been a lonely grump for long enough and he should shoot his shot, even if it was just for a summer fling.

The problem was, Penny Becker was more than summer fling material. At least for Zander. And he couldn't square that fact with the reality that he was desperate to see her again.

So he told Quinn the truth.

"I'm not ready to talk about it."

Quinn's eyes narrowed at him, but she nodded. "Fair enough. But you're not totally off the hook. If you won't talk about Penny, we *will* talk about the house."

"The house is fine. Yes, I'm a little bit shitty at home repairs, but I'm figuring it out. A real estate agent is coming tomorrow to get the listing started."

Her eyebrows shot up. "And?"

"And . . . what? Winter's room is almost done."

Her knee hit his. "And?"

"For the love of god, Quinn," Zander said, wondering why he'd chosen a best friend who was so annoying. "Just say what you're thinking."

She pulled her legs under her as she faced him. "When are you going back in his room?"

Zander stared between his knees. "Maybe we should talk about Penny."

"Too late for that, my dear. When we got here you told me you moved all his stuff into his bedroom. You haven't gone back in?"

"No, Quinn. I haven't gone back in. I've been busy."

"Busy avoiding," she quipped.

"You think I don't have more important things to do than sort through my grandfather's crap? I'll tell you what's in there—ratty furniture, clothes he would never throw away, and seventy-five years' worth of newspaper clippings."

Papou used to spend every morning at the wobbly round kitchen table, snipping articles out of the paper. Sometimes he'd wave one in Zander's face, telling him about some terrible crime two counties over, or the price of soybeans. His tone always implied that it was somehow Zander's fault, that if Zander would just shape up like everyone wanted, he could solve the world's problems.

"I should probably just have someone come in and put everything in that room in trash bags," he said. "Would save me some time."

Quinn groaned into her hands. "You are such a shit. What happened to your old song and dance about looking our demons square in the face and determining our own course in life? When you came with me to get my first hormones and I almost chickened out, you told me I'd be a fucking coward if I let the people who raised me define who I was."

"I said it in a loving way."

"I know you did, you jerk. And I'm saying this in a loving way. You're being a fucking coward." Her hand covered his knee softly, carrying the love and tenderness beneath her tough words. "You have unfinished business here. And it's not just selling the house."

"He's dead," Zander said flatly. "I missed my chance to finish any business with him."

Maybe he could have, if he'd come back in time. His mom had told him that his papou was sick. But she hadn't talked to her father in years and wasn't planning to visit. And if she wasn't going back, Zander had told himself, he didn't have to either, right? He and Papou didn't have a relationship; the old man wasn't awaiting the return of his prodigal, no-good grandson.

Quinn looked like she'd like to truly kick his ass, but before the argument could continue, he was saved by the front door opening again.

"You two aren't hiding out here, are you?" Candace peered at them from the doorway. She had Mallory's dark skin but looked her daughter's opposite in almost every other way. She was short and soft, her hair dusted with gray, cut close to her head. Even now, three weeks after a hip replacement, she was in slacks and a fancy blouse with a string of pearls.

"Um, no, ma'am, no hiding." Quinn stood quickly and wiped her hands down her jeans.

*Ma'am?* This was a new side of Quinn. It was cute to see how desperate she was for the Robinsons' approval. He'd make fun of her for it later.

"Quinn, again, please call me Candace."

"Yes, of course, Candace." Quinn nodded. "I think Mallory needs me in there, so I better, uh—"

Quinn slipped back inside as Candace lowered herself onto the porch swing behind him.

Zander rose. "Do you need some help?"

She shot him a look that could stop a bull in its tracks. "The next person who offers to help me will be sent to the next county. But come sit with me for a minute. We haven't had any time to catch up. Since you haven't been coming over."

Zander swallowed hard as he took a seat. Now he was tempted to call her ma'am, too.

Though now retired, Candace had been a doctor at the closest hospital, where she'd often worked nights. Her husband, Isaiah, was also a doctor—they'd met in medical school in New York City and moved upstate for a peaceful life for their daughter.

But Mallory hadn't thought much of the peace they were seeking. According to her, everything started going wrong when her parents enrolled her in ballet, where she eventually tore her hair out of the restrictive bun and refused to wear the special shoes and the ballet tights that matched everyone's skin tone but hers. As Mallory grew, so did her rebellions, and her parents responded to each incident by tightening the rules. Lower grades resulted in being grounded from seeing friends; nights out past curfew meant losing her phone and driving privileges. Eventually Mallory snuck around and defied them at every turn. The pattern persisted until Zander and Mallory skipped town.

They'd already divorced when Mallory reestablished her relationship with her parents, but Zander had seen them now and then on their trips to Boston. They had a cordial relationship, all things considered. But he realized now, swaying slightly in the swing with Mallory's mom, that he really didn't know her at all. She was his son's grandmother, but he'd wrapped Candace up in all his other mess from Sullivan's Glen, thrown it in the closet of his mind, and stuck a "not worth it" label on the door.

"You don't have to be scared of me, Zander."

He laughed awkwardly. "I'm not scared. Not exactly."

"I would understand, of course. I was angry at you for a very long time."

In the modest front yard, a red bird landed on a feeder. "I can understand that."

Candace looked sideways at him, something mischievous sparkling in her eyes. "Can you? I blamed you for taking my girl, for keeping her from us. When I didn't know where she was, or *how* she was . . ." She shuddered.

Zander squeezed his hands into fists, knowing he'd caused some of that painful quiver in Candace's voice.

Not that he'd do anything different if given another chance. He'd loved Mallory, and she'd wanted to leave, so they'd left. To eighteen-year-old Zander, it was the most uncomplicated, soul-affirming thing he'd ever done, and the catalyst for the rest of his life.

"But I know it wasn't just you," Candace continued. "We didn't know how to parent Mallory, not when that spirit she had didn't match with what we thought our life should look like. When Isaiah and I moved up here from the city, we had this idea of how things would go. It felt worth it to move farther from our families, even to choose a place with so few other Black families, to have this ideal life for Mallory, where there was fresh air and space, where she could be valedictorian and prom queen. Where she could have everything I didn't."

Candace stretched her legs out in front of her, crossing her ankles. "I couldn't let go of that vision, that idea of what our life would look like, of who my daughter should be. I held on so tight to it that I lost her, and it was the worst thing that ever happened to me."

Zander imagined losing Winter that way, and the unfillable hole he'd carry around each day. "I'm sorry I contributed to that."

Candace chuckled quietly as she patted his knee. "I know. But I also know we weren't what Mallory needed then." Zander finally looked away from the bird and at Candace, who had Mallory's coffee and cinnamon eyes. "But you were, Zander. You were there for her when I couldn't be. And instead of hating you for that, I've decided to love you for it."

Something broke open in Zander—small but heavy, cracking now to relieve the pressure in his chest. The child still in him lapped up the word *love* like an eager puppy, and from the knowing look in Candace's eyes, she might have known how rarely he'd heard it.

Zander pushed words past the lump in his throat. "Thank you."

It was quiet but for an occasional birdcall or a burst of loud laughter from inside. A stark difference from the urban soundscape of Boston, which Zander found he didn't miss at all.

Finally, Candace sighed. "That's enough touchy-feely for me. Care to tell me why you were seen sneaking off into the forest with Penny Becker last night?"

That certainly broke him out of his emotional stupor. "*What*?"

"I heard you two broke the rules and went off the path."

Zander rubbed his face as he tried to keep up. "We were fifteen miles away from here. Who even saw us?"

Candace's regal brows arched. "It's true, then?"

This fucking place. A guy couldn't engage in any innocent

shenanigans without being discovered. "Yes, I was at the fairy light thing with Penny, and yes, I may have gone slightly off the path looking for an owl."

"Mallory said you're helping with the Honey Festival."

"I am," he answered cautiously. "I'm keeping a deal I made with Winter, to really try to get to know this place and make it a great summer."

She nodded. "Penny Becker is a special woman. She means a lot to this place, and she holds up a lot of it on her own."

"I've gotten that sense, yes."

"There was a man, some years back, who was supposed to help her with it all."

Zander recalled their conversation in the forest, how much he'd wanted to hear more about Penny's past. "Henry?"

Candace nodded. "They met at some conference or other, and he came back here with her. He was a bright guy, always full of ideas, but definitely a free spirit. He'd leave town for a bit and come back. Then do it again. I'm not sure what kind of arrangement he had with Penny, but she seemed to welcome him back each time. But then Henry left again, and this time he didn't come back."

Candace straightened, watching him keenly. "You know why I'm telling you this?"

"Penny and I aren't—" he started. "We're just—" What *were* they, actually? "We're working on the festival together, that's all."

Except for when they were talking through open windows, sneaking through the forest, or kissing against her door.

"And I'm happy you're doing that. I'm just letting you know that Penny has a history of men leaving this place. I know your heart is in the right place, but for Penny's sake, you might want to proceed with caution."

He'd known he was playing with fire walking through the magical forest with her, kissing her like she was the fresh air he craved. He'd be back in Boston in just over two months, and no matter how much he helped with the festival between now and then, no matter how much he really *liked* her, at the end of it all Penny Becker would be here, holding the world on her shoulders all alone. Again.

Candace patted him on the shoulder, batting away his attempt to help as she slowly stood. "Just be careful, Zander. If you decide to do more than festival planning, make sure you both understand how much you can give."

When he looked back to the yard as Candace went inside, the red bird had flown away.

# CHAPTER 15

A woman stood in the long grass with Zander in front of the Bouras house. A pretty woman at that, auburn hair flashing in the sun.

Which was fine with Penny, because she was playing it cool after their not-date. It had been almost forty-eight hours since the kiss against her door, and he hadn't texted or called. But neither had Penny. Because she was playing it cool.

And because she had no idea what she was doing.

Penny didn't go around kissing people. As RJ had so kindly reminded her, she'd been celibate since Henry left two years ago. For all she knew, it was perfectly normal to kiss the hell out of someone and not follow up. Maybe Zander went around kissing people like that all the time. And Penny'd been insistent that it wasn't a date, so she couldn't blame Zander for not making the night out to be more than it was.

She *could* blame him for not responding to her text about festival planning.

After *begging* her to let him help out, he'd gone silent. They hadn't set up any formal schedule for going about festival business—something Penny now regretted—but they were close enough to go time that she couldn't afford to go two days with her messages left on read. Especially from her so-called co-planner. So after checking in with RJ about his progress with the orchard pests, she'd put on her big-girl panties to march over and see what the hell was going on.

And now there was a woman in the yard talking to Zander. She had pale skin, shiny reddish hair, a tailored navy suit, and she looked tiny next to Zander, whose blue T-shirt fit him perfectly, because one of Zander's most annoying qualities was filling out a simple piece of cotton perfectly. The woman wove one hand fluidly through the air as she spoke, clutching a clipboard at her side. As she spun to sweep her hand around, both she and Zander turned in Penny's direction.

For a flash, Zander's eyes brightened as his mouth pulled up into a wide smile, the kind she'd seen so many times the other night. But then his expression flattened as he looked away.

Penny tripped on the trail, just barely catching herself. Maybe it was a bad time, and she should go home, be patient. But what about Zander's sincere look in his darkened truck as he talked about elementary school math?

*When I decide to do something, I do it.*

The hell he did.

When Penny reached them a moment later, huffing from her speed walking, the redheaded woman smiled big. "Why hello, you just came out of the wilderness!"

"Just from next door, actually. I came to say hi and make sure Zander's phone is working. But if I came at a bad time—"

"Oh no," the other woman said. "I was actually just leaving. You're next door, at Becker Farms?"

"Sure am."

"Incredible piece of land you've got there."

"Sure is." Penny glanced to Zander, but he was staring back at his house, hands shoved into his back pockets.

Meanwhile, the well-dressed redhead slid a sleek business card from her clipboard and passed it over. "I'm Monica Reynolds, Zander's Realtor."

The card was slick between Penny's fingers. "Of course. To sell the house."

"As soon as possible, according to this one," Monica said in an exaggerated deep voice. "Suddenly had a fire lit under him today. You aren't looking to sell also, are you? Putting these lots together could really up the appeal for a buyer looking to develop."

"No." Penny left no room for argument in her tone. "Definitely not selling."

She was working her ass off to avoid it.

Monica smiled breezily. "Had to ask." She peered back down at her clipboard. "Okay, Zander, I'll let you know about the photographer coming for the pictures. It should be about two weeks or so, and meanwhile I'll send over those numbers for the contractors for the fence."

Finally, Zander looked up and nodded. "Great. Whatever it takes."

*As soon as possible.*

While Penny was still reeling from their good-night kiss, waiting for him to follow up about the festival as he'd promised, Zander was calling Monica the Realtor to rid himself of this place, stat.

"Don't worry." Monica gave Zander's substantial shoulder a little pat. "I think you'll make out just fine on this place. People are snatching up these properties like hotcakes. As soon as I mentioned we were going to list it, I started getting calls. Lots of buzz!" She gave a short nod to Penny. "If you ever change your mind about selling, you have my number."

Monica admirably navigated the grass in her heels. Once they were alone, Zander finally looked at her.

"Hey." He squeezed the back of his neck. "Sorry I, um, went MIA."

She held his eye contact. "A fence, huh?"

His brows furrowed. "Monica says it's a good idea. People like to know what's theirs."

"How beautifully capitalistic."

He shrugged, looking down again. "It is what it is."

She couldn't stop the harsh laugh. "What a poetic way to talk about a house that's been in your family for generations."

A thick swallow moved down Zander's throat as his feet shifted in the grass. "I've never lied about my intent here, Penny." His lids lowered in a slow blink before he looked at her again, brown eyes intense. "I'm here to sell this house and leave."

Penny threw back her shoulders and kept her face blank. "I hear you loud and clear, Zander. I get you wanting to sell the house," she huffed. "You don't want to live here. You have a whole life somewhere else. Fine." She nodded to the offending house. "But if you're just waiting to sell, why bother fixing it up? For all you know, whoever buys it will just knock it down and start over."

Zander went even more rigid. "I wanted Winter to have a place to stay."

"He does have a place to stay. With Mallory's parents. You probably do, too, if you want it. But you're here. Fixing the sink, playing house, and for what?"

"Because I needed to clear out all the old shit in this place, so I decided to stay here while I did it, it's that simple." He ran a hand through his messy hair. "I know this whole town is special to you, Penny. But it means shit to me, do you understand that? None of this can—" Zander's head tipped back as he stared at the sky. "None of this can mean anything."

The sting hit right in her sternum, and only gave her more fire. "Maybe not to you, but it means something to the rest of us." She pointed fiercely to the meeting of their property lines. "You know that bees fly up to three miles to find a nectar source? So whether or not you put up that fence, the bees will come and encounter whatever the next owner puts here. What if they mow all this down and put in a lawn and spray herbicides all over everything? What if they decide they don't like the bees that come for a drink and lace the water with poison?"

Zander's eyes stayed trained on the sky.

"But it's not just bees." Penny pressed on. "Families that have called this town home for years are leaving because they can't afford the property taxes anymore. Houses are getting snatched up as vacation rentals or second homes, properties getting split up and flipped while pricing everybody out."

Finally, he looked at her again, his eyes a storm. "And what do you think I can do about that? You want me to hang on to this place out of some kind of principle? Ignore the opportunity to have savings for Winter because I can't promise you the perfect neighbor?"

"No!" A sparrow spurred from the thick grass, shooting up into the blue. "You have every right to sell this house. You have every right to not look back. But you can't show up here and do whatever you want and pretend it doesn't impact things around you." She stepped toward him through the grass. "You may have left this place, but you're back now, and what you do matters to people. You don't have to love it here, but if you don't give a shit about it, don't pretend to. Don't pretend to care about the house, or about the bees, or about the Honey Festival. And definitely don't pretend to care about me."

Penny turned and stomped through the grass, cutting back through the trees and beehives.

Her mistake to think he cared about any of it. To think anyone could take on the work except herself.

*Just keep working.* She weaved through the trees, and didn't even stop to notice the bees going about their orderly lives.

*Just keep working.*

# CHAPTER 16

"Penny, please. Open the door."

She'd slammed the door in his face just a few minutes before, but it felt to Zander like a year. He'd totally fucked up.

When she stormed away after laying into him outside his grandfather's house, Zander's feet were leaden, his eyes blurry. And he'd just stood there.

Then a bee buzzed past his face, and the world whooshed back, leaving Zander to see it clear as day: he'd been a serious asshole.

Which was why he was now pleading his case at her door.

"Give me five minutes. You know we need to talk."

His next knock hit air as the door swung inward. Inside, Penny glared at him, cheeks bright pink. Her cutoff shorts were frayed just above the knees, and she was in a SUNY Buffalo shirt with the collar cut out so it hung over one shoulder, leaving a stripe of red bra strap visible.

It was so cute and sexy, and absolute torture.

Penny's hands framed her hips. "We need to *talk*?"

"Yes. Please."

"Would this be a real talk, or something we're calling *not really a talk*? If it's not really a talk, can I pretend later it didn't happen?"

Zander closed his eyes for a breath. "I deserved that."

"Or how about this?" Penny tapped a finger to her chin. "Maybe I can promise to help you with something, like maybe selling your house, something you're desperate to do. And I'll beg and you'll agree. But be careful, because though I can be pretty convincing, I might end up ghosting you."

Seeing the last two days through Penny's eyes was brutal.

"I fucked up. I know that. Please give me a chance to explain."

Penny scoffed and turned her back on him, but the door didn't slam behind her, so he followed her inside.

"Listen—"

"For the record." Penny faced him and pointed a finger at his face. "I'm not mad because of the kissing thing. For all I know, you kiss people like that all the time and it doesn't mean anything."

"Penny, it *did*—"

"I'm mad because you pushed all my buttons and told me about your stupid fifth-grade math test and then up and disappeared. And why? Because you were afraid it was going to be awkward? Afraid I'd cling to you after one kiss?"

"Two."

"*What*?"

Zander closed the door behind him, stepping in cautiously. "It was two kisses, technically. And I *have* been working on the festival. I got in touch with my buddy about the equipment rental and he's going to give us a discount. I also revised the vendor contract with new pricing and put together some ideas for the website, like a slideshow of pictures from past years."

Her glare faltered, but only for an instant. "And were you going to keep all of that to yourself?"

"I was figuring out how to talk to you. I was trying to develop some kind of plan to work with you on the festival while maintaining the space I thought we needed."

"Because you regret what happened?"

"No." He stepped closer, hands out. "No, not even in the slightest." With a sigh, Zander ran a hand through his hair. "I was a dick, okay? I know. I am so sorry. After the other night, with the lights and the kissing and . . . I was thinking about what to do, what to say to you, and then I had this very unexpected heart-to-heart with Mallory's mom, and she told me about Henry."

Penny's arms went across her chest. "What does Henry have to do with any of this?"

"Candace didn't say much, but she told me how he would leave and come back, over and over. Until he left for good. And I kept thinking about your dad, and your mom's dad, and then Henry and—"

"And *what*?"

"And how much I fucking like you, Penny. How I want to spend time around you and know more about you and—" He groaned, dragging a hand across his face. "And how kissing you was like realizing I'd been in the middle of the desert for months, and then suddenly someone reminded me what water tasted like."

He paced across her small living space. Penny's cabin was so *her* it hurt him to look—plants bathing in sunshine by the windows, a colorful throw on the couch, and a little sprig of wildflowers on her small wooden dining table.

"But I'm leaving," he continued. "I'm leaving in two months. And whatever I could give you, it would end then. And I couldn't bear to be another man who walks out of your life."

Penny's eyes narrowed. "So you decided the best course of

action was to ignore my texts and leave me hanging? To what, protect my feelings?"

"It was stupid. I should have just talked to you."

"Yes. You should have. And you know what I would have told you?" She stepped closer. "That I know what everybody around here thinks about what happened. How Henry would promise me he was ready to be here, ready to be part of the farm, and then a few weeks later there'd be a workshop in New Haven or a friend with a project in the city and he'd take off for weeks. And yes, I took him back every time, because I thought eventually he'd be ready to just stay, to really be my partner. And all of that is true."

She stared out the window. "They don't know that *I'm* the one who told him to stay away the final time. I finally realized he wouldn't change, and worse—that the times he was away were actually easier for me, because he was a shitty, selfish partner when he was actually around. And I was embarrassed I'd accepted it so long, and I asked him to leave." She pointed at Zander. "And he stood right there where you are and cried, and he begged, and he made promises. And I told him to go."

Penny shook her head. "So no, I don't have the best history with men. But I'm not some damsel in distress who needs you to protect me from myself. I have that covered. I'm a big girl."

Zander heated with embarrassment, horrified at how he'd decided what was best for Penny when she was clearly good at figuring that out herself.

"I understand, and I'm sorry."

She blinked, like maybe he'd surprised her. "Fine."

"But while we're setting the record straight." He stepped closer, and she didn't retreat. "I *don't* kiss people like that all the time. Not even close. I've basically been a monk for years, and now I can't get *you* out of my head."

She stepped toward him, her cheeks still pink and her breath coming fast. The lightning in her eyes didn't look angry anymore. It looked far more dangerous. Especially when she licked her bottom lip. "And that's my fault?"

"Yes!" His fists were so tight at his sides Zander knew there'd be half-moons all over his palms. "It's your fault for being so fucking irresistible, your fault I can't stop thinking about kissing you again." Electricity zipped up Zander's spine. "But it's *my* fault for wanting things I can't have, for lying awake at night fucking my own fist just thinking about how you smile or how your mouth tastes or what it would be like to slip my hand inside your T-shirt."

And that was maybe saying too much, but instead of throwing him out of her house, Penny stepped into him and stared up, lips wet and plush, defiance flashing in her eyes. "Who says you can't have those things?"

Before he could answer, Penny grabbed his hand as she lifted the hem of her shirt. She guided him beneath the fabric and flattened his palm on her warm stomach, then guided him across her soft skin, over the ridges of her ribs.

"Penny." He barely choked out the word. "This is a bad idea."

She wet her lips and nodded. "Probably."

The tip of his middle finger brushed the underside of her breast. She was so soft, so close. "I'm not that guy who runs toward a bad idea anymore."

"Come on," she dared. "I thought it was once a bad boy, always a bad boy?"

And who was he kidding? He had the chance to get his hands on Penny, and he wasn't passing it up.

"Fuck it, you're right."

He captured her mouth in his, took the kiss deep and hard

as her hand drew his up to cup her full breast. Zander moaned into her mouth as he worked her over, kneading her through the soft cotton of her bra and rubbing at her hard nipple with his palm.

"Need to feel you," he managed to mutter against her mouth.

"Yes." She nodded, scraping her teeth along his lip. "Yes."

Zander tugged at the fabric of the bra, yanking it down until Penny's breast fell into his open palm. "Fuck, you're perfect."

He thrummed his thumb across her nipple as her hands gripped his waist, pulling him with her. Zander had to trust Penny knew where she was going, because he was fully consumed by her—the fresh taste of her lips and tongue, the hard peak between his thumb and forefinger. It was all he could do to remember to breathe.

He was pushed down to the couch, where he watched in awe as Penny swung a leg over to straddle him. Without preamble, she moved on him, grinding against the aching ridge of his erection.

Above him, she whimpered and drove into him harder as they struggled to kiss in the midst of their frantic movements.

"I can't believe it," he gasped.

"Believe what?" She nipped at his ear, licked the side of his neck, still moving her hips.

"I think you might be as desperate for this as I am."

She pulled her face back to smirk at him. "Nah. I'm totally fine."

"Are you?" Zander released her breast and gripped her waist, pushing her back so there was space between them. Penny whined and tried to slide back across his thighs. "You're *totally* fine? You don't want to be grinding down on me right now? Don't want to feel my cock pressing against you right where you need it?"

Penny's eyes grew even wider. "Zander!"

"Don't pretend to be shocked, Penny." He squeezed her ass, just barely resisting yanking her back against him. He wanted to hear her say she needed it this much, too. "You wanted me to be bad. And I think you might like my dirty words."

He leaned forward, breathing hot air onto her neck before whispering into her ear, "I think you're probably soaking wet for these bad words, aren't you? So wet that if I slipped my hand into your shorts, I could slide my fingers right inside you and let you ride them while my thumb does perfect little circles on your—"

"Enough talk," she whined. "Just fucking do it!"

Oh, he would. He'd do that and much more. He'd spend the whole night with her spread out under him—

"Shit. Penny, god, wait."

Her eyes flew to him. "What is it?" Her expression hardened. "I swear to god, if you suddenly have another hang-up—"

"No. No more hang-ups." He smoothed her hair over her ear and rubbed his thumb along her bottom lip. "But Winter is coming to my place tonight. I finished his room, and he's coming at—" He looked over Penny's shoulder, heart sinking at the sight of the clock. "He'll be there in thirty minutes."

"Okay." She nodded. "That's okay. Thirty minutes is enough time." She pulled at the hem of his shirt.

"It's not." He stilled her hands while a debate raged between his brain and his other parts. "It's not nearly enough time for everything that I want to do to you."

Not time for everything, but definitely time for something. They were choosing to make a bad decision, and he didn't know if it would extend to another day. This might be his only chance.

He grabbed her hips and dropped her onto the couch on her

back, rising on a knee to hover over her. His fingers lingered at the button of her shorts.

"Can I?"

Her brows arched. "I thought we didn't have enough time."

"It's enough time for me to make you come."

She laughed, and it was so damn lovely he could cry. "Cocky."

"Yes, I am. Now tell me if I can unzip these shorts and put my hands on you."

"Yes, but hurry up about it!"

Zander dragged the zipper down slowly, watching Penny's face the whole time. He watched her bite her bottom lip as his hand slid between her legs, then her body arch as he cupped her over her underwear.

"I was right. You are *so* wet for me."

"I said *hurry up*."

"So feisty, Penny Becker." Zander moved his hand beneath her underwear and ran his fingers through her curls, then deeper, where everything was smooth and wet. He teased at her entrance with one finger, moving away each time her hips tried to take him in. "Everyone around thinks you're so perfect, but they don't know what I do. They don't know how bad you can be."

He slipped one finger inside where she was hot and tight for him, then followed quickly with another, dragging his fingers in and out of her willing body. It would be easier with her shorts all the way off, but he denied himself that temptation. Odds were low he'd actually pull himself away if he saw her naked and spread for him.

"Tell me how it feels." He sped up his movements as his thumb brushed over her clit.

"So good," she said through her breath.

"What do you need to get there?"

"Your thumb. Side to side."

He did it slowly at first, watching her breasts press against her shirt as she arched off the couch. Then faster, finally giving up the sight of her to taste her neck, her jaw, and her mouth again.

"Yes," she moaned. "Like that."

His motions were steady as Penny squirmed beneath him, but then her hand was on his stomach and reaching lower, popping the button of his jeans.

"*Penny*."

"Let me touch you, too. It's not fair otherwise." She pulled down the zipper and palmed him over his boxers. "I want to."

He groaned helplessly. "Fuck, of course."

Penny's fingers worked under his waistband to wrap around him, then froze. "You're uncut. I've never—" He felt her swallow under his mouth. "I've never, um, encountered this. What do I do?"

He chuckled against her mouth. "Same penis rules apply— almost everything feels good. Just—" She squeezed, dragging his foreskin up and down around his cock. "Yep," he choked. "You got it. Just keep—ahhh."

He wasn't going to last, not with her writhing beneath him and her hand wrapped tight, so he doubled his efforts, fucking her with his fingers as his thumb strummed her clit.

"Zander," she gasped. "I'm gonna—"

"Hell yes you are. I'm right behind you."

Zander's forehead fell against her as he thrust into the tight sleeve of her hand, matching the rhythm with his fingers inside her. Penny's body tightened around him, mouth hung open in a long moan. Her hand on him faltered as she came, and it was that—knowing he'd made Penny Becker lose control—that sent him over the edge.

"Baby, fuck, I'm about to—"

Penny kept her hold on him as her other hand wrenched up her shirt, exposing her pale belly, her luscious breasts spilling from her red bra. It was more of her than he'd seen before, and he struggled to memorize every inch as Penny pulled him closer.

"Here," she said. "Come for me."

And she was beautiful—sweet like sunshine—so he really shouldn't.

"Come on," she teased him with a smile. "You know I like to be bad."

With a groan that shook his body, Zander gave her what she asked for, decorating her stomach as he came.

The next few minutes were a blur. First was heavy breathing, then a slow disentanglement. Zander had trouble taking his eyes off her, the evidence of what they'd just done on Penny's skin pleasing the caveman in him even as he reached for the box of tissues on her coffee table and cleaned her off gently.

"I have to go," he said finally, redoing his pants. But what he didn't say—*What just happened? And will it happen again?*—rang loudly in his head.

Penny smiled gently as she finished putting herself to rights. "I know. I have work to do anyway. I can't spend all day having orgasms."

"Of course not. So, um, text me your email and I'll send over what I've been working on these last couple of days."

When he stood, Penny did too. Her hair was an absolute mess, and it filled him with ridiculous pride. And as much as he wanted to have a State of the Situationship conversation with her, his kid was going to show up at the old house any minute, so it would have to wait.

"Come over tomorrow? We can review those vendor numbers and start making the map for the tents. I'll feed you lunch."

"Are you sure? I don't want to interrupt father-son time."

"You kidding?" Zander headed toward the door. "Winter will be excited to see you. The kid thinks you are way cooler than me."

"I mean." She shrugged. "He *is* a smart one."

Zander reached for Penny's hand and pulled her into a hug. His hands rubbed down her back as she relaxed into him. "Thanks for letting me in and hearing me out. And I'm sorry."

She spoke into his chest. "You're forgiven. But don't be a dick again."

"I won't." He kissed the top of her head, then each cheek, and finally her mouth. "See you tomorrow, Penny."

Then Zander walked back through the grass, smiling at every bee he saw.

# CHAPTER 17

"I just think we could all use a little break is all I'm saying." Penny's mom held out an open palm, the lines of her hands dark with dirt. She always eschewed gloves when gardening, a preference she'd gotten from Mimi and passed on to Penny. "Maybe a few days in a cabin somewhere farther upstate. Oh! Or we could go to Niagara. We haven't done that for a while."

Penny swallowed a sigh as she passed over a peppermint seedling, its fuzzy leaves emerging an inch or so from its peat pot. "I don't have time for a vacation, Mom."

"I don't mean right now. Maybe after the apple harvest this fall." Ruth scooped some more soil from the hole before dropping in the plant, covering it up, and patting the earth around its baby stem. There were more efficient ways to plant a garden—Penny had researched all of them, even presented her mom with a plan for placement and shown her methods using new tools and systems, but her mom had laughed them all off.

"What's the point of all of this?" she'd asked, shaking her head. "If I'm just working for efficiency? I want the plants in my hands, honey, and the dirt under my fingernails."

"Mary Sue went on one of those cruises for vacation," Mimi

piped up now from her lawn chair at the edge of the herb garden, where she sipped sweet tea and swatted at mosquitos. "They all sit around and knit all day, from what she explained. Why you'd go on a boat to do that I don't understand. Knitting is about as boring as watching a fly in a puddle of honey, and I don't imagine it's much better when you're at sea. I reckon I would rather be on one of those singles cruises where everybody's looking to have some fun."

Penny shot her a smile. "We could not set you loose on one of those. Think of the hearts you'd break!"

The lines on Mimi's face all came together as she laughed, capturing decades of shared smiles etched through time.

Penny had a list of things to do before going to Zander's for lunch, but when her mom invited her to spend some time in the garden with them, she'd found herself saying yes. Head and body still reeling from her encounter with Zander the day before, getting her hands in the ground was exactly what Penny needed.

"Oh, or we could go east," her mom mused. "To the city, maybe, or down to Baltimore. It would be a little cold in the fall. It would be nicer to go a little earlier. Remember that guy I knew who ran a crab restaurant down there? He always said Maryland crab was the best."

Penny's hand flexed around the spongy peat pot of the next seedling, making some soil spill out the top. "Things will be busy here," she said, noticing the bite in her tone and pulling it back, speaking out of a tight smile. "But you could go for sure."

Ruth tsked and shook her head. "You know, honey, the world won't stop turning if you let yourself take a break."

"No." Penny huffed a laugh as her thoughts tipped and tumbled, falling right into one of those potholes Quinn had described. The one worn by years of Ruth promising Penny everything would be fine, then letting Penny do the work to make it so. "The world would still turn. It's only this place that would fall apart."

Her mother rolled her eyes. "You know that is—"

"Let's not, okay?" Penny handed her mom another plant without looking at her. "I know how this conversation goes. I should work less, take a break, trust the universe to pay all the bills."

Maybe she should and let them see what happened. Hell, maybe she should throw her little baby peppermint on the ground and shout for the other Becker women to hear: *I took out a shitty loan and we can't pay it back. If I stop working now, we'll lose everything! How's that for the world turning?*

Penny marveled at her mom's ability to look at everything through warped glass, somehow seeing only the positives. An untimely freeze in the orchards? Just nature's pruning. A flat tire when the truck was laden with goods for a market? An opportunity to notice the wildflowers blooming at the side of the road. A man who moved so quickly through her life that he was gone by the time she got pregnant, and plainly turned down an invitation to come back and meet his daughter? A sperm donor who'd given Ruth a gift.

But could the ever-optimistic Ruth Becker find a silver lining to the disaster Penny had stepped into? Not likely.

"I would love"—Penny bit out the words—"to not have this conversation with you again, Mother."

The lawn chair creaked under Mimi. "Penny girl, tell me this: What exactly crawled up your ass and died?"

"Nothing, Mimi."

"Mm-hmm." Mimi's eyes narrowed. "Something is going on with you. Your mom told me you even suited up for a bee inspection the other day. I haven't seen you suit up in ages."

"It was just PMS," Penny grumbled.

Mimi huffed, and they worked in silence for several minutes, Penny pulling over flats of plants and handing them to her mom to put in the ground. Each peat pot was warm in her palm, full of possibility, roots ready to snake their way through the dirt. Her tension eased with every plant she held, until Penny found herself lost in the easy movements of her mother's weathered hands doing what they loved best.

"So." She was often the first one to let her temper rise and also the first to make amends, so she broke the silence. "Zander Bouras is going to take on some of the Honey Festival planning."

Penny wasn't eager to discuss the Zander situation with her family, but it was better that they heard it from her. Ruth had spies all over town, and the only thing that would pique her curiosity more than Penny letting Zander help would be Penny keeping a secret about letting Zander help.

Ruth looked up with big eyes, clearly trying to play it cool. "Is that so? Aaannd . . ." She drew out the word. "How did that come about?"

They'd both shifted to a new row in the garden, and Penny rose to grab the flat of basil, its leaves broad and deep green. "He helps start restaurants back in Boston, so he has a lot of experience that's useful. He's also going to help RJ see if he can step up his baking stuff, try to make a business of it."

"Is he?" Ruth glowed. "Isn't that wonderful!"

"Always knew that boy had a big heart," Mimi added. "You don't cause that kind of trouble without a big well of passion. He's like his grandfather that way."

"Like his grandfather?" Penny squatted as she watched her grandma. "The way Zander talks about him, his grandfather sounded cold, not passionate."

It was safer to change the subject, but Penny was too eager for more information about Zander. Seeing the different sides of him—devoted father, unrelenting flirt, bad boy—was like examining the rocks she and RJ used to collect during days spent at the nearest lake, where complex worlds existed under every turn.

Mimi ran a finger along the condensation of her glass and looked into the distance, toward the Bouras house. "You can be both," she offered. "Both passionate and cold. Sometimes that passion turns inward and all but eats you up. I never knew Nikolai too well, mind you. Always kept to himself. But anyone could see his love for Elsie, the care he poured into her." A smile drifted across her face. "Planted her rows of flowers in front of the house, all pinks and reds because those were her favorite colors."

Mimi sighed and tucked a wisp of hair behind her ear. "A part of him broke when Elsie died so young, and he didn't manage it well. Not with their daughter, and not with that boy, either."

No, he hadn't. The bits Penny had heard made her want to grab Nikolai Bouras by the shoulders and curse at him. Just as strong was the urge to travel back in time and actually try to talk to young Zander, to be a friend to him, to be someone who gave him a chance.

When the phone in her back pocket buzzed, Penny had a guess as to who was messaging her, because Zander had kept up a steady stream all morning.

First, it was *How'd you sleep? I had great dreams but none of them did you justice.*

Then, *You're still coming, right? I told Winter and he is ready to talk to you about "drone congregation areas," whatever that is.*

Later, as she was headed out to the garden, came her favorite one: *Please tell me it's not true that bee dicks are ripped off when they have sex.*

Now, she gave in to the urge to pull out her phone but kept on her game face. No ridiculous smiles, no simpering sighs, nothing to give her away.

ZANDER B *I know we said 12:30, but you should come anytime. we'd love to see you asap.*

She grinned at the phone. Was it Winter who wanted to see her ASAP? Or Zander? What did "we" mean? Had Zander also kept thinking of their hot make-out session? Did he want to do it again?

"Penny," her mimi called. "What's happening on your phone? You look like you're doing quadratic equations over there."

"Nothing, Mimi." Penny rose and brushed her hands off on her jeans. "Mom, are you good with the rest of the planting? I, um, have a meeting."

Mimi shook the ice in her tea. "A meeting, huh? I wish my meetings made me blush like that."

Penny touched her cheeks, surely blushing even more. "It's just warm out here."

"I've got it, hon," her mom assured her, basil in hand. "Thanks for your help. Head on off to your meeting."

Penny was almost to the trail when her mother called out.

"And say hi to Zander for us!"

# CHAPTER 18

"I don't want to give you every detail about yesterday, Quinn. I want you to use your special fashion magic to tell me what fucking shirt to wear."

Zander slammed the drawer of the shaky dresser he'd taken over for the summer, waiting for it to finally fall apart.

"How am I supposed to tell you what shirt to wear when I have so little info?" Quinn asked through the phone wedged against Zander's ear. "I don't know what's going on with you two!"

"I don't know what's going on either." For all that Zander and Penny had managed to do with their few minutes the day before, talking about *what* they were doing, or if they were going to do it again, wasn't one of them. "Whatever we're doing, it's a terrible idea. I'll be back in Boston in two months."

"Maybe, but you're here now. And so is she. And, Zander, I love you, but you can be very annoying in your mission to always be the best guy for the people around you. You deserve to do things sometimes because *you want to*."

He yanked open another drawer. "Sure, but is that fair to her? To start something I can't finish because I *want* to?"

"I think what's fair to Penny is up to her, not you."

Which was exactly what Penny had told him yesterday.

"Ah," Quinn said. "Your silence means you know I'm right. Penny is acting on her own free will, but we still want to make you impossible to resist."

Zander stared at the dresser, pushing a dime across decades of pale rings from sweating glasses. "What if I'm reading too much into it? What if it was just a hookup for her?"

Quinn's voice gentled. "And it's not just that for you?"

"No." He didn't know what it was, what it could be, but it was more than a hookup. Or he'd like it to be. But with each passing moment since he'd walked away from Penny's front door, he wondered more if it was one-sided.

"I think the walls of this house actually suck out my self-esteem," he told Quinn. "It's like I hear his voice, asking me what I'm worth."

Quinn sighed. "Paint the walls and tell that voice to fuck off. Did you bring that pink shirt you got in Provincetown when we went to the folk fest?"

"That barely fits me."

"Exactly. Put it on. And call me later to tell me *everything* or suffer the consequences."

Zander shoved his clothes around until he found the right shirt. "I will, I promise."

"And, Zander. You're worth a lot."

He smiled big at the phone. "You're being sappy."

"Whatever. Call later."

He was halfway down the stairs when a knock came at the door. He hollered to Winter that he'd get it, then took one slow breath before opening the door to the view of Penny framed in sunshine, biting her lower lip.

"Hi." She was in snug jeans and a loose flannel shirt. Her

hair fell in twin braids, and her thighs were streaked with dirt. One small dark smudge marked the curve of her cheek.

Zander pulled the door closed behind him as he stepped onto the porch, close to Penny. So close he could smell peppermint, basil, and fresh soil. So close he could wrap his fingers around one of her braids if he dared, which he didn't.

But he did swipe at the dirt on her cheek with his thumb, wiping it clean. "Hi. Been gardening?"

Her cheeks pinkened as she touched where his thumb had been, and she tugged at her shirt and stared at her pants. "I'm a mess. I was helping my mom put in starts. I should have cleaned up."

"No. You look . . ." Like he should slip his hands into her back pockets and see which parts of her skin smelled the most like peppermint. "Good. Fresh from the garden is a good look for you. I'm glad you could come early."

Penny smiled as her eyes drew a path down his body, lingering on his chest and shoulders. *Good call, Quinn.*

When she looked at his face again, she shrugged. "I may have been looking for a way out of another circular argument with my mom."

"Anything you want to talk about?"

She gave a full-body sigh. "I've just been thinking of patterns and potholes. You know, those same conversations and experiences that you have so many times—"

"They become potholes you might fall into. Believe me, I know all about them."

"It was something Quinn said that day at the coffee shop."

"Ah, yes." Zander laughed. "When she accosted you and pleaded my case."

Quinn was still waiting for a thank-you.

"Yep, that time," Penny answered. "I keep thinking about this pothole thing. Like today my mom was talking about taking a vacation like she always does, and I responded like I always do, saying there was too much to do here. We're like a broken record."

"Do *you* want to go on a vacation?"

"I don't know." Penny turned, looking into the trees she'd walked through to come over. "I mean, sure? But she doesn't get it that things aren't that easy. Especially this year."

"Why especially this year?"

Penny looked back to him, mouth slightly parted, like there was something just on the tip of her tongue. "Forget it." She swept her braids to her back. "I didn't mean to start complaining. We've got work to do."

Something else was up, something that made Penny look a little desperate whenever she talked about the stakes of pulling off a great Honey Festival. Something he wanted to push but didn't, because this was Penny's life and he was only a blip in it, and he had no idea what they were to each other.

"Come on in." He opened the door just as Winter yelled, "Aww shit!"

Penny covered a laugh with her fist.

"Dude." Zander shook his head at his kid, leaning onto his elbows with his Switch in his hand. They'd had a *Mario Kart* tournament earlier—Winter wiping the floor with Zander, as he always did—and his kid was playing some new game now that moved too quickly for Zander's mid-thirties brain. "Language, please."

"You and Mom use that word all the time."

"Yeah, but we—"

"Have developed the self-control to know when to use it and when not to, and you don't want me being in the habit," he parroted, still not looking up from the game. "*I know*. Chill."

*Just don't react*, Mallory had taken to telling him. *Winter's hormones are a mess, and he's going to push to see what we do.*

Zander pushed some of his frustration out in a slow breath as Penny stepped into the house behind him. "Penny's here. We're going to work on the festival stuff a little. I was going to make some sandwiches. Will you come in and join us in the kitchen?"

The mention of Penny's name pulled Winter's eyes off the screen as a smile appeared on his face. "Dad's actually helping you, huh?"

"He actually is." Penny shot a dazzling smile to Zander before refocusing on Winter. "I'd love your input, too. A couple of years ago we started having a kids' tent with activities and stuff, but you probably know better than me what kids actually like."

Winter shrugged, but another smile was creeping its way up his face. "Yeah, I guess."

Zander led Penny through the open doorway to the kitchen, flooded in midday sunlight. Like always, he did a double take when he entered the room, seeing it then and now.

Then it was drab and stuffy, with newspapers on the table and the ancient drip coffee machine gurgling on the yellowing linoleum counter. His body had always tensed upon entering, crossing the room for cereal and milk and waiting for Papou to mumble something from his spot at the table. One morning when he was seventeen, a classified ad had been cut out and stuck to the door of the ancient fridge: a job listing for a landscaper with a local company, entry level, shit for pay. He'd wanted to swipe it from behind the magnet and toss it in the trash, but he also wanted money and a reason to be out of the house. And there was a hope that if he saved money to bring back to his mom, she might see how he could be helpful in the summers and not just a burden.

He'd gotten in three good weeks of work, sweating his ass off in the humidity, before getting in a fight with his boss that resulted in a call to his grandfather to come pick him up from the jobsite.

"It's nice in here." Penny's voice rolled over the rough edges of the memory. "Did you do all of this?"

He had. Bright yellow walls, green linen curtains from a thrift store two towns over, and an eclectic painting of a glimmering peacock that had made Winter laugh. There was a floral fabric tablecloth, a small jar of wildflowers, and the detritus of Zander's weeks in Sullivan's Glen spread onto the counters—the electric kettle he'd brought from Boston along with the waffle iron and his set of kitchen knives, and a dish rack full of colorful Fiestaware that he'd splurged on when picking up basic cleaning supplies at the store.

More than he'd *needed* to do once he covered the basics by watching enough YouTube videos to fix the dripping kitchen pipes, cover the worst of the wear and tear on the walls with fresh paint, and replace the flickering bulbs with ones constructed in this century.

"Yeah." He shrugged. "Thought it would be nice to make it a little homier for Winter. Even if it's temporary."

Penny's smile wavered. "Right. Totally."

"Anyway." He motioned to the table, where he'd been looking at the maps from the festival setup the year before. "I was starting to place vendors based on the applications we've gotten back. I thought maybe you could look at what I have so far and see if it looks okay, and we can go from there. Then I have some contracts for you to sign for the tent and table rental."

As Penny took a seat, Zander pulled out items from the fridge. "I was going to do turkey sandwiches, but we also have supplies for PB and J, or I have some hummus I made if you'd rather just that and veggies. I have stuff for a salad, too, and a tub of minestrone soup I picked up."

He might have gone a little hard at the store this morning, knowing Penny was coming over. He'd been so busy wondering what she might want to eat, he'd barely noticed the way the clerk—a woman probably close to his mom's age—had looked him up and down like he might have stolen goods stashed in his hoodie.

"Turkey's good." Penny shuffled papers around for a moment before tsking. "We can't put Neat Knit next to Light Up My Life, it'll be a disaster."

"Why not? And do you like mayo?"

"Yes to the mayo. And we have to separate them because Janice, who owns Neat Knit, is Noreen's cousin's ex and there's some bad blood there."

Zander dropped two pieces of sourdough in the toaster. "And Noreen is . . ."

"Noreen owns Light Up My Life. She sells candles with inspirational sayings on the containers, like *Live, Laugh, Love* and *Dance Like No One Is Watching*."

"I see." Zander worked on constructing the sandwich, hoping he was using the right amount of mayo and perfect leaves of lettuce, because he wanted Penny to really like this sandwich. "And Janice and Noreen's cousin had a particularly bad parting?"

"Well." Penny lowered her voice. "If you believe my mom's telling of it, Janice's husband, Antonio, suggested they open their marriage. And when they did, Janice had a lot more takers than Antonio, and suddenly the arrangement didn't look so good to him and he tried to shut it down. But at that point, Janice was way happier. And when she left him, his whole family kinda ganged up on her, including Noreen."

"Seriously?" Zander cut the sandwich down the middle and placed the triangles on an orange plate, then added a garnish of sliced strawberries. "All of this is happening in Sullivan's Glen, and somehow I'm still a matter of public interest? I can't hold a candle to Janice and Noreen."

"Yes, but you're new. Or new again. We small-town gossips love fresh blood."

"Do you?" He slid the plate in front of her and dropped into a chair to her left. "What are the local gossips saying about me lately?"

Either it was his imagination, or Penny shifted his way a few inches. "Mostly they have questions for me. They seem to think I have some special insight."

He lifted his brows. "I wonder why they'd think that?"

Under the table, Penny's knee brushed against his, sending a jolt right up his thigh.

Less than twenty-four hours ago he'd had his fingers inside her, had left her looking obscene with her shirt pushed up to her neck as he finished on her pale skin. But this—their knees touching, the sandwich he'd made for her on the table—was deliciously intimate. Kitchen intimate, the best kind.

"And what do they want to know?"

"What you're like now, what kind of father you are, why you're back." She hesitated, then looked at the table. "Why you didn't come back sooner."

"Ah." He swallowed hard. "And what do you say?"

"That you're a perfectly normal person, if a little stubborn." Penny's eyes found his again. "That you seem like a great father.

That you're back to help your family, to sell the house." Her hand slid over his, so light on the backs of his knuckles that he barely felt it. "And that I don't know why you didn't come back sooner, but I imagine you have your reasons, and that those are your business."

He was saved from having to respond to her generosity by Winter wandering into the room, eyes still on the screen of his device. Penny's hand slipped away like a breeze.

"Hey, bud. Let's put that down now, okay? You're in a room with other humans."

Winter hummed in response but didn't look up, and he slumped into the chair across the table from Penny.

"Winter."

Still not looking up, Winter answered with a gruff "What?"

Zander held back a wince. It burned each time his kid used that tone with him, like Zander was the enemy. "I asked you to put that down."

"In a minute."

"No." He let out a long breath. "Now, please. You're at the table with us. You know we don't do screens at the table."

"Unless it's your screen," his son mumbled. "Then it's fine. Because you're *working*."

Each successful restaurant launch had come with greater demands for Zander's attention, and he'd fallen into the bad pattern of returning emails and texts all the time. A pattern he was happy to disrupt with this break from work over the summer.

"Okay," he said. "You made your point. Now put it away, or we'll have to reassess how much gaming time you have each day."

This, finally, got Winter to look up. "And then what am I supposed to do? Hang out with all the friends I don't have here?"

It hit like a punch to Zander's chest. "Hey, buddy, we can look for—"

"Forget it." Winter stood, slamming the gaming device on the table, making the jar of flowers wobble. His hard, closed look made Zander ache. He could see how much his kid was trying to be tough, how much conflict brewed behind his eyes. It was like looking back in time into a mirror.

"I can see you need some space," Zander said calmly. More calmly than any adult had ever spoken to him when he was being a pain in the ass, which wasn't saying much. "Maybe you should take a break in your room. When you're ready to come back down, I'll make you some food."

They stared at each other for a moment, but then Winter stormed out. Zander let his face fall into his hands. Penny—whom he'd shopped for and cut a sandwich into perfect triangles for because he was trying to show her that he was worth her time—had just watched him have another stupid fight with his kid.

"I'm sorry about that," he said finally through a lump in his throat.

Penny's voice was soft beside him. "Don't worry about it. That's normal family stuff."

He looked up. "Is it? I think that's half my problem. I don't know what's normal. I read books, and I talk to my therapist, but it's like I'm making the map as I go, you know?"

She looked at him kindly, generously, and it only made him feel worse.

"I've pissed so many people off in my life, Penny. I've had grown men shout at me in the middle of a busy kitchen. I've had my own mom tell me I wasn't much more than a drain on her bank account. But when Winter looks at me like that? Like he can't stand me? It scares me so fucking much."

Her hand covered his again, and this time Zander let himself flip his palm over and watch as she threaded her fingers through his.

"What scares you?"

"Mal swears this is all normal. I know logically she's right." He slowed his breathing to the rhythm of Penny's thumb rubbing his knuckles. "I'm just so scared of him deciding I'm not worth it."

Of Winter rejecting him the same way he'd cut off his mom and Papou.

Penny looked at him for a minute, then pulled her hand free and stood to move to the counter, where she started constructing a sandwich. He watched her build the layers, cut the whole thing into triangles, and pull a blue plate from the dish rack.

She lowered the plate in front of him and returned to her seat. The sandwich was maybe the best thing he'd ever seen. "When I tell the gossips you seem like a great dad, I mean it. You're showing up for Winter, giving him the love you should have gotten more of yourself. You can't see into the future and know what your relationship will always look like, but you're breaking patterns. You're creating something different for him than what you were given, and you should be proud of yourself."

Stunned, Zander blinked back the heat in his eyes. When he opened his mouth to say anything—*Really? Thank you? What am I to you?*—no words pressed through.

Penny smiled and nodded to the festival map. "Now eat something, and I'll tell you why Carrie's Homemade Jewelry can't even be in the same row as Rasheed's Ten-Minute Massage Stand."

Zander cleared his throat. "All right. But if a juicy scandal isn't involved, I'm going to be sorely disappointed."

# CHAPTER 19

ZANDER B  *Winter is back at Mallory's. Are you free for dinner tonight?*

ZANDER B  *And for the record, this would be a date.*

Penny read the texts again as she paced the small footprint of her cabin.

A date, a date, a date.

Zander would be here any minute for their date.

He'd texted her that morning while she was working at a farmer's market two towns away. She'd gasped so loudly at that message that a customer worried his credit card was declined. By the time she was able to respond, the market was over and she had two more texts waiting.

ZANDER B  *Please tell me if I'm coming on too strong.*

ZANDER B  *Penny?*

A date with Zander was a bad idea. He was fun, and hot, and made Penny feel lighter in his presence. And while making out with him on her couch had been, *wow*, really amazing, chatting at his kitchen table was just as special. But did she have time for any of that this summer? Or the wherewithal to watch him leave when it was over?

"Text back," RJ had said bluntly, staring over her shoulder without shame. "Say yes. You deserve it."

"But—"

"But nothing, Pen. Don't overthink it. Let yourself have this. You deserve nice things."

And dammit, she did. So she'd typed back a yes before she could think better of it. Which now left her pacing the living room in a dress that was maybe cute or maybe way too much.

When Zander's truck rumbled out front, Penny was too amped to stand inside, so she grabbed her bag and stepped out to meet him. He was still in his car, looking into the visor mirror and, from what Penny could tell, talking to himself. His lips moved and he nodded and then, adorably, he fist-bumped his own small reflection. When he made a move to exit the car, he caught her watching and shook his head with a smile.

"I was, uh, giving myself a pep talk," he said a moment later, after hopping out of his car to walk her around to the passenger side. No one had ever opened a car door for Penny, and there was something almost shy about how Zander did it, looking away from her like she might laugh at the gesture.

"Am I that scary?" she asked, brow raised.

"No." He jogged to his side and slid in. They were down the drive and turning onto the main road when he spoke again. "You're not scary. But the idea of being on a date, especially with you, is a little, um—"

"Nerve-racking?" she offered. "Exciting? Terrifying?"

"Yeah." He shot her a relieved smile. "Yes, all three."

"So, where are we going?"

Another smile. "You'll see."

They rode in a comfortable if weighted silence as Zander took a road into the hills outside town. When they passed their third *Private Property—No Trespassing* sign, Penny tucked her feet under her to face Zander. "Are we supposed to be here?"

"Not technically." He turned onto a small dirt road almost imperceptible in the trees. "But we're not hurting anyone, and it'll be worth it."

The grin he shot her way made Penny squirm a little in her seat. When the hem of her dress shifted higher on her thigh, Zander's gaze tangled in the bunching fabric until he cleared his throat and returned his attention to the road.

The trees thinned as Zander drove into a large clearing that was all dirt except for three large concrete slabs, the kind that marked the first phase of construction.

"These have been here since I was sixteen." Zander shut off the car as he nodded outside. "I found them one night taking my grandfather's car on any back road I could find."

He jogged around to her side again, and Penny undid her belt slowly so as not to beat him to opening her door. Once outside, she spun to look around—three would-be houses were poised on a bluff overlooking the valley below. There were tracts of farmland like checkerboards, lower wooded hills, stripes of vineyard rows, a few shimmering lakes in the distance, and in the center . . . the township of Sullivan's Glen.

"I think I remember Mimi talking about this place," Penny said, pulling at memories. "It was supposed to be some luxury development, but the builders got in a fight with a local conservation group, and everything sort of froze." A breeze played with the bottom of her dress. "It's beautiful up here."

"It is." Zander watched her for a moment, then let out a breath and pulled items from the trunk of his car. Soon a blanket was spread on the ground, along with a quaint picnic basket and a bottle of champagne. He popped the cork and poured the champagne into two small mason jars as Penny lowered herself to sit.

He handed over her glass and clinked his against it, his eyes never leaving hers.

She grinned. "Here's to trespassing."

Zander laughed as he sipped. "To being a little bit bad."

The bubbles tickled her mouth and throat as Zander watched her over the rim of his glass.

He cleared his throat as he pulled out a loaf of bread, a chunk of cheese, and a bundle of plump red grapes, laying them out on a large cutting board. "Um, help yourself."

Penny stretched her legs in front of her and ripped off a piece of baguette, recognizing that unique crack of crust of Sullivan Bakery bread. "So. Did you bring a lot of girls to this spot?"

"No, actually. I always came here alone."

"What would you do?"

He shrugged, looking out at the view. "I'd sit and brood. I liked the idea of looking down on everything, like somehow it made me bigger to see everybody so small."

"Does it feel like that now?"

Zander looked out in silence for a minute, then shook his head with a sigh. "Honestly? No. It still looks small, but I don't think I need to feel big anymore." He chuckled lightly. "I do see a lot of memories, though."

She scooched a little closer to him. "Like what?"

He pointed down at the valley. "See where Main Street leaves Sullivan's Glen and heads east, then bends around that lake?"

Penny knew just the spot he was talking about. She could

drive all the roads of the county with her eyes closed, but she moved closer anyway, leaning in to look down the length of his arm. "I see it."

He shifted slightly, leaning his shoulder against hers. "That's the farthest I ever got on foot before the old man pulled up behind me. I could hear his car coming from a mile away."

"Where were you going?"

"Beats the hell out of me. Just gone, I guess. My teenage mind was mostly impulses and reactions. A repetition of the fight-or-flight cycle."

Penny followed his arm as it swung left. "I climbed that water tower once," he said with amusement. "I had this idea that I could graffiti a romantic message to Mal up there."

"I thought you didn't like heights?"

"I learned that one the hard way. I made it up the ladder by talking to myself the whole time, but once I was up there, it was very hard to talk myself down."

"Wait." Penny swiveled to look at him. "I remember this! The fire department sent someone up there to get you. Everyone said you refused to come down, so they had to harness you to someone to make you leave."

Zander looked sheepishly at the ground. "It was a little less *wouldn't* come down and a little more *couldn't* come down. Not that I shied away from letting everyone think I was just that troublesome. What about you? What do you see when you look down there?"

Penny looked west to east, tracing the contours of the valley. "More memories than I can count. And a lot of farmer's markets." She pointed to spots all around the valley as she listed them by name. "But mostly, I just see home." She drew her hands back into her lap, feeling suddenly self-conscious. "That's kind of cheesy."

"It's nice." Zander reached for her slowly and took her hand in his. "I think that's a feeling some people search for their whole lives."

"Is that how Boston feels for you? Like home?"

Zander's thumb passed over the back of her hand. "Not quite," he said. "It is home, but I don't know if it feels like home, if that makes sense."

"Yeah." Her voice was a little breathy. Zander was only holding her hand, but her entire body was very aware of every centimeter shared between them.

"But Penny?" His gaze dropped to her mouth. "I don't want to talk about Boston right now."

She swallowed. "You don't?"

"No." He leaned closer, putting his other hand on the blanket beside her hip.

"What do you want to talk about?"

He looked down to where her dress fluttered a few inches above her knees. "I want to talk about how this dress is making me a madman."

"Oh?" Her voice cracked. "I was worried it was too much."

"It's not." He released her hand and wrapped his palm around her thigh, the press of his fingertips hot through the thin fabric of her dress. "It's just right." Zander came closer, until his breath was hot in her ear. "But I can't stop thinking about sliding my hand under it, finding out if you'll be as wet for me as you were the other day."

She licked her suddenly dry lips. "I was starting to think that day might have been a dream."

"Mm." Zander hummed against her neck. "Me too. It felt like one. Can't stop thinking about it." His hand slid up her leg, where his thumb teased at the crease of her thigh before drawing back down toward her knee. He pulled back to look at her. "I've been wondering what it meant to you."

She wouldn't let herself look away, even as her face heated further. "I've been wondering what it meant to *you*."

He smiled, leaned in, and brushed her nose with his, whispering against her mouth, "It meant something, I know that much."

"It meant something to me, too."

Then Zander kissed her, slowly and thoroughly, like a walk through the forest, as sunshine shone through gaps in the trees. It was the kind of kiss she wanted to live in for a little while.

He drew a hand up and into her loose hair. "Kissing you is better than I remembered."

She wrapped a hand around his neck, urging the kiss deeper as Zander moved over her. Small rocks poked at her back through the blanket as she lay beneath him, but it didn't matter, because Zander's hand was under her skirt now, his mouth working at her shoulder, then trailing down the strap of her dress.

He tongued her skin along her collarbone and scraped his teeth on the rise of her breasts, then caught her gaze with his deep brown eyes. Above him, wisps of clouds streaked against the just barely pink sky. "Come home with me tonight?"

She nodded mutely, teased by the hand gripping her bare thigh. "Okay."

His eyes searched hers. "Sleep over?"

More nodding, then a shift of her hips as she tried to ease the ache building between her legs. "I can't promise much sleeping. And I'll have to get up early for the Johnstown market."

Zander's mouth descended on hers for a moment; then he nipped at her bottom lip. "I'll get up with you and go help."

"RJ will be there."

"It'll be easier with all of us, right?"

It would, but she could not believe he was talking about the farmer's market right now. "Zander, please shut up and move your hand a few inches higher."

His laugh was dark and tempting, just like his fingers as they crept up her thigh. "Someone is very eager."

But just as Zander pressed his palm where she needed it, there was the roar of an engine and the bright glare of headlights. Zander pulled away his hand and angled his body in front of hers as she sat up.

A car door slammed, and a figure stepped out, their face impossible to discern against the bright shine behind them.

"You folks are trespassing on private property." Penny recognized the voice, and it made her skin crawl. Especially when it spoke next. "My, if it isn't Zander Bouras. It sure will be my pleasure to arrest your ass."

# CHAPTER 20

In all the times Zander snuck up to this spot as a teenager, he'd never encountered a cop.

So it was just his luck that one was here now, when he was about to strike gold under Penny's dress. And whoever this guy was, he had a bone to pick with Zander.

Zander helped Penny to her feet, still keeping her behind him. "Hey, man," he called, shielding his eyes. "Can you turn off the headlights? You're blinding us."

"Step over here please." The cop motioned to the side of the car. "And move slowly."

"Jesus Christ," Zander muttered. He kept contact with Penny as they followed directions. "We were having a picnic, not committing international espionage."

Penny pushed out from behind him and stomped ahead. "Brad, what the hell? Why are you being such an ass?"

"Penny, geez." The whining wasn't too far off from how Winter sounded when Zander told him to eat his vegetables. "Will you just cooperate and show some respect?"

Out of the glare of the headlights, Zander had a better view of the guy. He was tall and thin, his gray uniform pants cinched by a leather belt. His pinkish skin looked pallid in the glow around the car. When Zander made eye contact, the guy stood taller. "I'd say it's nice to see you again," he said with a sneer. "But it's not."

"I'd say it's nice to see you again," Zander replied. "But I have no idea who you are."

The cop scoffed, disorientation flashing across his face.

Penny's fingers brushed Zander's between their bodies. "It's Brad Jeffries."

"Brad?" Zander squeezed the bridge of his nose. "I thought we already encountered Brad."

"This is the other Brad. He and Brad Preston hung out together, and everybody called them—"

"The Brads. I remember now." Skinny Brad Jeffries was always trailing after his friend, talking a big talk and thumping his chest. But he'd run off as soon as Zander punched his buddy.

"Enough." Brad stalked toward them, keys jingling. "I heard you were back, Zander, and I knew it was just a matter of time before you were up to the same old shit. I've been keeping my eye on you."

"Keeping your eye on me?" Zander shook his head, disgusted. "There aren't kittens you could be saving or old ladies to help across the road? Maybe innocent motorists to profile?"

Penny grabbed for his fingers. "Hey, it's okay."

"It's not okay. This is total bullshit and he knows it. But fine—" Zander threw up his hands. "We'll pack up and get out of here, okay?"

"'Fraid not." Brad shook his head dismissively. "I think considering you're trespassing, and acting suspiciously, I better take you in for questioning."

"Excuse me?"

"In fact, there's been some weird stuff happening around town. Trash cans knocked over and such. Could be an act of vandalism by someone with an old axe to grind."

Penny stepped forward. "Cut the shit! You know that's the raccoons. Everybody knows it's the raccoons."

"Come on, Penny." Brad gave her a sleazy grin, the kind that deserved to be wiped right off his face. "Don't jump in trying to help. I think a guy like Zander Bouras can take care of himself, don't you?"

Zander made a move forward, but Penny cut him off, nearly blocking his view of Brad. "Of course he can!" she shouted, hands balled in fists at her sides. "Of course he can take care of himself! He's been doing it forever. He was taking care of himself when other people should have been doing it for him. He was taking care of himself when your mom was whining to the parks commissioner just so you wouldn't get benched in Little League games!"

Brad's face went red. "She did not."

"She did and everyone knows it," Penny spat. "You sucked at baseball! And you suck now, using your power to try to intimidate us, to poke at Zander just like you all used to. He's a grown man. It's embarrassing, Brad, and you should be ashamed of yourself."

Zander stepped beside her. "Penny, you don't need to—"

She spun on him, face pink and twisted in anger. "I've *got* this, so please just shut up."

And this really wasn't the best time, but her fury—for him—had Zander half hard again.

"This is how it's going to go," Penny said back to Brad, her finger in the air. "We're going to pack up our picnic and drive away. And not only are you *not* going to take Zander in tonight, you're not going to say a single word to him for the rest of the summer. Do you understand?"

Brad sputtered and stepped back, staring at Penny with his jaw hung open. "Why would I do that?"

"Because if you don't, I'll tell Jenny about all those trips you make to the Red Garter outside Lewisville. What do you think the odds are that when your wife hears your paycheck is going into those backroom poker games, she'll cut you off from her parents' money, hmm?"

His eyes went double wide. "You wouldn't."

"I would. And I've got plenty more material if I need it. Sometimes there's a benefit to having a mother who needs gossip like it's oxygen."

Brad Jeffries gaped like a suffocating fish as Penny turned on her heel to pick up their blanket. Zander followed silently, taking items as she passed them over and stowing them back in the basket he'd found at an antique store on Main Street. Penny shook out the blanket and bundled it up, her hands shaking just enough for Zander to notice. Without acknowledging Brad, Penny stalked to Zander's car. A minute later, they were heading back down the dark road.

Zander counted passing trees through the silence as his head swam.

"I'm sorry," Penny said quietly, a different woman from the fierce warrior who'd stared down Brad. "I shouldn't have spoken for you. I just got so angry, and—"

"Penny." He closed a hand around her knee. "Do you think I'm mad?"

"I don't know." She worried her lip as she looked at him. "You're not saying anything, so I guess I assumed—"

"No one has ever stood up for me like that, ever. So it's a lot to wrap my brain around. Not to mention." Zander tightened his fingers on her knee. "You were so sexy laying into him, I am using all my self-control to keep from pulling over right here and fucking you in the back seat of my car."

"Oh." Her leg shifted beneath him. "You could. I have a condom in my bag."

Jesus ever loving—

"Don't tempt me, Penny." When the dirt road approached the asphalt, Zander slowed to a stop and turned to her, tipping her chin up with his finger and staring into her blazing blue eyes. "When I fuck you, you're going to be naked and in my bed, and I'm going to touch and taste you everywhere until you're begging to have me inside you."

She blinked and swallowed as Zander's chest swelled with satisfaction. Penny Becker liked dirty talk, and he liked giving it to her.

"Not to mention," he added, "our friend Brad will have to come back down this road soon, and I'm not about to give him a show."

"Oh yeah." She peeked behind them, where the road was blessedly dark. When she looked back at him, she swiped her bottom lip with her tongue.

He wanted to kiss her. But odds were low he would be able to stop, so Zander eased the car onto the larger street. "You really tore him a new asshole."

Penny barked a laugh. "Oh my god, the look on his face!"

"I thought he might pee himself when you mentioned the poker games."

"You know the best part? I wasn't even sure. It was just a rumor, but I went for it."

Zander joined in her laughter. "In that case, I'd say you just garnered a confession. Did you really have more dirt on him?"

She shook her head. "No. But I assumed there was more dirt, because he's one of the Brads."

"And the Brads are the worst."

"The worst!" she shrieked.

And then they were both cracking up, Zander gasping for breath as Penny wiped tears off her cheeks.

"I've got to hand it to you, Zander. I've never had a date quite like this one."

"Likewise, Penny. Likewise."

# CHAPTER 21

Zander opened the car door for Penny again when they got back to his place.

But instead of helping her out, he leaned inside, slanted his body over hers, and crashed their mouths together.

Penny cupped his face as Zander took the kiss deep, like he was making up for every minute of the drive they'd spent not touching. She let it overtake her, pushing aside her to-do lists and responsibilities until her brain registered only the echo of champagne on Zander's lips and the pressure of his hand sweeping over her waist to unclick her seat belt.

He broke the kiss with a groan and pressed his forehead to hers. "Was it just me, or was that the longest drive ever?"

Penny laughed as Zander tugged her out of the car, closing her door before pushing her against it. His mouth went to her neck, where he scraped his teeth against her skin with perfect pressure as his hands gripped her hips. Penny snaked her hands beneath his T-shirt and let herself explore the broad softness of his stomach and the thick hair on his chest.

He moaned and pulled back, releasing his grip on her hip to run his fingers gently over her cheek. "Is this all okay? I haven't done this in a long time. I haven't *wanted* to do this in a long time. And now it's like the floodgates are bursting."

Penny moved his hand under her dress, watching his jaw drop open as she pushed his fingers against her underwear. "You're not the only one with bursting floodgates."

His face tipped back in a laugh that filled the darkening sky above them, where a few swallows dipped and dove. Then his fingers dragged up and down, pressing into her through the fabric, and he wasn't laughing anymore. The intent in his eyes had shifted to something predatory.

"Come on," he said gruffly. "We need to go inside."

After grabbing the picnic supplies from the back, Zander guided Penny into the house. "I just need to put this stuff away," he said, riffling through the basket. "Because I plan to be busy for the rest of the night." He was throwing cheeses into the refrigerator when he stopped and turned. "But you didn't eat much. Are you hungry? I should feed you."

She watched the furrow deepen on his brow, the nervous twitch of his fingers, and thought of the urge she'd had lately to parade this man through the streets. To take him from shop to shop, showing everyone who he was now. Probably who he'd always been deep down: someone who was sensitive, kind, and generous to a fault. A person with such a big heart, it was easy to bruise.

"I'm sorry."

Zander's face fell, one hand gripping the back of his neck as he watched her. "Sorry? What for? Penny, if this is moving too fast—"

"No." She cut him off with a shake of her head. "It's not that. I'm just sorry that I never tried to know you during the summers that you were here. I'm sorry you were going through something and didn't get the love and support you deserved."

"Penny." He sighed her name like a song, coming close enough to run his fingers over her hair. "It's okay. It was rough sometimes, but it wasn't all bad. I had friends in Detroit, even if they were terrible influences. I had good times with my mom when she was doing well; I had teachers who'd slip me books I might like and beg me to do the slightest bit of work so they didn't have to fail me. And I had Mal, and then I had Winter. And he gave me the chance to decide what kind of person I was going to be, how I was going to define myself."

"Is it selfish of me," she asked, "that I'm glad you had to come back?"

His lips brushed her cheek, then her ear, where he whispered, "I'll tell you a secret." His swallow was slow, like he was preparing for something. "Sometimes I think I'm glad I had to come back, too."

Before she could ask anything more, Zander's mouth trailed across Penny's jaw, finding her lips again to kiss her slowly, like a discovery. Tender, like a thank-you.

He drew back and held her face in his hands. "We should talk about what this is."

This. The two of them, and the bad idea they kept jumping into with fervor.

"I don't want to pretend it doesn't mean something to me," he continued. "This feels like way more than a hookup or a fling. But I'll be back in Boston in less than two months, so I also don't want to pretend this can be something it's not."

Come the end of summer, he'd be back in Boston, and she'd be dealing with whatever happened after the festival. If they managed to pull it all off as she hoped, maybe she'd be finally addressing the loan and finding fresh footing. If not, she'd be managing the fallout. Either way, she'd do it alone.

Nothing with Zander changed any of that, and maybe it was better that way. Better to know when something would end, and her normal life would start back up. And until then, she could take hold of something good, and fun, and freeing.

It was tempting to call it a fling. Easier on her heart at the end of the summer. But Zander was right—it felt like more, and Penny couldn't help but believe she deserved to see it as more, too. Even if it wouldn't last.

"So we let it be real," she said with a solid resolve in her chest. "Even if it's temporary."

A thumb brushed her cheek. "Real, but temporary." Zander nodded, but his frown persisted. "It's going to be hard, when the summer is over. I don't want to cause you pain later."

Penny shrugged. "Sometimes pain just means you had something worth missing. I've spent so much of my life taking care of things, weighing pros and cons and making the right decisions. Maybe I should . . ." She bit her lip and fluttered her eyelashes. "Be a little bad?"

Whatever resistance Zander was still holding wavered as his eyes narrowed on her mouth. For a moment, he just stared; then he looked back at her with a grin.

"You want to be bad, huh?"

Penny warmed at the obvious shift in his mood and dark intent in his eyes. "I've always been such a good girl." She pushed out her lower lip in a pout. It was a little ridiculous, but it made Zander's nostrils flare. "Maybe I need to try something different."

He pressed a thumb on her bottom lip. "Maybe you do. Get on the table."

"The—what?"

His brows arched. "You never told me whether or not you were hungry, but I just realized that I am. Starving, in fact."

Zander brushed against her as he plucked a small jar of wildflowers from the table and set it down on the counter; then he crowded her space as his hands slid up her bare arms.

He toyed with one of the thin straps of her dress, looking at Penny with hooded eyes. When she nodded, Zander pulled both straps down her shoulders. He removed her dress slowly, watching each inch of her skin as it was revealed, bending to taste the curve of her neck, the swell of her breast, and, in a move that made Penny gasp his name, closing his teeth on her nipple over her bra.

When the bunched fabric of her dress gathered at her hips, Zander tugged it over and down, whispering a low, growled "fuck" when the material fell to her feet.

He brushed her lips with his. "I believe I asked you to get on the table."

"But—" She finally registered his last words, about being starving. "You *wouldn't*."

His chuckle was dark and enticing. "I would."

He closed his hands around her waist and lifted her to the edge of the table, then smiled and ran his fingers over her hips. "I want to make sure we do this all the right way. Like I said before, it's been a while since I've been with anyone. All my tests are negative."

"Mine, too." Penny let her legs fall open to make more space for him. "I'm on birth control, but I want to use a condom to be totally safe."

"Sounds good." Zander's hands drew up her waist, then lightly brushed against the sides of her breasts. "What about other stuff? Do you like oral? If yes, are you comfortable without extra protection for that?"

Penny reached back to undo the clasp of her bra, then shrugged the whole thing off as Zander's gaze devoured her. "You mean is it okay if you go down on me on your kitchen table?"

"Yeah, Becker." He palmed her breasts, plumping them in his hands as he licked his lips. "That's exactly what I mean."

And maybe Penny should have demurred, but Zander had her feeling free, like she could be anyone when it was just the two of them. So she spread her legs wider in invitation. "Only if you promise to change the tablecloth after."

A bark of a laugh. "You have yourself a deal."

He bent his head, bringing his lips and tongue to one nipple, then the other, always glancing up, gauging her reactions, adjusting his pressure and speed until she was grappling with the back of his T-shirt.

"You're overdressed," she whined.

He caught her mouth in a fast kiss and yanked his shirt up and over his head, letting it drop to the floor. Zander's chest and stomach were broad and soft, covered in dark hair she wasted no time in touching. "You're beautiful."

He ran his hands reverently up her thighs, letting his thumbs just barely touch her underwear.

"Christ." Zander shuddered as his fingers touched where she was damp and needy. He pressed his palm against her. "Tell me this is for me." With a tug and a whoosh, her underwear was tossed to the side. Then Zander pulled up a chair and took a seat, hooked his fingers under her knees, and dragged her to the edge of the table.

"This is—" Penny gasped. "I've never done it quite like this."

He grinned from between her knees. "I do like to leave an impression."

Penny couldn't muster an answer, because Zander started touching her, running his thumb through her wetness, then using his hands to expose her to him, groaning before he dove in.

"Jesus," he murmured against her. "So sweet, just like I knew you'd be."

His mouth moved on her desperately, as if seeking the satisfaction that only her writhing could bring. His movements and sounds, his pure enthusiasm, confirmed he was enjoying this as much as she was. Which was a whole hell of a lot, especially when he hoisted her leg over his shoulder to go deeper, fucking her with his tongue like he'd been born for it.

Zander grasped Penny's ass, holding her body to his mouth like a holy offering, as she massaged her own breasts with one hand while the other grasped Zander's hair, urging him on. It had been two years since she'd been in bed with Henry, but longer since she'd been this hungry for it, chasing an orgasm that started in the tips of her toes and crackled like lightning through her body. When his tongue finally landed on her clit, swiping as she whimpered his name, she knew she wouldn't last much longer.

Then Zander closed his lips around her and sucked hard as he slid one long, thick finger inside her, and Penny's climax hit her fast. Shooting stars streamed across her vision as she shook in Zander's strong grip.

Slowly, she drifted back to reality: the hard table beneath her, the bright yellow cabinets, and Zander, showering her face and neck with kisses, telling her she was beautiful, thanking her for giving that to him. Penny let herself float, blessedly relaxed.

After a moment she cupped his face and pulled him in for a deep kiss, getting a possessive thrill from the taste of herself on his lips.

"So," she said with a smile. "What's for dessert?"

Zander offered her a hand and pulled her off the table, then ran a palm down her bare spine. "Why don't you come upstairs with me and find out."

# CHAPTER 22

When their feet hit the upstairs hallway, Zander used his hands on Penny's hips to guide her to his doorway, then pressed her against the wall for a long, lingering kiss. "Give me one second, okay?"

She nodded, eyes still a little glazy, like she was waking from a dream. Funny, since they'd been acting out *his* dream down there—undressing her, exploring her body, spreading her before him on the table. Making Penny come had been every bit as mind-altering as he'd expected.

He dropped a kiss to her forehead and slipped into his room, flipping switches and smoothing out the bedspread, and returned to her as quickly as he could. When he pulled her inside, he watched her face as she took it in.

Penny's blue eyes twinkled as they reflected the strings of lights he'd hung on the walls and ceiling. He'd done his best to put some in clusters, imitating the—

"Fairy lights," she said quietly. "It's beautiful."

He wrapped his arms around her bare waist, pressing his chest to her warm back. "I thought you'd like it. And lucky for both of us, I just got a new mattress. It's the kind that expands when you open the box. Winter thought it was amazing."

Penny laughed in his arms as he smoothed the golden water-fall of her hair to one side, exploring her neck for a slow kiss. He lost himself again in the softness of her body, ignoring questions in his own head about why he'd buy himself a nice bed when his goal was to sell the house and get out, or why he'd invested in all the small improvements that made this whole place feel more like a home.

It was for Winter, he'd told himself with every step. And in this room, for Penny. To give her a taste of magic in her busy life.

Zander shuffled them toward the bed, but before he could toss Penny onto his brand-new navy comforter, she spun in his arms and began laying hot kisses along his neck, then trailed her tongue along his collarbone as her hands slid south to the waistband of his jeans. The button popped open easily—no surprise, as Zander's erection had been straining against it since she'd stepped out of her house earlier in that dress. Penny pulled down the zipper and dipped her hand inside, pressing her palm against him through his boxers.

Zander shuddered as his knees went weak.

Penny's fingers closed around him, giving him a soft squeeze over the fabric. She moaned into his neck as she maneuvered inside his boxers to wrap her fingers around his full length. Whatever flash of insecurity she'd had the other day was long gone, and she moved now with the confidence of a woman who regularly held bees in her bare hands.

But then she was out of his arms, dropping to her knees.

"Penny—"

"Let me." She pulled at his jeans and boxers, bringing them to his ankles. "I want to learn how to make you feel good."

It was a struggle to stay upright as he shucked off his clothes while Penny ran her curious fingers up and down him, but he managed. When her tongue stretched out to lick him experimentally, he had to weave his hands into her hair for grounding.

Her tongue danced around the head of his erection, barely flirting with the edge of his foreskin.

"That's it," he encouraged. "If you lick just under the foreskin, it feels really good."

When she did, fireworks shot up his spine. His fingers played in her hair, staying gentle, making sure she had room to pull away. She covered his whole tip with her mouth as her hand gripped him, and when he responded with a light tug on her hair, she moaned loudly around his cock.

Everything she was doing felt so damn good, but he still noticed the concentrated furrowed line of her brow, her classic determination to do something to the best of her ability.

"Relax, baby," he soothed, loving the way the pet name rolled off his tongue. "You're doing so good. It all feels amazing. Fucking incredible."

If the way she then took almost his full length into her mouth was any indication, the praise pleased her.

"Just like that." Zander tried to keep talking, but forming words was hard when he was engulfed in the sweet heat of her mouth as she squeezed his base. "But I'm gonna come in your mouth if you keep it up."

This earned him another moan that sent vibrations through his body, but she released him and looked up. The sight of Penny Becker's blue eyes locked on him while she was on her knees almost sent him over the edge. "Don't come yet. I want—"

He rubbed a thumb across her cheek as he studied her wet, swollen mouth. "You want what, Penny?"

He knew, but sometimes he was a selfish bastard, and he wanted to hear her say it.

But she only raised her eyebrows. "I thought you'd have me begging for it."

With a growl he hardly recognized, Zander pulled her up and kissed her. "Get on the bed."

When he turned back from his bag in the closet, condom in hand, she was spread out on her back, hands behind her head and a smile on her face. The full view of her body—supple, soft, and strong as hell all at once—made him stumble. He dropped the condom on the bed and crawled over her. "You ready to beg yet?"

Her body arched into him as she smiled. "Not quite."

"So stubborn." He tsked. "Almost like you already forgot how hard I made you come downstairs. Maybe I should remind you."

He entered her with one, then two fingers, moving slowly to make sure her body would be ready to take him when she finally asked. He used his other hand on her breasts, squeezing her nipples as she writhed beneath him, so entranced by her body and its reactions that he barely registered Penny reaching for the condom and tearing open the package.

He encircled her wrist and pinned it over her head, foil packet still in her fingers. "I think you're forgetting something."

Penny pouted defiantly, her full lower lip pushed out. "I don't beg."

Zander pulled the condom from her hand, ripped it open, and rolled it down on himself as she watched. When she snaked her tongue along her lip, he pumped his cock again for good measure, going impossibly harder as Penny's eyes glazed at the sight.

"Tell me what you want," he said gruffly, squeezing himself.

Her gaze flicked to his face with understanding. He didn't just want to hear it, he *needed* to hear it. To know she was choosing this, choosing him. Her pout softened to a smile. "I want you inside me. Please. Please, Zander."

*Please, Zander.* He wanted to hear it from her all night, breathless and on edge.

He rolled to his back, pulling Penny so that she was draped over him. "Ride me, Penny."

Her chest heaving, Penny straddled him, taking him in hand. They both watched as she held him in place and lowered herself slowly.

*Holy. Shit.* She was so tight around him that Zander felt it all over his body, squeezing at his lungs and heart.

Penny closed her eyes and bit her lip, and Zander stopped her with a hand on her hip. "You okay? Go as slow as you need."

"It's so good," she said dreamily. Her eyes opened to shine on him. "It's so good, I want to go slow. Want to treasure it."

Her body moved slowly over him, taking him in another inch. Penny's hair streamed over her shoulders as lights sparkled behind her. It was beyond his imagining—that he'd have her like this at all, let alone here, fairies alight around her in a room he no longer recognized. It suddenly seemed too much to hold, like it could crumble in his grip.

"I don't deserve this," Zander said quietly.

"You do." Penny lowered herself farther. "You do." Her hands went to his face, and she kissed him as she brought her body flush to his. "You do deserve this. So take it."

And he did, thrusting his hips up into hers as he set their rhythm, lifting her and taking her deep, then rocking his hips against hers.

She was a vision, rising and falling on him, some kind of honey-blessed goddess.

"You feel," he moaned, "so, so good."

As Penny pressed her hands to her chest, Zander slid a hand between them, finding the ripe nub of her clit. She gasped as she hit his finger, again and again.

"Oh god," she moaned. "Oh god, oh god."

"Just like that." He urged her on. "Use my hand, use my cock. Come for me like this."

Her movements became more desperate as she chased her orgasm, grinding down on his fingers and rolling her hips.

"Zander." Her head tipped back. "God, Zander."

"I've got you, Penny. Come on, baby."

He saw the climax on her face first, her expression going taut as she moaned his name. Then he felt it around his body, squeezing him, holding him tight as she rode it out.

But it was her eyes opening again, looking at him full of fucking wonder, that put Zander over the edge. He flipped them with ease and hooked an arm beneath Penny's knee to open her wider, then drove into her.

She gasped a sharp "yes" with each thrust, her nails grappling for a grip on his back as he lost himself in her, burying his face in her hair as he came hard. He might have shouted her name, or a string of expletives, or a prayer. It was all lost in the bliss of his orgasm.

Zander gave himself the deep pleasure of relaxing over Penny for just a few seconds, then made sure to hold the condom in place as he rolled off. It was a damn pleasure to look over and see her flushed and relaxed, her entire body splayed like a happy starfish.

"Wow," she said after a minute, turning to him with a lazy smile on her face. "I'd kind of built that up in my head, and I think it might have been as good in reality."

"Might have been?" Zander climbed over her as she giggled,

then showered her face and neck with kisses as she screeched. He let up only when she yelled, "Okay, it was better!"

He told Penny how to find the bathroom down the hall, then dealt with the condom. After stepping into fresh boxer briefs and grabbing one of his most comfortable T-shirts in case Penny wanted it, he sat back on the bed, stupidly arranging himself to look dashing when she came into the room. Soon she was back in the doorway, flushed and naked and biting her lip.

"So." Her foot made circles on the old wood floor. "What happens now?"

"Whatever we want." He stood and brought the shirt to her, pulling it over her head and arms. It was almost worth losing the sight of her incredible body to see her in his clothes. "We're defining what this looks like for the summer. For my part, I hope you'll spend the night. Then I want to help you at the market. After that, I hope to see you as much as I can."

"You kind of have to see me a lot anyway, if you're going to keep helping with the festival stuff."

"Even better." He wrapped Penny in a bear hug and threw them both down on the bed as she giggled. "I'm going to insist you eat dinner soon, but first I want to cuddle."

Penny nestled against him. "You really are a softie underneath, just like Quinn said."

"Geez, that woman. Giving away all my secrets."

"How's she been doing here with Mallory's family?"

Zander reached for Penny's hand and held it above them, tracing each of her fingers as he talked. "She's doing really well, actually. I thought she'd go bananas living with Mal's parents, but being around them, feeling like a family, is giving her something she needs. Something I'm not even sure I realized she was missing."

Quinn had always had rough edges, something that had drawn

Zander to her in the first place. And even here, with the summer sun tanning her cheeks as she worked from the Robinsons' porch, Quinn was still Quinn—fierce and full of attitude. But whether it was being in love with Mallory, or the copious amounts of Isaiah's comfort food, his friend was blooming, and Zander was happy to see it.

It was almost like Sullivan's Glen wasn't the worst place on earth.

"The other day," he said, staring at the outline of Penny's hand against the backdrop of the fairy lights, "I went into the library to grab a book for Winter. Thought maybe he'd want to read about bees once he watched every YouTube video in existence. The same librarian was still there."

"Patricia Hewing."

"Good ol' Miss Patricia. The minute I walked in, I knew she recognized me. I half expected her to throw me out."

Penny gasped. "If she did, I will go down there and—"

"Simmer down, my little knight. She didn't throw me out. She *hugged* me."

Miss Patricia had pulled Zander into a hug much tighter than her wispy frame implied possible, leaving him nothing to do but pat her on a bony shoulder.

Much to Zander's surprise, for every Brad in Sullivan's Glen, there had been a Miss Patricia. Someone who told Zander they were glad he was doing well, who said Winter was growing like a weed, or who asked after his mother, though he didn't have much to report. There'd even been an old man lingering at the hardware store whom Zander couldn't place until he was reminded that they'd laid down a few tennis courts together in the neighboring town the summer Zander had managed to hold on to a job for an entire month.

"Nice to see you in one piece, son," he'd said, patting Zander hard on the back. "Some of us are survivors, I reckon."

Now, Penny threaded her fingers through his. "So what you're saying is, this place isn't the worst."

"We-ell," he said, dragging out the word. "I'm not ready to concede the point. But it did get markedly better tonight."

"Oh yeah?" She rolled toward him, biting her lip. "What was the best part?"

He bopped her nose. "Definitely giving it to the latest Brad."

She laughed. "I guess it's fitting that you took out Brad Preston and I took out Brad Jeffries. Together, we've taken down the Brads!"

"King and queen of Sullivan's Glen!" Zander proclaimed.

And even if it was a fantasy, for tonight, Zander let it feel true.

# CHAPTER 23

"These are the maple scones, those are blueberry, and those"—RJ pointed to another paper plate covered in baked goods—"are honey ginger. Using Becker Farms honey, of course."

Penny grinned. "Of course."

RJ piled one of each on Penny's plate, which overflowed already with a salted chocolate chip cookie, a slice of rich zucchini bread, and a piece of rhubarb pie. The combined smells—sweet and salty, rich like butter and sunshine—overwhelmed her senses.

"This is a lot of food."

"Well, yeah," RJ responded, building a plate for his mom. "That's the entire point of a taste-testing party. So you guys can vote on which ones I should pitch to Brewtopia and Scatterbeans."

Penny's plate held only a sampling of what RJ had brought to the park, where they'd arrived early enough in the day to claim two tables. One was dedicated to RJ's goodies—cookies, pies, and scones among them—while the other held an array of foods brought by everyone else. Penny was particularly excited about Zander's homemade hummus, the Robinsons' barbecue ribs, and Mimi's potato salad.

Just beyond the tables, the *Vote Here* poster board was propped on the easel Penny usually took to market. After reluctantly agreeing to try out RJ's ice-skating skills class a few weeks before, Winter had warmed considerably to him, even agreeing to set up the voting system, complete with ballots and colorful markers.

"Personally . . ." A deep voice sent goose bumps along her arm as a familiar body sank onto the bench next to her. A *very* familiar body, one she'd come to know almost as well as her own. "I'm a fan of the honey ginger. Something about that honey that melts right on the tongue." His voice lowered at her ear. "Reminds me of something else I love to eat."

Her face flaming, Penny glanced behind her, where RJ was presenting his treats to his mother, Ruth, and Mallory. Closer to the lake, Candace, Isaiah, and Mimi held court in lawn chairs, watching with smiles as Quinn used a clothes hanger to blow giant bubbles with Winter and two more kids from the rink. Luckily, none of them were paying the slightest attention to her.

She knocked Zander's knee under the table. "Do not dirty-talk me at a family-friendly picnic."

"Me?" He pressed an offended hand to his chest, right over the tight pink T-shirt he'd worn to torment her. Their real, if temporary, relationship was under wraps from Winter, so they had a strict no-touching rule when he was around. One Zander loved tempting Penny to break. "I'm only talking about food, Penny."

Grumbling, she took hold of her plate and scooched away from him. "You're a very bad man."

He laughed and slid down the bench after her. "Yes, but you like it so much. Especially this morning in the shower." His grin was wicked. "Betcha never did *that* with Henry, huh?"

And now her face was surely the color of the rhubarb pie, because *that* had been getting on her knees and pushing her breasts between her hands to . . .

When Penny fanned herself with a napkin, Zander chuckled triumphantly. "Yeah, I thought so."

Before she could douse Zander's head with lemonade, RJ saved them both, returning to load up another plate. "Okay, okay." He arranged everything just so, then made a cookie and a scone trade spots. "This is going well, right? People are gonna like the food." He put down the plate and wiped his hands along his track pants. "What if they don't like the food?"

"Bro, they will *love* the food." Zander offered up a fist bump across the table, which seemed to soothe RJ immediately. "That rhubarb pie is ridiculous."

Zander and RJ had regular meetings about RJ's budding business, and sometimes Penny sat in to taste test while working on her own projects. She loved being in the background, watching the balance between Zander's experience and RJ's excited-puppy instincts. When Zander suggested that RJ pick some items to take around to local cafés and bakeries, RJ'd panicked about which treats were fit for the job. Thus the Fourth of July picnic turned taste-testing party.

"Kinda cool having the whole gang together, huh?" RJ nodded to everyone enjoying the July day as the lake glistened just down the field. Penny's family had spent many Mondays there in her childhood, taking a few hours' rest after a weekend of markets. She hadn't been back in a long time.

"Winter seems to be getting along well with those kids," Zander noted, watching them laughing and jumping through Quinn's giant bubble rings. "Thanks for bringing them along."

"Of course. He's doing great in the clinic, and these jokers have all connected. Non-jocks tend to find each other in jock-dominated environments." He winked. "Ask how I know."

Later, everyone would spread blankets near the bank as people in their summer homes celebrated the Fourth of July from their docks, setting off fireworks that would fill both the sky and the mirrored surface of the lake below.

Not that Penny intended to see any of it. Her plan had been to come for the tasting and quietly slip back to work. All her time spent with Zander—festival planning and *otherwise*—had farm chores piling up. And she needed to run all the numbers again—her latest market sales along with Zander's forecasting of festival proceeds—to assess whether she had a chance of avoiding foreclosure.

But when Zander begged her to stay and relax—adding to the chorus from her mom and Mimi—what could Penny say? She was now committed to lying to all three of them about the stakes of this summer, and her guilt for the omission weighed on her as heavily as the loan itself.

So she'd acquiesced, and now—in the sun, surrounded by RJ's pastries, Zander's familiar warmth next to her, and the beautiful web of their families around them—she couldn't regret it. With Zander's help gathering permits and rustling up extra vendors, the Honey Festival was coming together well. He'd even developed record-keeping systems that would save her time for years to come.

Assuming it would all be enough, and that there *were* years to come.

A loud, very obvious clearing of a throat announced Mimi's presence. She wore an old button-down and jeans, with a Finger Lakes Wine Tour hat snagged from the Becker Farms lost and found last fall perched on her head. Penny's grandmother had been lively today, cracking up Mallory's parents with stories about the old days in Sullivan's Glen, half of which were likely fabricated.

"RJ, honey, I've been sitting here waiting for my cookies for half a century. Is this a taste-testing party or a gabfest?"

"Sorry, Mimi." RJ fluttered his thick eyelashes at her, a trick that had been working for him coming on three decades. "Here, this plate is special made for you."

Mimi inserted herself between Penny and Zander, then tore off one corner of a blueberry scone and tossed it in her mouth. "Ooh boy." Her eyes closed as she smacked her lips. "Flipping frogs, kiddo. This is amazing. This one help you?" She elbowed Zander, shooting him her biggest smile.

"Um, no, ma'am," Zander answered. "It was all him."

Mimi shook her head ruefully. "Zander, I told you no *ma'am*-ing me. Makes me feel too old. It's Cynthia or Mimi to you."

Zander's fingers tapped along the table. For someone who joked about being a bad boy, he turned into mush in front of Penny's mom and grandmother. It had taken them all of two days to realize something was happening between him and Penny, and he'd been promptly invited to dinner, where he'd spent most of the time complimenting Ruth's rudimentary cooking before insisting on doing all the cleanup.

In other words, he'd been a hit.

"Yes, okay," he said now. "Um, Mimi?"

"That's more like it." Mimi shot him another smile, then narrowed her eyes. "It's shocking sometimes, how much you look like him. Especially that gorgeous hair of yours."

Zander sent a hand through his hair. "Who, exactly?"

"Your grandfather, honey. You know he was in that house when I first came to town, don't you? His parents were still there at the time, but they retired soon after to a home somewhere or other. Once they left and Nikolai was alone in that house, oh boy!" She slapped the table. "Women came for miles, I swear to the goddess. Hoping for a touch of that silky hair."

"Mimi!" Penny chided. She kept her tone playful but watched

Zander's reaction. Though they'd been together as much as possible these past two weeks, Zander had still barely talked about his grandfather.

She knew that reminders of him existed around the house, and Penny found them herself from time to time. A few nights before, she'd asked Zander if he had any wineglasses. "Second cabinet over," he'd called from his spot at the stove as he cooked a Bolognese.

She'd pulled out two stemmed glasses and then spotted it in the back of the cabinet—a green glass, stout and heavy, with decorative edges. Soon it was in her hand, held to the sunlight coming through the window, casting green shadows around the kitchen.

"It was his," Zander had said, gaze shifting between the shimmers of green. "He'd sit in the evenings and play solitaire and drink ouzo. One drink a night, never a drop more. He told me he'd know if I ever snuck it out of the bottle. I never bothered trying."

Then Zander returned to cooking, and Penny had placed the glass back in the cabinet, carefully stowed like most of his memories.

Now, his face was open, curious. "I didn't know he had women fighting over him."

"Not after Elsie showed up, mind you." Mimi shook her head and looked into the distance, where sun flashed on the lake. "From what I understand, they met at the fire department spaghetti dinner. I believe he was smitten."

"Did you—" Zander swallowed, then continued. "Did you know my mom?"

Across the table, RJ had stopped plating up his desserts. Mimi took another bite of her scone before answering.

"Not well, I'm afraid. She was born a little after Ruthie, and I had my hands full. Elsie had helped me some when Ruth was born, and I'd tried to return the favor, but they were always a private family. Especially after Elsie passed." She laid her hand over Zander's on the table. "Your mom was a beauty, though. I'd see her sometimes hanging outside the high school when I went for Ruth's band concerts, a flock of boys ready to do her bidding." She patted his hand. "I understand she's had a hard time of it."

"Um, yes, ma'am—Mimi." Zander's voice was a little scratchy. "She and I haven't talked in a while. I needed to draw some boundaries."

"Sounds wise to me." Mimi stepped over the bench gingerly, reaching for her plate. "I reckon sometimes we need distance from things to let ourselves love them."

The table fell silent as she walked away, until finally RJ groaned. "I hate it when she does that. Just drops a wisdom bomb and walks away from the rubble." His attention flipped between Zander and Penny before he filled another plate. "I better make some deliveries. Make sure you two vote!"

Penny scooted over until her body pressed against Zander's. "You okay?"

"Yeah." He drew in a breath, then laughed quietly. "Yeah. Just sifting through the rubble. I forget sometimes that people here knew my mom and papou, probably more than I ever did."

Penny nodded but didn't press, instead watching Zander's face lighten as he watched Winter, who stood like a pencil as his new friends tried to draw a bubble down over his head. "Who knew preteens would still like bubbles, huh?" he said. "Maybe we should rope Quinn into a bubble station at the kids' tent."

"Good idea. Did I tell you Ash said they can do the pop-up

tattoo shop?" Penny asked, nibbling at her cookie. "I think we can squeeze them in between Get Your Rock On and the Singing Grannies."

"Tattoos, huh? Maybe I need to get one."

She laughed, eyeing his ink-covered arms. "Where would it go?"

Penny let her gaze linger on his tattooed arms. She knew all their stories now: the snake twisted around his arm was done one late night in Detroit when he'd found sixty bucks in cash floating down the sidewalk in the breeze; a chef's knife on his bicep as a celebration when he graduated from the line at his first restaurant job; a *Now Open* sign to mark the first food truck he'd helped to start. Her favorite was the snowflake on the underside of his wrist, which he'd gotten on Winter's first birthday.

Penny traced the webbed lines of it with her finger, lost in the pattern until he cleared his throat.

"You're breaking the rules, Becker. If you keep touching me, I'm going to have to pretend to get a call about a festival emergency that you and I have to solve immediately, and then we'll never get to vote on RJ's desserts."

She scratched her short nails along his exposed forearm. "You're all talk. You'd never abandon RJ like that."

"You're right." His fingers landed on her thigh under the table, gripping tightly. "We wouldn't have to leave. Maybe I'll just take you for a little walk over there." Zander nodded to the thick forest bordering the grass as his mouth dipped closer to her ear. "Have you flatten your hands on a tree as I pull these cute little shorts over your ass." He teased a finger beneath the fabric. "Get on my knees behind you and lick that sweet little—"

Penny slid away and clenched her thighs together. "You wouldn't."

With a chuckle, Zander smiled and arched his brow. He definitely would.

She shook her head, trying to regulate her breathing. "You're ridiculous. We literally shared orgasms three hours ago."

"Like that matters," he scoffed. "I can't get enough of you."

Even as Penny laughed him off, an uneasiness twisted in her chest. She couldn't get enough either, but August was coming up awfully fast.

Zander cleared his throat as Winter plopped down at the table. His hair was frizzy in the humidity, gray T-shirt splattered with soapy water from the bubbles. He ripped apart a scone and tossed half in his mouth.

"Whoa, man!" Zander exclaimed. "These are delicacies, take a breath."

Winter shrugged, ignoring his father to address Penny. "I was telling Adam and Jazz about the bee stuff, and they're wondering if they can come see everything."

"Of course." Penny sensed Zander smiling her way, but she didn't peek at him. There was something in Zander's expression each time she interacted with Winter, like maybe his brain was working ahead, imagining a future that wasn't possible.

Kind of like hers did sometimes.

"How about you get their parents' numbers, and we can figure something out, okay?"

"Cool." He finished the scone in one go. "Dad, Jazz wants to play Frisbee. I told them you weren't bad."

"Wow, kid, thanks."

"So." Winter rolled his eyes. "Come on."

"Oh. *Oh*." Zander practically glowed. "You want me to play Frisbee with you? Of course." He was already rising, nodding his head, and brushing his hand across Penny's back before bounding after Winter.

She was watching them play, finding that Zander leaping for a Frisbee was sexy in a way she hadn't expected, when RJ came back to load another plate. He stood behind Penny, observing the scene, then sighed.

"Pen, they're kind of the best."

RJ's hand closed over her shoulder, and Penny let her head fall against his arm with a sigh. "They kind of are."

"I'm going to miss them."

"Yeah," she whispered. "Me too."

# CHAPTER 24

"The apple blossom is the best."

"No, bro. It's wildflower all the way."

"Whatever, J. You just have broken taste buds."

Zander chuckled from his spectator's spot in Penny's honey shed, where he watched three tweens debate honey varietals as Penny, bright-eyed and smiling, recapped the last jar. Her warehouse contained shelves of supplies, two industrial sinks, and a few long worktables, all sparkling clean and organized. This was where she spun and processed the honey from the Becker Farms hives, and where she was ending the tour she'd set up for Winter, Jazz, and Adam.

"But how do you know this is just from wildflowers?" Jazz asked, dipping another wooden spoon into the open jar of wildflower honey.

Since the Fourth of July picnic, the trio had been nearly inseparable, splitting their time between exploring the woods, yelling at video games, and messing around on the ice. Winter had remained abundantly *cool* about making friends, so Zander went along with the vibe that it was no big deal, even though he thrilled at the sight of his kid finding people who made him laugh.

Of course, making friends here meant Winter was no longer counting down the days until they left Sullivan's Glen, and Zander suspected that his son's mood might crash when it was time to return to Boston. It was possible that Winter wouldn't be the only one who would have a hard time with the transition.

"We know where most of the nectar is coming from based on what's blooming at any given time." Penny sat across the large table, the sunglasses on her head holding back her spill of golden hair. "Plus, once bees have a taste of a certain kind of nectar, they'll keep collecting from that plant as long as it's blooming. So if a bee leaves the hive in the morning as clover is blooming, and she collects some of its nectar, she'll spend the day finding more clover, then do it again the next day and the next day, until the bloom is over. It's a cool system called floral fidelity. It's what makes bees such great pollinators, because if they stopped off at a bunch of different plants every day, they wouldn't necessarily be moving the pollen around where it needs to go."

*Floral fidelity*. Penny had mentioned it before when she was telling him how the apiary in the apple orchards ensured that the trees would be properly pollinated for a good harvest. And while it was a biological concept, not a romantic one, it made Zander feel a kinship with the bees. Because once Zander had had a taste of Penny, he couldn't imagine wanting anyone else.

"Dad, can Jazz and Adam come over? Jazz brought new Pokémon cards we wanna go through."

"Sure. You all can walk over and I'll help Penny clean up. But don't make a mess. Monica is sending someone over to take pictures for the listing later today." Something she'd asked to do a week ago, and that Zander had avoided, telling her for days he hadn't had time to clean up.

The kids all muttered thank-yous to Penny as they gathered up the honey she'd given them to take home.

Once they were left alone, Zander worked his way to Penny and wrapped his arms around her waist as she recapped the wildflower honey.

"Just one second, missy. I didn't get a taste."

"I think you've had enough honey in the past few weeks to last a lifetime."

"Please." He pouted into her neck. "Just one more."

She spun in his arms and peered up with those eyes he couldn't get enough of, an endless blue that messed with his equilibrium, whisking the solid ground from beneath his feet each time.

Back in Boston, Zander'd had a pretty good run of things. He had a healthy relationship with his co-parent, enough friends to meet his needs, a positive if hormonally strained relationship with his kid. Yeah, his apartment was cramped and the city was a little loud. And his once-reasonable work schedule was more demanding of late, sometimes keeping him up at night. But he had a good life. A life he was proud of.

Then Mallory dragged him back to Sullivan's Glen and he met Penny Becker in a clearing full of bees, and now he was all fucked-up thinking about things he had no right to think about. Like what the trees around the house would look like in the fall, or how the storefronts of Sullivan's Glen might be decorated at Christmas.

And, more dangerously, he yearned to know how Penny would fare through all of it—welcoming people to the farm to fill their baskets with apples, or tucking inside with a blanket for the season's first snowfall. Would she stand outside her cabin in the spring, watching the first flowers press up through the dirt and remember when Zander kissed her on her doorstep?

Pushing aside the questions he couldn't answer, Zander caged Penny against the table, picking up the jar of honey in one hand and a wooden sample spoon in the other. He'd had plenty of samples, but was fixated on tasting it just like this, so he scooped up a glob of shiny golden honey and smeared it along her lower lip.

She grinned, then pouted her lips to make his work easier. Zander marveled again at how devastatingly well-matched they were. Penny was as fierce in bed as out of it, stepping up to his every flirtation and dirty suggestion. And though she had the sort of strident independence that made it hard for her to accept help washing the dishes, she let go when they were together in bed, often ceding control to Zander and letting him take care of her like he craved.

When both her lips were gleaming, he moved in for his taste, dragging his tongue through the honey and then sucking the rest into his mouth. He reveled in the sweetness—Penny, the honey, one and the same. It was a crime he hadn't yet sucked honey from her pink nipples or made sweet streaks to lick off her inner thighs.

But he couldn't do that now, much as he'd love to mark the honey shed as one more place where he'd made Penny come. He had to return to the house soon to check on the kids, but first he had an idea to pitch to Penny.

Penny chased the kiss, but Zander kept her at bay with hands on her shoulders. "Before I go, I want to talk about something. I have an idea for the festival."

Her brows pulled together. "As in, the festival that's in two weeks? Are we still in idea mode?"

"I know it's kind of late in the game." Zander walked around the table, collecting used tasting spoons and tossing them in the large silver trash can near the door. "But hear me out. Imagine this." He pulled a paper from his pocket and unfolded it, flattening it out on the table. It was a crude drawing of the festival—several blocks of Main Street dedicated to rows of vendor booths, with performance stages at each end, and a children's area in the adjoining park that surrounded the town square.

"I want to put a culinary station here." He tapped the basketball courts in the park. "Think several cooking stations, set up with cooktops and portable counters, kind of like in those cooking shows. And we can have local chefs and folks from farther away, too. I have a buddy in the city who said he thinks he can make it, somebody else who said she'd come from Toronto. They can do cooking demos, using local ingredients, real farm-to-table stuff. And the best part? We can have a special focus on honey, give everybody ideas on more ways to use it, then send them straight to Becker Farms to pick it up."

He bounced on his heels, eager for Penny's thoughts. He'd begged to be part of festival planning to prove himself to Winter and his old doubters in the town at large, but now Zander was invested in how the whole thing turned out. And while his expertise and connections were clearly a help, most of his work had been toward Penny's vision.

But this plan spoke to his interests and skills, a way to really bring himself into the Honey Festival.

As Penny stared at the crude map, Zander continued. "I thought of this the other night with RJ, actually. We were hanging out while he was making pies, and I realized how much fun he was to watch, how people would probably line up to see him in an apron."

And once he'd started thinking about it, it seemed perfect. He put together restaurants for a living, and he could do it here, building a master kitchen at the Honey Festival.

Penny stared at the map, not meeting his eyes. "This sounds like a big thing," she said tensely. "And we only have two weeks left."

"I know. But we have everything else sorted out, and I really think we can pull it off."

Her fingers traced along Main Street. "It would mean getting another permit."

"I can handle that," he answered quickly. "Dolores down at the township office likes me. I think I can get it expedited."

Penny blew out a long breath. "Cooking stations like on TV sounds fancy. What would that cost?"

"It would be a few thousand to rent everything, and some of the chefs would need some money for travel costs. But before you—"

"Tell you that we don't have thousands to spare? You know this is all happening on a shoestring."

"Sure, but with higher vendor fees, there's some extra money that we could—"

"There's *not* extra money, Zander. I need—" She shook her head. "We need all of that."

"I can show you the breakdowns. It's not like I haven't thought this over."

"I can tell you've thought it over," she said sharply. "You didn't want to clue me in?"

Zander narrowed his gaze on her, struggling to read her reaction. "I wanted to come to you with a plan, Penny. I'm clueing you in now."

He circled the table, but when he reached an arm toward her, Penny ducked his touch and headed toward the door. "I just—" she started. "I need some air."

Zander followed her outside, where rows of apple trees spanned out around them like a fan, hive boxes stationed throughout. The trees were purposefully kept short to allow for an easier harvest, each crown of leaves dotted with young fruit.

"Penny." He approached where she stared into the tangle of limbs. "It's a good idea. People could get excited about the demonstrations; then they'd want to buy the products. It's a win-win."

Golden hair whipped over her shoulder as she turned. "It's a brand-new idea out of nowhere that I haven't planned for, and it's going to cost a bunch of money. Where's the win exactly?"

He stumbled back, confused. "What is going on? This isn't that big of a deal."

Penny laughed, but it wasn't the light trill that Zander heard in his sleep. "Maybe you should go talk to my mom about it," she said. "She'll be happy to tell you about all her great ideas that aren't a big deal, except how they would cost us money and be more work for me once she caught sight of the next exciting thing."

"So because your mom has pissed you off over the years you won't even listen to my idea?" An old, defensive ugliness rose up in him, pushing out before he could yank back the leash. "You'll let me find you discounts, let me call in favors, but when I have my own idea, it's not worthwhile, is that it?"

"Zander."

"Or maybe I'm here to help you be bad, not actually use my brain, too."

Her glare turned icy. "That's not what I said."

"No, you said I could help you with this. You said we could be co-planners. I'm just trying to help."

"I never asked for your help! This isn't *our* festival, Zander, it's *mine*. Because I'm the one who stays here after. I'm the one who deals with the consequences, over and over." Penny thumped her finger against her chest. "I'm the one who cleans up after everybody's great ideas. And I can't risk it. I can't use the small cushion we made on another idea, not now."

Penny's body was tightly wound, her mouth pinched and angry. Just yesterday he'd woken before her—a small miracle in itself—and watched the sunlight move across her room until it glowed against her hair and face. She'd stretched and sighed, then peeked her eyes open at him and smiled, and he just *felt* it: a sense that Penny Becker would be in his marrow forever, no matter where he went next.

That intimacy was flimsier now, wispy like the clouds crossing the dome of sky. Penny looked a million miles away.

"Listen," he said calmly. "I get that you're used to doing a lot on your own, but you don't have to right now. I'm here—"

"Zander, stop pushing this—"

"Why? Why are you shutting down like this? Why can't you just consider it?"

"Because this festival is important and I can't let you fuck it up!"

Zander's lungs emptied. A choked laugh escaped as he shook his head. "Because that's what I do, right?"

Zander stalked away a few steps, clenching his hands and shaking out his arms. He loathed these moments, when the damaged parts inside him beat against his chest, screaming to be let out.

*Then fuck your festival and fuck this place*, he'd yell, letting the righteousness burn up the embarrassed heat in his chest. It would feel so damn good.

And if he let it out at Penny now, he could leave town in a few weeks and not look back, not ache with the *what-ifs* or *maybes*, not stare at his phone and wait for her to text. He would have burned up all the goodness between them.

She was basically asking him to do it.

But then a hand was on his shoulder, followed by Penny's forehead pressing just between his shoulder blades. "I'm sorry. I'm sorry, I'm sorry."

She wrapped around him from behind, holding him in place, hands splayed across his chest, where it burned. The instinct to break out of her embrace rose up, but Zander pushed it back down, and the rise and fall of Penny's breath steadied him. Those damaged parts didn't control him anymore.

She nestled her head against him. "That was a horrible thing to say. I didn't mean it like that. Not at all. There's just stuff that I . . ." Penny squeezed him. "Zander? I'm sorry."

When she said his name again, quietly, like a question, he turned in her arms and pulled her into his chest, letting that fire die down as he breathed in and out.

There was more going on with Penny than Zander could see, that much was obvious. She'd thrown up her shields and knocked him down in the process. And even if he didn't know entirely why, he'd done it enough himself to know that it wasn't about him at all. He was well-versed in the art of pushing people away. And he wasn't about to let Penny get away with it.

"If you want me to quit and leave you to do this alone," he told her, "you're going to have to try harder. Because I'm not willingly leaving your side until I have to." He rubbed a hand up her back. "We don't have to do the culinary station. It was just an idea."

Penny peered up at him. "It's a good idea. I just . . . I fell into a pothole. A really big one."

Zander ran a thumb over her soft cheek. "Those things are everywhere."

"Yeah." She sounded so sad. The sky reflected in her eyes until Zander got lost in the blue. "I guess they are."

And he longed to see all of hers, everything that wore her down: the experiences with her mom that made Penny feel like Becker Farms was entirely on her shoulders, whatever happened with Henry that left Penny so tight-lipped about him. He'd learn each turn and dip, look ahead and help her steer clear. And days when it couldn't be helped, when she fell in, he'd be there to pull her up and steady her again.

But being here to keep Penny steady was as likely as seeing Sullivan's Glen bursting with the oranges and golds of fall. In other words, not at all.

# CHAPTER 25

The hollow hoot of an owl wafted through Zander's window as he rolled over in bed again.

It wasn't his first sleepless night in this room, not by a long shot. His very first night there, fifteen years old and scared as hell about why his mom had shipped him away, and if she would be okay without him, he'd kept himself awake in this little room for hours, listening to his papou move about the house.

He'd studied the peeling paint on the ceiling and watched the blinking colon on the digital clock. Finally, he'd thrown his worn black backpack over one shoulder and tiptoed down the street, ready to take off.

He hadn't made it far, of course. Papou drove up behind him after about ten minutes. Zander could still see the long shadow his adolescent body cast against the road as his grandfather parked behind him before storming out of the car, cursing in his mother tongue, which Zander had never learned, and yelling at him to get into the passenger seat.

Later, he'd sometimes read all night, holding his book beneath the bedside lamp that had appeared in his room one

June. Sometimes he stayed up all night just to have an excuse to sleep well into the next day, minimizing time spent with his papou.

After another hoot from his friend outside, Zander abandoned his bed and took a few creaky steps to the window to stare out into the darkness. In retrospect, the last two summers there hadn't been too bad. His grandfather had managed to secure jobs for Zander here and there, and he and Papou had reached a detente, wherein they lived in the same house while ignoring each other as much as possible.

Papou still mustered up an occasional lecture, especially when word filtered through town that Zander had been seen sneaking around with Mallory.

*Leave that nice girl alone*, he'd said. *You don't want her to end up like your mother.*

Zander's fingers curled into tight fists at the memory, so he took a long, calming breath and grabbed his phone from the nightstand for a distraction. He clicked on his messages with Penny automatically, smiling at their exchange of good-nights a few hours ago.

ZANDER  *I miss you in my bed.*

PENNY  *It's probably good I couldn't stay. I need some actual sleep so I can work tomorrow*

ZANDER  *and why wouldn't you get enough sleep with me?*

PENNY  *you know the answer to that*

ZANDER  *mmm, maybe I need you to tell me, though*

PENNY *good night, Zander*

ZANDER *good night Penny Becker. Sweet dreams*

They'd moved on from the argument at the honey shed, though there was an extra thickness between them now, something unsaid. She had asked him to go over the culinary station details again, and together they agreed to a scaled-down version where local chefs, RJ included, could show their skills.

They were just over a week out from the festival, which meant three weeks until he packed up to return to Boston. Three weeks out, and he still hadn't accomplished his goal for the summer of selling the house. Cursing himself, he swiped to his messages with Monica, his real estate agent. They'd been piling up for a few days.

MONICA *Good afternoon! I dropped the For Sale sign at your house since you said you wanted to put it in yourself at the end of the driveway. Have you been able to get it up?*

MONICA *Good morning, wanted to check in about the sign. Also, the listing went live today! I'm feeling good about this!*

MONICA *Good afternoon! I spoke to my friend today and he said you never called about the fence installation. Wanted to let you know that's totally fine. I think we'll have enough interest anyway, and the new owner can always alter the property as they see fit.*

MONICA *Good morning, Zander! I hope these messages are coming through. I have great news! I already have a bite on the listing! It's a couple from the city looking for a good getaway spot. They'd love to tour the house ASAP. Let me know if there's a window tomorrow. Thanks!*

MONICA *Following up about tomorrow. My calls went to voicemail. We don't want to miss this!*

Now, bleary-eyed, he finally typed a reply:

*Sorry, Monica. I got wrapped up in some things. Unfortunately, tomorrow won't work, the house is a mess from some projects I've been doing. I'll let you know about timing later this weekend.*

Monica was trying to do her job, and Zander was no help at all. The sign was still leaning against the front porch, the fence idea all but forgotten. His papou's room was still untouched; how Monica had made it work for the photos, he didn't know, but she'd probably be horrified to show the house with a dead man's coat still hanging over a chair upstairs.

And now he had people excited to see the house.

Wasn't that exactly what he wanted? Getting this place off his hands was supposed to be the silver lining of his summer in Sullivan's Glen.

So why did he cringe to think of strangers walking through the house—assessing, measuring, standing in the kitchen where he'd made souvlaki with Winter, where he'd laid Penny on the table their first full night together? Would they stand in this room and look out at the field below, planning a fence or another building? Hell, maybe they'd knock the whole thing down and start fresh.

The idea made him wildly, irrationally angry.

At the sound of a long creak in the hallway, Zander's eyes flew to the door. Winter peeked in, his face swollen with the signs of sleep, hair smushed down on one side. He was in athletic shorts and a T-shirt from last summer's science camp, and it was stretching at the shoulders.

"Dad?"

"Buddy, what's up?"

Winter stepped in, rubbing at his eyes "I, uh, couldn't sleep. I'm . . . it's . . ."

"Come here." Zander returned to his bed, where he folded himself to a sitting position on the mattress, wishing he'd splurged on a bed frame, too.

Winter sat several inches away, hands cupping his bouncing knees.

"What's going on?"

"You don't talk to your mom anymore."

"Um, no. No, not right now."

Winter had been given a cursory explanation of the situation: Zander's mom was sick and not able to have a healthy relationship with him, and while Zander loved her, for his own sake he needed some space. And keeping this boundary now helped protect her from her tendencies to sabotage relationships when she wasn't doing well.

"Do you think you will, ever again?"

Zander asked himself that question all the time. "I hope so."

Winter's attention stayed glued to the floor. "You didn't talk to your grandfather, either."

"No, I didn't. We didn't have a great relationship, and I didn't think he wanted to hear from me."

That's what he'd told himself all those years. That he'd been doing his papou a favor by not bothering him anymore, and that the old man had been stuck with Zander long enough and just wanted to be free of him.

He never allowed himself much time to wonder if it was true.

Winter's body stayed slumped over his knees, but he looked over to Zander. "What if *we* don't talk?"

"Who?" Something inside Zander cracked. "You and me? Bud, that won't happen."

"It happened with your mom. And your grandpa. I never even got to meet him."

It was one thing to answer to his own conscience, another completely to answer to his kid. "I know, and that's on me." He sighed, swallowing hard as he kept his eyes on his son. "When you and your mom started coming back, she offered to reach out to him so you could meet him. But I told her not to."

"Why?"

Zander steadied his voice. "I was afraid he wouldn't want to meet you, and that would have made me so angry I wouldn't even have known what to do with the feelings. And I tried to put that anger away a long time ago. I chose to ignore the situation altogether, which was not the brave thing to do."

He scooted back on the bed to sit cross-legged. When Winter did the same, Zander nudged his son with one foot. "Where's this coming from?"

Winter shrugged, but his chin trembled. "What if that happens to us? What if we stop talking?" he asked again.

"That's not going to happen to us."

Winter's eyes widened, looking almost pleading. "How do you know? What if it does?"

Zander closed a hand on his son's knee, squeezing hard. "Because I'm going to make sure I am always there for you."

"But you can't always be there! What about when you die? Or Mom dies? Because you will, you both will. And what will I do then?"

"What has you thinking about that, buddy? We're fine, we're all totally fine and healthy."

"But you won't always be!" His voice cracked. In his lap, his hands twisted together. "You won't always be, and then I'll be alone!"

One tear spilled out, then another. Jesus, this was a lot. These were the kinds of questions that kept Zander up at night. It hadn't occurred to him that Winter's angst would cut this deep.

But his kid was smart and sensitive and observant, and he was growing into a *person*. A real person in his own right, who slammed doors and played with bubbles and worried about losing his parents. He was processing a world that always seemed to be spinning out of control, and his father—fifty percent of Winter's family until not so long ago—didn't exactly provide a model of how to keep people in your life as you grew up.

His instinct was to bundle Winter up, pull him to his chest, and promise him that everything would be okay. They would never ever fight, and Zander would defy the laws of human existence to stay in his life forever.

But he wasn't about to make promises he couldn't keep.

Instead, he tipped his head down to catch Winter's eye. "Hey. I understand, okay? Living is *so scary*. I feel that in my bones every day. It's really normal to feel like this."

After Winter was born, sometimes Zander stayed awake at night just watching him, making sure he was breathing, until Mallory dragged him away to make him sleep.

"There are some things about life we can't change, like how it ends. But we can do a lot in the meantime. Make sure we love each other as much as we can, make beautiful things, see beautiful places."

"But what is the *point*?"

"Bud, that is the major question of human existence," Zander admitted with a light laugh. "And I don't know the answer. But right here"—he tapped his chest—"I still feel like there's a point, you know?"

Winter shrugged. "I guess."

"And there are a ton of belief systems out there you can explore if that helps. Your mom and I never did the formal church thing with you, but a lot of people find meaning and answers in that, and that's valid, too. There's a ton out there to explore."

Winter raised an eyebrow wryly. "You'd take me to *church*?"

The church would have to be super liberal and queer-friendly, but they were out there.

"I'll take you wherever you feel like you need to go, Winter, whether that's church or counseling or meditation class."

"Meditation?" Winter sneered.

"Don't knock it till you try it. The point isn't for you to turn out just like me or your mom, but for you to be you. And we're here to support that."

Winter yawned. "Life is weird."

Zander slung an arm around him. "Dude. It is so weird. But so amazing, too, right? I mean, have you heard about how bees mate?"

"Dad—"

"The male bee's you-know-what gets ripped off, bro."

"Dad!" Winter laughed, then yawned again as he eyed the open bedroom door.

"You want to lie down in here?" Zander asked tentatively. It had been almost a year since Winter climbed into his bed in the middle of the night—not that he was keeping track. "See if you can get some more sleep?"

Winter shrugged, not meeting Zander's eyes. "I guess."

Zander climbed to the other side of the bed and crawled

under the light blanket as Winter stretched out beside him on his stomach, facing the other way.

"You want me to scratch your back like the good old days?"

Another shrug. "I guess."

Slowing his own breathing, Zander ran his short nails along the back of Winter's T-shirt, moving over his bony shoulder blades and down his spine.

"Is this what's been on your mind lately? When you've been . . . upset? Worrying about your mom and me being gone?"

His son answered quietly. "A little. I've been thinking about it, I guess. And just . . . I feel strange. Like, all over. And really sad sometimes for no reason."

"That's all normal." And something Zander and Mallory would keep an eye on, especially the sadness. "If you want support beyond your mom and me, you know we'll find it for you, okay?"

"Okay."

Zander scratched up and down, then in slow, shrinking spirals.

"It's hard to imagine now," he said softly, "but your life is going to get bigger and bigger. You'll have people you love and who love you, and a whole life outside your parents. You have so much amazing stuff ahead of you."

Zander knew how a life could transform, how it was possible to move forward from one set of circumstances and build up the next. How, even at thirty-five, surprising things could happen.

His son was still, but Zander kept up the movement of his fingers along his back. "And for as long as we can, your mom and I will love you so fiercely that you'll think we're *so* annoying."

Winter shook with laughter beneath Zander's hand. "I know."

Then Winter's body twitched in the last surrender to sleep, and sometime later, with his hand still on his son's warm back, Zander's did too.

# CHAPTER 26

"All I'm saying is, someone should have warned me. You know I'm lactose intolerant."

"Babe." Mallory shook her head at Quinn, affection all over her face. "We told you it was a dairy festival. I'm not sure what you expected."

"I expected dairy to be present," Quinn huffed. "Not"—she motioned around the table to RJ's grilled cheese, Mallory's cheesy fries, and the beer and cheese soup that Penny was sharing with Zander—"ubiquitous."

RJ sighed. "We tried. Didn't we, Pen?"

Penny shrugged and stirred her soup, congealing in her bread bowl. It *was* a lot of cheese. "We did tell you the Dairy Festival goes hard."

Zander laughed beside her and drew a hand along her spine. It had been his idea to do "festival espionage" by attending as many festivals in the surrounding counties in one weekend as they could, so Penny and RJ had joined them all at the Dairy Festival after the morning farmer's market.

Penny knew the espionage plan was Zander's way of distracting her from her anxiety as their own festival approached.

The nights they slept together, Penny tossed and turned, her mind spinning with last-minute details and a parade of *what-ifs*, until Zander interceded. He'd wrap an arm around her waist and tuck her into him, running his hand through her hair and shushing her gently. More often than not, his touches turned more demanding, and he'd scatter Penny's thoughts by snaking a hand between her legs, suggesting that if she still wasn't asleep, maybe it was because he hadn't fucked her hard enough earlier, and he better try again.

"Well," Quinn mused, drawing Penny's mind out of the gutter, "I preferred the Kite Festival. Less tummy troubles for me."

"It was the gnome thing for me," Mallory chimed in. "What was that called?"

RJ spoke through a mouthful of bread and cheese. "Gnome Knob."

Which was less of a festival and more of a display of garden gnomes, but Penny wouldn't argue the point. After Zander had dragged Winter to that one, he'd begged off the Dairy Festival, especially when Adam invited him fishing for the day.

Zander's palm spread across her back like it belonged there. In the weeks they'd been seeing each other, his touch had come to feel as natural on her skin as sunshine. And since their argument in the orchard the week before, it was even more present, like Zander was holding on to her like a kid with a balloon, worried she might float away if he let go.

"You okay?" Zander's voice was soft by her ear. "Don't tell me you're lactose intolerant, too?"

"No," she said lightly. "Bring on the dairy. I'm just tired."

"You're working too hard."

But it wasn't the work exhausting her. The beehives relaxed her and the markets gave her energy. Penny herself drained her own energy, hurting herself with the secrets she kept. A secret made real by the weight of the simple piece of paper in her back pocket, the one that had arrived in yesterday's mail.

RJ stood and circled his hips in a stretch. "Pen. I need more food, come with me."

"That was your third sandwich," she answered. Not that she hadn't seen him consume far more over the years.

His eyebrows lifted. "Penny, friend, come with me for a minute."

Which meant she was about to get a lecture. One that started as they walked toward a food truck specializing in cheese curds.

"I love you, but you look like hell." At least RJ cut to the chase. "You have shadows under your eyes and a drag in your step."

"Wow, thanks."

"I know Zander is keeping you up at night, but sex is supposed to make you glow, not"—he motioned to her—"look like this."

"Please," she muttered. "Don't hold back."

"Are you guys fighting? I know you had that lovers' spat about the culinary station—which, by the way, I'm glad you folded on, because it's going to be amazing."

"I didn't fold." They joined the back of the food truck line behind a dozen people also angling for fried cheese. "We compromised. And no," she continued. "We're not fighting. That's a thing that a couple would do, and we aren't—"

"Oh, you *so* are. You two are attached at the hip, and he looks at you like you're a big jar of honey he wants to gobble up."

"I'm just being realistic about what's going on," Penny said. "Whatever it is, it's not going to last. I'm not going to expect anything more."

He tsked. "Because people keep disappointing you."

"RJ, can we not? Let's just buy more cheese."

"I will buy more cheese, thank you very much. But I will also say this, Pen. That man—" He nodded back to the table, where Zander laughed as Mallory talked and waved her hands in the air. "He isn't the kind of guy who disappoints people. He's not your dad, or his dad, or Henry."

"Maybe not," she admitted. Looking back, Penny knew she'd lashed out at Zander in the orchard to all but challenge him to walk away. And he hadn't. "But that doesn't mean he won't still be back in Boston in a couple of weeks." Her stomach twisted at the thought, and not just because of the soup.

"I know. And if you guys go your separate ways then, I get it. But you said you'd be real with each other while he was here, and you haven't been."

"That's not true," she shot back.

"He doesn't know what you're really going through right now, so he doesn't know how to support you. It doesn't take a genius to know how much Zander wants to be trusted and needed."

"So, what? I'm supposed to lay out all my dirty laundry so he gets to feel needed?"

"No, Pen." RJ shook his head, like he was so, so tired of her bullshit. "You lay out your dirty laundry because *you actually need him.*"

She glanced back to Zander, now on his phone as Quinn and Mallory chatted, faces close together. He had a couple of days' worth of beard growth and a smile on his face.

When her phone buzzed in her pocket, she pulled it out to see a text from him.

ZANDER B  *Can your line move any slower? I need you. These two are being SO gross.*

Penny typed back *Sorry, you can't rush good fried cheese.*

She slid the phone back in her pocket, shuddering when her fingers brushed the paper folded there. She'd read it enough times the day before to know it word for word.

NOTICE OF DEFAULT

*You have thirty days to remedy past-due payments before we
will be forced to formally begin the foreclosure process.*

She'd shoved the notice in her pocket this morning so it would be unavoidable, stuck with her all day. So that just maybe she'd find a way to pull it out and show it to Zander, to come clean and shed the last barrier between them.

But so far she hadn't mustered the courage.

Penny sighed, looking back to RJ. "He really thinks I'm great. He thinks I'm smart and pretty and he gives me credit for making everything work." She hated thinking about how Zander would look at her if he knew that she'd made a stupid decision and put Becker Farms at risk, or that she still hadn't worked past the semipermanent boulder in her throat to tell her family about it. "We can just finish the festival, and then he can go back, and I can be sad here. Whatever happens after, whatever I have to do about the farm and whatever I have to tell my mom and Mimi, he never has to know."

From the look RJ gave her, Penny wondered if there was cheese on her face. "I love you, Penny, but that's a really stupid plan, and it doesn't do either of you justice."

She willed back the heat behind her eyes. "I want to be better and I want to be honest, but I don't know how. I've spent all this time trying to keep everything together, telling my family, telling

Zander, telling everybody that everything is fine. They all think I have my shit together. That's kind of my thing."

His eyes narrowed. "Having your shit together is your thing?"

"Yes! It's who I am." Who she'd always been, from the early days of showing her mom and Mimi how useful she could be, how much she was worth the work.

RJ's hands landed on his hips. "You're defined by having your shit together?"

"Don't you think so?"

He shook his head stubbornly, having the gall to look angry at her. "No, I don't. I think you're defined by a hell of a lot more. I wish you could see that."

Penny sighed and shuffled ahead in line. RJ wore his heart on his sleeve and saw the world through rainbows, but that wasn't real life. "I love you, RJ, and I know you've been around forever, but you don't really know what it was like when I was a kid, how stressed out everyone was. And my mom would joke sometimes, you know? About how if only my sperm donor had stuck around, we'd have more hands to help."

"Pen—"

"And she *was* kidding. Because she always joked like that, like it didn't mean anything." Like Penny might not have feelings about knowing nothing about half of her DNA. "But what if he *had* stuck around? Wouldn't it have been easier on them? Easier than being stuck with—"

"Penny, *stop*." RJ's big palms cupped her shoulders, squeezing hard. "I'm not going to even let you say that shit, okay?"

She blinked up at him, her words catching up to her. They'd come spilling out in frustration, pouring through the fissures that were creeping through her as the festival approached.

And even though she'd been the one to say them out loud, the words were like strangers to her, appearing at the door for the first time.

RJ leaned close, speaking quietly as the festival action milled around them. "You know that's bullshit, right? They would choose you over keeping that deadbeat around any day of the week. And you don't have to work your ass off to prove you're worth it."

"I just—" she started, struggling for words. Of course she knew that. But she also knew it was her existence that had made her father leave, that she was the defining factor in her mom being without a partner. That feeling was true, too. Just as true as the fact that even as she strived to prove her usefulness, Penny loved Becker Farms and the work she did there.

"This is a lot for the Dairy Festival."

"I know it is, babe." RJ looked at her sympathetically. "And I didn't mean for it to get so deep, though I can't say I'm sorry it did. But I think there's a reason it's coming out now."

"Because I'm so close to the Honey Festival and maybe everything falling apart?"

RJ shook his head with a gentle laugh. "No, Pen. Not because of the damn Honey Festival or the loan or any of it. Because of a certain Greek god who's come into town and swept you off your feet."

"RJ, I told you—"

"You're not a couple, I get it. But he *sees* you, for far more than your work and your competence and your ability to, as you say, *keep your shit together*. And I think you feel it, and it's doing something to you, something really good. All I'm saying is, I think with him you're safe to—" RJ's attention snagged on something behind her. "Speak of the devil."

Zander's low laugh crawled up Penny's spine and moved

into the space next to her. "I'm an angel now, remember? I've hung up my leather jacket to plan wholesome town festivals."

Nerves still rattling in her stomach, Penny forced a laugh. "You didn't actually have a leather jacket, did you?"

"Okay, no. But it would have looked really good, right?" His fingers brushed hers. "Hey, can I steal you for a second?"

"I was, um, waiting with RJ."

RJ pushed Penny out of the line. "Go ahead. You'll only make fun of how much I order anyway."

Zander entwined their fingers and tugged her away, going in a wide circle around the food trucks and heading toward a large white barn. Penny concentrated on the warmth of Zander's hand and the cloudless blue of the sky as she settled from her conversation with RJ.

"What are we—" Penny's back hit the warm wood as Zander caged her in with both arms, taking over her senses and pushing out the distractions. Zander didn't make Penny forget everything, but he expanded her field of vision to include more. Like the golden glint of sun off his coffee-and-amber eyes, or the press of old wood on her back.

Or the small downturn of his mouth now, the slightest twitch.

"You okay?" he asked. "I developed my plan to steal you with naughty intentions, but then it looked like you and RJ were having an intense conversation."

"It was . . ." She swallowed, tipping her face up into the sun. It was all too much to explain, especially when Penny had no idea how or where to start. She would start, eventually. Just not right this minute. "We were just arguing about the price of his pies."

Zander's eyes narrowed on her, like he knew it was bullshit. "He should charge more."

"That's what I was saying. Now." She bit her lip and gave him the innocent eyelash flutter she knew drove him wild. Because a driven-wild Zander was just what her spiraling brain needed. "What was that about your naughty intentions?"

Zander's tongue pushed at his cheek as he studied her, and Penny worried he might call her bluff. But after a moment he stepped into her with a grin and buried his face in her neck, scraping his teeth along her collarbone. "I saw this barn earlier and started having dirty thoughts."

"Oh yeah?" She slid her hands under his shirt, promising herself she'd find a way to talk. Later. "Like what?"

"Like taking my cute farm girl, sneaking up to the hayloft, and making a mess of her."

His broad hand grabbed her waist, then snuck around to her ass. Zander groaned as he took a handful, digging in his fingers before slipping his hand into her back pocket. The same pocket with the notice of default.

Penny winced, sucking in a breath and slamming shut her eyes like the ink might infuse its meaning directly into Zander's fingerprints.

He stepped back, brow furrowed. "You okay? What's wrong?"

Penny could bat her eyelashes again, drag Zander back to her, and pull them both away from the truth in her pocket.

But as she looked up at him, the final fissures broke open. The act she'd kept up as they planned the festival side by side, spent hours together in bed, walked through fairy lights and looked at gnomes was about to come crashing down.

Because Zander looked at her with absolute care, like he'd move a mountain for her if he could, like she was something worthwhile. Worth keeping. Against all odds, this man had taught himself to love and trust, to care so much, even when he hadn't always been given that same gift.

He deserved to see all of her, even if it meant he might not look at her like this anymore.

"Can you come home with me?" she asked. "RJ can go back with Quinn and Mallory. I just . . . Can we go now?"

"Of course." Zander rubbed a thumb over her trembling lips, watching her closely. "Of course, Penny. Whatever you need."

Before she could think better of it, Penny threw herself at Zander and pushed her face into his broad chest.

"I need *you*."

# CHAPTER 27

The drive back to Sullivan's Glen took forty minutes, during which Zander had a stomach full of cheesy soup and a million questions in his head.

The most dominant was one he'd been asking himself for weeks: What the hell was going on with Penny?

He'd worry she was breaking things off early, but for the way she'd clung to him by the barn, saying the three words he wanted most from her.

Well, the three words he wanted second most. The others were too much to ask for when he'd be leaving town in three weeks.

Penny remained quiet as she pulled her truck into her drive, and as she sat on her front porch. When he sat beside her, she popped back up and paced in front of her cabin. Four steps in one direction, turn, four steps in the other.

"Penny, why—"

"You know something I've noticed about you, Zander?" She said it pointedly but didn't slow. Four more steps, another turn. "You're a pain in my ass. You helped at the market when I said I didn't need you to, even though I clearly did. You convinced me to let you help with the festival when I was determined to do it on my own. When I work through mealtimes, you show up at the bee yard with a sandwich and glare at me until I eat it." She stopped and stared him down. "And I know you keep resetting my alarm so I sleep later."

He didn't deny it. "You need more rest."

"I'm awful at asking for help," she said, spinning for another four steps away. "In case you haven't noticed."

Zander chuckled ruefully. "I've noticed."

Penny slowed, looking into the trees past her cabin. "When I was a kid, Mimi and my mom were so busy. They had this place to run and a kid to raise, and I just wanted to be helpful. I felt like—" She swallowed and pursed her lips. "I think sometimes I thought it was my fault. Like, my mom got pregnant with me, and my father didn't want to be a dad. So he left, and then they were stuck again, picking up the pieces. Because I was part of the equation."

Zander rose. "Penny—"

"They never said that." She looked at him now, biting her lip. "I'm sure they never even thought it."

Still, his heart clenched for the girl trying to make sense of it all. "But you did."

She nodded. "I just sort of realized that today. I've been thinking about it, trying to figure out when I started trying so hard, when I became like *this*, and that's part of it. I wanted to prove to them I was worth it—worth not having anybody to help. Prove to the whole town, maybe, that he was a fool to leave us. And asking for help, admitting sometimes that I didn't know what I was doing, that would ruin it."

Penny paced again, wearing a line into the short grass. Energy sizzled just below her surface, like a racer at the starting block. "But the thing was, my mom just let me. She'd talk about how I should take breaks, but she never offered to do any of the work for me. And Mimi has needed her help for a while anyway, so——"

"So a lot was left to you."

"Yeah. And then Henry." Penny sighed. "Henry had this vision. This vision of what this place could be like, what we could do here. And I thought I had found someone to share it all with." She laughed a little, but Zander heard the tightness in her throat, like it was his own. "It was dumb, how easily I fell for that vision."

"That isn't dumb," he argued, moving toward her. "It's the most natural thing in the world to want that."

He'd let his own dreams of building a life with someone go when he and Mal split. Their divorce had been the right thing, but with a child to focus on and a life to keep in one piece, Zander hadn't imagined he'd find another partner who would fit well into his untraditional family. Until recently, he'd figured it was impossible.

"Even with Henry." Penny came closer, until she was just a couple of feet away. Sunshine glowed off the long braid over her shoulder. "He had his own ideas, but he never helped me with mine. And I never asked. Because I suck at that. But with you, Zander." Her lips parted as her long exhale mixed with the shuffle of leaves in the breeze. "You don't make me ask for help. You don't wait till I'm desperate. You don't assume I'm fine. You just step up. Even when I get pissy about it."

Zander reached out and closed two fingers around the end of her braid. "It's not a hardship. Especially because you're pretty sexy when you're pissy."

She laughed, but she was blinking away tears. "Good. Because I think I'm about to get really pissy. I want——" She cleared her throat and started again. "I want to tell you something. I want to ask you for help." A single tear tracked down her cheek. "But

I don't know how. It's like I don't even know how to start. So I need you to, like, do your thing."

"My thing?"

"Yeah. The thing you're so good at, where you're a pain in my ass and make me accept your help even when I'm really stubborn."

"*That's* my thing?"

"I mean, it's one of them."

"I have a lot of *things*, Penny."

"Well, this is one of them!" She huffed. "I'm serious. Just—" She waved a hand at him. "Do it! Help me!"

He watched the rapid beat of Penny's heart in her throat. "You're asking me to be a pain in the ass?"

"*Yes*."

"Okay." He dropped her braid and circled her slowly, thinking back to the times he'd broken through with her—helping at the market until she agreed to the beekeeping lesson, arguing about the festival in the sunlit bee yard.

Those moments all had something in common—they'd started with a fight. With Zander pushing Penny's buttons.

But how could he pick a fight with Penny when he didn't know just what he was helping with? He played the day back: Penny had been fidgety, distracted, prone to long looks at the sky. She'd been talking seriously with RJ and had looked almost scared when Zander appeared at her side. She seemed ready for anything by the barn, but . . .

"You tensed up," he said. "When I put my hand in your pocket."

He'd panicked that he'd done something to hurt her—been too rough or forward, assumed too much. But Penny hadn't hesitated until his fingers slid into her pocket and touched the corner of a piece of paper.

Zander stopped in front of her. "Show me what's in your pocket."

Her jaw tensed. "I don't have—" She shook her head. "No."

Suspicions confirmed, he stared her down. "I know there's something there. I felt it when I was groping your ass against that barn. You tensed up when I touched it, so we stopped. If that piece of paper wasn't important, I'd be fucking you in a hayloft right now."

"Somebody's cocky."

"Come on, Penny. You know when I do that thing with my tongue behind your ear, you spread your legs for me."

Her luscious lips pouted. "Not always. Sometimes I get on my knees for you—"

"Christ." Zander dragged a hand across his face. *Focus*. "Stop distracting me with sexy stuff."

"You brought it up—"

He extended his hand. "Give me the paper."

"No."

"You know I could take it. I'm bigger than you."

She narrowed her eyes. "I'm faster."

"Maybe." He shrugged. "But my legs are longer. What do you think, should we test it?"

"You wouldn't dare."

Zander grinned. "You're right, that would be too easy. I'm going to get you to hand it right over."

Her nostrils flared. "The hell you will."

"Come on," he pushed. "What could it be?" He tapped his chin. "Are you secretly married?"

"No!"

"Did you win the lottery?"

"I wish," she scoffed.

"You're heir to the throne of a small European monarchy?"

"Also no."

Penny stepped backward, but he followed. "Maybe it's your high school transcript, showing all those perfect little A's you got when losers like me were barely getting by."

Her eyes went hot, shimmering an angry blue. So lovely and fierce. Just like every time he'd called her perfect all summer. Like something stung each time he said it. Something that betrayed the label, something only she knew.

"Or maybe," he continued, stepping close, "it's a certificate of appreciation from the Sullivan's Glen township council, acknowledging what a shining star you are in your community." He arched a brow. "I think mine got lost in the mail."

Penny crossed her arms over her chest. "They don't even make those."

"I bet they would, for you. Sullivan's Glen's golden girl, the one I was supposed to look up to."

"I am *not* the—"

"The perfect Penny Becker." He enunciated every word.

"Don't *say* that."

"Why not? Everybody knows it's true. My grandfather sure did. He spotted it when we were just kids. You were the perfect one—"

"Stop it."

"But me?" He forced a laugh. "I was just the fuckup."

"Shut up!" Her voice broke. "You are not a fuckup! And I'm not perfect, I've never been perfect!"

Penny's chest heaved as her eyes went sharp and angry, a storm moving across calm seas. Zander wanted to hug the hell out of her, but she *wanted* this. She'd ask for his help in the only way she knew how.

So he shrugged like an asshole. "Prove it."

"What?"

"Prove you're not the perfect girl everyone says you are. The shiny, perfect Penny Becker everybody loves. Prove you're not just what my papou always told me."

"Fine!" She yanked the paper from her pocket, closed the distance between them, and slapped it into his hand. "Fine!" she yelled again. "You want proof? There. Look at that. It's going to tell you that I have a big fucking loan out on this whole place, and that if I don't pay it in thirty days, they're going to start foreclosure. How's that for perfect, Zander? Perfect Penny Becker is about to lose the family farm." Penny swiped at her cheeks angrily. "You want to know the best part? They don't know. My mom and Mimi. They don't know I put their house at risk, the life they built for all of us. They don't know that I let Henry talk me into some stupid idea that didn't amount to anything but ballooning interest rates and a mess I can't dig myself out of!"

Penny breathed hard as Zander circled around her words—*big fucking loan*, *they don't know*, *some stupid idea*—until he could piece it together. Her air of panic about the festival, her ominous comments about the future, the way she'd shot down his expensive culinary station idea so quickly: it all clicked.

"This is why when you talk about the Honey Festival, you seem so desperate. You need it to be successful so you can pay toward the loan."

Penny drooped like a thirsty flower, the fury he'd helped her work up draining from her face. He ate up the space between them and wrapped his arms around her, rubbing a hand on her back as her face pressed into his chest.

After a moment she stepped away and walked slowly to sit on her front stoop. Zander followed, sitting beside her and pulling out the paper she'd thrust at him. Hearing it all from Penny's perspective was what mattered, so he kept the page folded and handed it back to her.

"I'm proud of you for telling me."

She grumbled, "You didn't give me much choice." Then, quieter, "I'm sorry I didn't tell you. I was afraid you wouldn't like me if you knew how much I messed up."

He tugged her braid. "Don't you remember, baby? I hated you when I thought you were perfect. I like you so much more now because I know you can mess up just like me."

Silence settled for a moment, broken only by the drumming of a woodpecker somewhere nearby. Zander rubbed Penny's back and watched an occasional bee fly by, and eventually Penny started to talk.

She told him about being deeded her family's property, about Henry's plan to ferment cider and the ways it had gone awry, about being saddled with a debt she was too ashamed to reveal. Zander held her hands as she told him about the piling-on of additional challenges—slower sales, her grandmother's health, and a poor harvest the year before.

"I made the payments for a while," she explained. "Until I couldn't. And then the interest rate went up, and I was just—it was dumb, to trust Henry with so much. He said it would all work out, and I wanted so badly for it to be true. I thought maybe I had a partner, you know?"

Zander nodded even as he burned from the inside, ready to go after every man who'd ever walked out of Penny's life.

"But the lender was shit and the builder was shit," Penny continued. "And then one day I was like, 'You know what? Henry is shit, too. This would be easier on my own.' And now here I am. I'd hoped that the festival would do well enough that

I could start managing the loan again and I'd never have to tell my family. It's sad that my goal was to keep it secret forever, but it's the truth. But then RJ—he's the only one I've ever told about this—he told me today that by not telling you what was happening, I was keeping you from seeing all of me."

She sniffed. "And I've been doing that with my mom and Mimi, you know? By not letting them know what's going on, I'm not letting them know me. Then I get mad at them for not knowing, and I shut myself off more and—"

"And it's a really big pothole."

"Yeah." Her gravelly laugh was halfway to a sob.

Zander wanted to see the loan contract, to examine her books. He wanted to look into this shady lender and track down Henry and make him pay. He wanted to solve every problem Penny had ever had. But that had to be up to her.

"You said you needed help. Is there something specific you need from me?"

"Actually, yes." She stood and wiped her palms along her jeans. "I need you to walk me to my mom's house. I need you to stand there while I go inside, and then I need you to stay there for five minutes in case I try to run back out."

Zander rose and took her hand. "I can do that. I can definitely do that."

It was a quiet walk, everything in the trees resting in the midday heat. They passed the gardens, where squash vines wound between staked tomatoes. Penny stopped to pick a sprig of peppermint and squish it between her fingers. They didn't talk, because they didn't need to. He knew Penny was preparing, and he was doing just what she needed. And somewhere deep in his chest, something was cracking open as Zander did some preparation of his own.

When they got to the house, he kissed her face where it was still damp with her tears, then gave her a friendly nudge up the steps.

And five minutes later, he headed for home, a sense of urgency propelling him down the path he'd worn through the grass. He moved quickly around his living room and up the steps two at a time, until he was standing in front of Papou's bedroom door.

He hadn't opened it since that first week in Sullivan's Glen.

But if Penny Becker could turn a corner today, maybe he could, too.

# CHAPTER 28

Penny had expected some yelling. Crying, too. She wouldn't have been surprised if some fists shook, or if a beloved teacup shattered on the floor.

Any of that would have been preferable to the silence at the Becker kitchen table.

"You heard me, right?"

She'd been talking since storming into the house to surprise her mom and Mimi in their recliners. After ordering them into the kitchen, where any conversation of consequence took place, Penny nearly balked and canceled the whole thing. But then she walked to the window to see Zander standing guard in the yard as he'd promised.

And she pulled out the letter, flattened it on the table, and started her story.

As she spoke, she studied the worn wood of the kitchen table and its decades of scratches and dings she knew from feel alone. Every piece of this house held a history like that—the doorway where her mom had measured Penny every year, the cabinets Mimi'd refinished one spring after a particularly good season, houseplants trailing years of happy vines. Though Penny's old bedroom had been converted into a landing place for odds and ends, she knew it still had the piles of blankets she and RJ had used to make forts, and the little hatch marks she'd drawn next to her bed as a terrified eighteen-year-old counting down to the days until she'd leave for college.

More memories lived outside in the bee yard and the orchard, in the fence repairs and irrigation lines and piles of red baskets stowed away, waiting for the next season of apple pickers to come through. They were signs of life, and signs of work, because the two had always been intertwined here. And Penny loved it all so, so much.

Sometimes she forgot why she worked so hard. But it was all right here, in the table nicks beneath her fingers. She didn't want to lose this place.

No one interrupted as she talked, a rarity for the Becker women. By the time she'd said it all—about the cidery and the loan and the scammy builder and how she'd kept it all to herself— her throat was raw. And the table was silent.

"Mom? Mimi? Say . . . something?"

Her mother stood and walked slowly to the cabinet, lifted out a glass, and moved to the fridge. She clinked in ice, then filled it with the peppermint iced tea she brewed with leaves she dried each fall.

"This sounds," she said finally, "like something I would have done."

At the table, Mimi laughed roughly. "You did do something like this, honey. Back when Penny was just a wee thing. You got your bee in a bonnet about hiring out the hives in the winters, hauling them down to Georgia and whatnot. Thought it would be a great adventure for you and Penny."

"That's right." Ruth leaned against the fridge with a faraway look on her face. "I read about beekeepers who did that, keeping the hives active year-round. But we needed the trucks for it, and extra equipment, and money to hire folks to help while I spent the winter there."

"And we went to the bank together and pitched it to 'em," Mimi added. "I think they would have rejected us if old Griffin hadn't taken a liking to me."

"Wait," Penny interrupted. "We trucked the bees to Georgia? Why don't I remember this?"

"Well." Ruth blushed. "Because it never happened. I tried to save money buying the trucks for cheap, and they both ended up needing so much extra work, we didn't even get them going that season. By the next year, you were gearing up to start kindergarten, and I didn't want to take you away from all that. The idea just kind of petered out. I eventually sold the trucks to Carson down at the scrapyard."

"Petered out?" Penny stared at her mom. "What about the loan?"

Mimi sighed. "We were in a hard way for a while there, stretching everything pretty thin. I did have to go into the bank and bat my eyelashes at Griffin a few times, asking for an extension. But we made it through."

Penny looked between the elder Beckers, then back at the letter on the table. "Okay. But this isn't like that. They're threatening foreclosure, Mimi."

And her grandmother, the woman who'd brought in the very first bees to Becker Farms, *laughed*. "You did go big, Penny. I'll give you that."

Ruth clucked in agreement. "I wouldn't expect anything less from her."

Penny rose, almost sending her chair sailing back. "Do you

hear yourselves? Did you spend too much time in the sun today? Are you both suffering from head injuries no one told me about? I just told you that I took out a loan without telling you, that I kept it all secret, and that now in thirty days they'll start foreclosure proceedings on our *home*! What the hell is wrong with you two?"

Ruth set her tea down on the table. "What would you rather I do, honey?"

"Scream!" Penny demonstrated. "Yell at me! Throw a coffee cup or something. What is wrong with you?"

"Nothing is wrong with me," her mom replied with a firm voice. "I heard every word you said, and I'm reacting in my own way. I'm not a yeller, Pen, and you know that. Why would I want to make you feel worse when you clearly feel terrible already?"

"Because I deserve it! Because I messed everything up!"

Her mother just shook her head, remaining infuriatingly calm. "Hate to break it to you, honey, but you're not the center of the world, and neither is Becker Farms. Of course this is upsetting, and scary, and honestly, quite a surprise. But screaming about it won't do anything. We're going to be okay."

"We're going to be *okay*?" Penny bellowed. This was worse than wailing and broken teacups. This was insanity. "How can you always say that, Mom? *We're going to be okay*," she mocked. "*Trust the universe*. It's always some shit like that. But you know what, the universe hasn't been the one doing everything all these years. It's been *me*." She thumped her chest. "And now that it's me who messed it up, who's going to come in and save the day? I'm supposed to just throw up my hands and trust the universe? Is that what I should tell the lender when they come to take the house?"

"Now, Penny," Mimi started. "Don't say things you'll regret."

"No, Mother." Ruth shook her head. "It's fine. You're right, honey."

As Penny's mother released a breath, her shoulders slumped forward. She looked older, tired, and Penny hated it. She loved this woman so much—her weathered hands and penchant for gossip and way of finding every silver lining—and . . . and found her so damn irritating at the same time.

"I've always let you do too much," her mom said. "But right from the start, sweetie, there was no stopping you. I would have had to tie you to the couch to keep you from those bees. You seemed almost frantic about helping out, and I just saw it as a part of you."

"It is," Penny answered. "It is part of me. I really love the work but I also think I worried about . . ." She hesitated, not wanting to yank in another element that would only make everything more fucked-up. But then she thought about those potholes, where everyone did the same things again and again. Maybe it was time to do something different.

"I think I worried that it was my fault that we were doing it alone, because my, uh, dad left when you were pregnant, and everything seemed so busy and hard and I wanted it to be worth it for you." When her mom and Mimi simply stared, slack-jawed, Penny barreled forward. "And I know it's a ridiculous thing to think. I know it's not true at all, but it wiggled its way into my brain and it sucked that I could never talk to you about it, because you just joked about him being a sperm donor and that was that. It wasn't anything we could ever discuss."

She sniffed wetly and wiped at her face, knowing her cheeks were bright red and her eyes probably no better. "And I'm sorry," she said. "I'm sorry if that's hard for you to hear, or if I shouldn't have brought it up. I'm sorry—"

"Will you stop it!" Penny's mother slammed her hands on the table, making her glass teeter dangerously. "I swear to the lords above, Penny Lee Becker, if you so much as even start to apologize one more time, I will—"

"Okay, *okay*!" Now it was Mimi shouting, rising from her chair. "No one is apologizing anymore, and no one is getting worked up here. Ruthie, you sit your ass down. Penny, go grab a tissue. You look something awful."

Avoiding her mother's furious glare, Penny went for the tissues. "Thanks, Mimi."

Her mother's hand shot out. "Come 'ere, Pen."

Dreading her mother's anger and hurt, but knowing she'd brought it on herself, Penny sat next to her mom.

"Penny, honey, I am so sorry. I grew up with such a hole in my heart, wondering why my own dad didn't stay. I thought . . . thought if I could make it a joke for you, make *him* a joke, it might hurt less. It was cowardly of me, honey, and it obviously didn't work."

How had Penny never seen it? Everything she'd gone through as a kid—the questions, the pining, the wondering—her mom had experienced it all first, and was left to ferry Penny through it all again.

And maybe she'd messed up with parts along the way, but what was Penny expecting? Perfection?

"You are worth a hundred of that man," Ruth continued, squeezing Penny's hand. "A hundred times over. I might joke about the sperm donor part, but I have never joked about you being the greatest gift anyone could have left me with."

"It is true," Mimi said from her seat. "Never did like that joker myself. Best thing he ever did was leave your mama alone and give you those pretty blue eyes. Our Ruthie never did have good taste in men."

Ruth shot her mother a look. "Okay, Mom."

Mimi lifted her hands defensively. "Not that I did much better." Her expression softened. "But I'd do it all again for you, Ruth."

Ruth smiled back and blinked away more tears. "And I'd do it all again for Penny."

Penny picked up her mom's glass and took a long drink, letting the brisk peppermint cool her down. Just a couple of hours ago she'd been eating cheese soup and keeping all her secrets to herself. Now, here she was, fifty pounds lighter but no closer to a solution.

"I want to talk about all of this more," she said finally. "We *need* to talk about all of this more, but right now"—Penny stared at the letter, still spread in the middle of the table—"we kind of have a bigger problem to deal with. Like what we're going to do if the festival isn't enough to help with the loan."

"Honey." Ruth squeezed her daughter's hands one last time, then leaned back into her chair. "I don't think you're going to like my answer."

"Whatever you do, do not tell me to trust the universe."

"Mother." Ruth spoke to Mimi. "Tell Penny what happened when my dad left."

"What happened when Frederick left?" Mimi shook her head. "I fell apart, didn't I? I had a huge plot of land and a newborn, and I just about thought my life was over. Packed my bags so many times, ready to just walk away from it all."

Penny's heart squeezed. "Mimi."

"I'll tell you when I turned a corner, though. Elsie Bouras brought over a great big casserole, enough to feed an army."

"Elsie Bouras?"

"That's right." Mimi nodded. "She and Nikolai had just been married. My, she was a beautiful, bright-eyed thing. Reckon she must have seen me pacing the porch, holding this damned colicky baby, crying my eyes out." Her gaze drifted to the window. "Elsie had a gift for helping. She never came out and acknowledged that I was suffering and alone. Never asked me to pour my heart out to her. She just brought food over every day and held Ruthie while I ate."

Penny blinked back more tears as she swallowed thickly. "She sounds like Zander."

Mimi hummed, still looking outside. "I don't know if it was Elsie or someone else who got the word out that there was a half-crazed woman on this land with an orchard going wild, but people just started showing up with tools and tractors and the know-how I needed to get moving."

Penny reached across the table to cover her grandmother's soft hand with her own. "I didn't know that story. Why didn't you tell me?"

Mimi shrugged. "I don't reckon it's anything spectacular, is it? Just neighbors helping neighbors."

"Tell me something, Pen." Her mother called her attention back. "When we had that freak freeze last year, who put the heaters and fans out in the orchards?"

"The football team." Colin, the high school coach, had heard Penny talking about the job of warming the orchards while she was getting a coffee on Main Street. That night a line of bulky teenagers had arrived ready to work.

"When you were just a toddler, and your mimi and I had to spend every weekend at markets, where did you go to play?"

"Miss Randal's house." It always smelled like pine trees and cough syrup.

Ruth smiled smugly. "That's what I'm talking about when I say trust the universe, honey. I mean that people have your back, even when you don't realize it, starting with us in this room. And no matter what happens to this building or this land, we have each other."

As practical and panicked as Penny was, she couldn't deny the rightness of her mom's words. Through everything life had thrown at them—sperm donors coming and going, seasons changing, orchards freezing, and all the rest—Becker Farms had survived because of the Becker women. And, Penny realized, the universe of people around them.

And if Penny had anything to say about it, that wouldn't end now. Her family was the heart of Becker Farms. But the land and the bees that kept it blooming were the heart of Penny herself. It was work, but it was also her life, and she didn't want to let it go.

"I don't want to lose the farm, Mom. I love it here."

"Well then"—her mother laid her hand over Penny's and Mimi's, so the hands of all three Becker women were stacked—"I guess we'll handle this like we handle everything else. Together."

# CHAPTER 29

When Zander finally swung open the door to his papou's old room, nothing happened. No gust carrying long-stored memories, no shivers down his spine. Only old beige furniture and glints of dust dancing through shafts of sunlight. Stilling at the threshold, Zander felt the phantom of Penny's hand on his back, soothing him. And he stepped inside.

His fingers cut twin trails through the thick layer of dust on the bed frame, the dresser, and the dark wood desk where his grandfather would sit, flipping through mail. It didn't matter if it was junk or not, Papou always opened every piece and read it front to back, then piled all the letters together on his desk.

Threadbare clothes filled the dresser. Zander pulled out one brown button-down and shrugged into it, pulling it down over his T-shirt. Just as he'd suspected, it fit him perfectly.

At the window, he pushed back the tan curtain and looked down. He had the perfect view of the front porch and long driveway.

The desk held a framed photo of Papou and his wife, arms around each other and smiling in black and white. They were young, maybe early twenties. Zander's grandmother—though he rarely thought of her that way—had long straight hair and a turtleneck. She looked like his mom when she'd been younger and healthier—big brown eyes and high cheekbones that raised her whole face with a smile.

Zander lowered himself into an old wooden swivel chair that groaned under his weight. The seat beneath him tipped, sending him into a weightless fall before something creaked and caught.

"*Christ.*" Despite having moved slowly through the room, Zander's heart thundered. He watched the slight tremor in his hands as he pulled open drawers, looked through old mail, bills from over a decade ago, empty pill bottles, and Christmas cards from people whose names he didn't recognize.

It was all so mundane. Years of paper and dust on the dresser. Just normal life and signs of the passage of time.

At least now Zander knew he could let this room go like the others. Empty it out and organize it into piles—donate, throw out, recycle. Make it ready for its next life. Finally call Monica about the showings and put up the *For Sale* sign outside.

As he pulled out the last desk drawer, papers shifted to reveal a glossy photo between some old newspaper clippings.

A photo of Zander.

He lifted the whole stack out, flattening it on the desk with a brush of his palm.

AFRO-CUBAN DINER WOWS OLD TOWN

It was the article from *Bon Appétit* from about four years ago. There was a photo of the restaurant's chef, Anton, with members of the kitchen crew. Tucked in at the side of the photo, smiling big, was Zander.

It had been his first splashy project, garnering national press and elevating his name as someone to know in the New England restaurant world.

And it was in his grandfather's desk drawer.

Zander sifted further through the papers from the drawer. There was a cutout *Boston Globe* review of another restaurant he'd partnered on, and a printout of Zander's bio from the website Mallory had helped him build.

The room held no computer, no printer. Where the fuck had this piece of paper even come from?

A few minutes later, the desk was covered in yellowing restaurant reviews and computer printouts, Zander's face was wet, his heart a confused mess.

A younger Zander might have been relieved, happy, or even smug to see the evidence of his grandfather's attention laid out like this, so plain to see.

But now it only made him deeply, achingly sad.

Zander rose from the desk, the chair skidding behind him as he broke for the door. He'd never understood the man who'd made a life in this room, and he understood him even less now. He had a lifetime of questions that would never be answered.

But though he'd never get answers from Papou himself, maybe he could find answers somewhere else.

Ten minutes later he knocked on Ruth and Cynthia Becker's front door.

When Penny's grandmother peeked outside, her eyes went wide, then softened.

"Penny's not here, honey." She looked past him, to the trees. "She just left a few minutes ago. I think she was due for a long hot bath and a cup of tea."

He longed to know how Penny's conversation had gone, how

she was feeling now that she'd unloaded the burden, what help she might need with her next steps.

But that wasn't why he'd come.

"Actually, ma'am, I'm here to talk to you. I'm hoping you can tell me about my grandfather." Zander let out a long breath and steadied his voice. "You talked like maybe you'd known him a little, and I thought maybe—but I'm sorry, if it's a trouble, I can—"

"Zander." Cynthia's tone brooked no argument. She nodded to two porch chairs arranged between pots of blooming flowers. "I told you to call me Mimi. Now sit down, honey. I've only been waiting for you to ask."

Cynthia closed the door behind her and took a seat. Zander sank into the other chair, trying to steady his tapping legs by pressing his hands into his knees. After a moment, Cynthia was the first to break the silence. "You want to tell me what brought this on? You've been here all summer, and you haven't asked about him once."

Guilt gnawed at Zander, pushing at that same bruise that ached when he thought about how long he'd stayed away.

He swallowed past the feeling. "I was looking through his stuff. I found some clippings about me—work projects and everything. It—" He grabbed for words to describe his extreme disorientation, the way his heart felt all mashed up. "I'm confused."

Cynthia nodded. "You didn't think he cared."

"He didn't act like it."

She watched him thoughtfully for a moment, then looked over in the direction of his house. "He and I were never close. Even though we lived next door to each other, he was a hard person to know. His parents were—" She sighed, shaking her head, then looked to Zander. "Nikolai would have seemed like a teddy bear compared to them."

Zander swallowed. "That's saying a lot."

"I don't think he got many examples of joy. His parents weren't a love match, and they put enormous pressure on him as their only son. I'm glad he got some fresh air when he met your grandmother. Elsie just laughed at him when he was grumpy. They really had some magic.

"She was his sunshine, and it seemed like he couldn't find it again without her. When your sweet mama started acting out, he just disappeared into himself. I tried reaching out to him, but he wouldn't have it. I think he felt he was failing Elsie by struggling so much with your mom, and that just made him close up even more."

"I can't make sense of any of it," Zander admitted. "It was easy when I was young to just assume the worst about him. That he was a cold asshole who didn't care about me or my mom."

"And now you're questioning that?"

"He *was* a cold asshole. And as a kid, that's all I saw. I was so mad at everybody, so confused about what I was doing wrong and why nobody seemed to want me, and he just became the center of that. But he had to be more than that, right?"

"What do you think?"

"I don't know what to think," he admitted. "I know that when I was doing all that shit here every summer—stealing tractors and messing with the public pool—people thought I was just some punk kid. To them, it was probably that simple."

Mimi caught Zander's eye and held his gaze. "But you were more than that. I imagine you were hurting, quite a lot."

"I was," he pushed out. "In ways I didn't even understand then, and it made me so self-destructive. But the thing was"—and this was something Zander had spun around in his head over and over, something he couldn't make sense of—"he could have told my mom I couldn't come, that I couldn't stay for the summer. He could have told her I was more trouble than I was worth and that I had to stay in Detroit with her."

Cynthia nodded. "Probably so."

Zander tugged at his own hair, wishing something could just be fucking simple. "But he must not have, because I was here. And I had a bed, and food in the fridge, and he found me jobs when he could, and he left stupid articles for me on the stupid kitchen table."

And every time Zander had snuck out the front door and down the driveway, trying to run away, his grandfather had been close behind. Because his papou was always watching, standing alone in that drab bedroom looking out his window.

"God." Zander slammed his eyes shut as his face fell into his hands. "I think he was doing his best."

Cynthia's hand, light as the breeze, curled over his shoulders. She held it there as he fought for a breath, then spoke quietly. "I think he was, too. But Zander . . ." When she paused, he lifted his face to look at her. She didn't have Penny's eyes, but she had her smile, the one that settled something in his veins. "You still deserved better, honey."

She rubbed down his arm and took his hands in hers. "He was doing his best, and you *still* deserved better. From Nikolai and from your mother."

Zander stared at Cynthia, breathing slowly. It was a heady truth, sharp and soft at the same time, and he didn't have a place to put it, not yet. For now, all he could do was sit in the rubble of her truth-bomb, knowing that sometime the dust would settle.

He studied Cynthia's small hands closed over his, each line telling its own story.

He'd never touched Papou's hands. That last summer, when

Zander managed to buy his own car and stood triumphantly in the kitchen, telling his grandfather he was getting out of that shithole, the old man had silently offered a handshake.

But Zander'd only scoffed and gone outside, letting the screen door slap shut behind him.

"He deserved better, too." He tipped his gaze up to Cynthia, determined to look someone in the face as he said it out loud. "I should have come back. I did so much work to heal and be better, and I should have used some of that to get over my own shit and come back."

Tears welled over his bottom lids, but he didn't bother wiping them off. Instead, he watched them land where his hands were joined with Cynthia's. "My mom couldn't be here. She couldn't handle it. But I could have. I should have let him meet Winter, I should have come, I shouldn't have let him die alone."

There was the rough scrape of a chair, and then Cynthia's arms were around him, pulling his face into her shoulder. Dragging in deep breaths, Zander let himself break open.

He'd cried to Mallory and Quinn. He'd cried on his therapist's couch while she handed him tissues. But he'd never cried like this, held by someone's mother and grandmother, who smelled like baby powder and peppermint and knew just how to rub his back.

He wondered if this was how Winter felt in Zander's arms. Like he was safe, if just for a few minutes. God, he hoped so.

Zander leaned into Cynthia for another breath before pulling away. He sniffed and wiped his face. "I regret so much, but he's gone. I can't do it differently. I don't know what to do with that."

"I'm not one to say what you should or shouldn't have done, Zander. But I know we can't redo the past." Her light hand brushed hair from his forehead. "What's done is done, and we're stuck carrying that regret with us, and sometimes it can be quite a weight. The best we can do to help ourselves is stop the next regrets before they can form."

Zander rose.

Earlier he'd felt an urgency to open that door, to revisit the past. But now, he could think only about the future. "Thank you, Mimi. I appreciate all of this more than you know."

Her smile had a mischievous twist. "Going so soon? What's the rush?"

"I, um . . ." Zander rubbed the back of his neck. "I think I need to go talk to someone. Prevent a future regret."

"I reckon you do."

## CHAPTER 30

Penny heard Zander before she saw him. His heavy footfalls were unmistakable, just like the kick in her heartbeat whenever she recognized them.

After leaving her mother's house, Penny went for a walk, weaving between trees and pausing to touch each trunk and drag her fingers across the bark. Then she drew a hot bath and sat in it until her skin was red, looking back at the day through the steam rising from the water.

Penny knew this was a before-and-after day: one of those rare moments when life turns a clear corner, like the first time Penny held her own bee frame in her hands, or when she told Henry not to come back to Sullivan's Glen. But the scary, exciting thing about those days is not yet knowing what comes after.

After throwing on a tank top and her most comfortable terry-cloth shorts, Penny sat on the porch with a cup of tea to listen to song sparrows as they trilled from the trees. She tried to relax, but her whole system felt primed and jittery, ringing like a bell.

Zander appeared from behind her house, hands tucked into the front pockets of his jeans, face flushed. He was so beautiful—a gentle bear in the woods, smiling at her shyly in the sunshine.

"Hey."

"Hi." She sucked in a shaky breath and stood, leaving her mug on the porch.

Zander stayed in the clearing, simply *looking* at her. His gaze started curiously—a scan to see that she was all right and in one piece—but soon melted into something else. Something that burned at the edges of her senses as he wet his lower lip. Something that sent that bell inside her clanging as his chest rose and fell.

Penny stepped off the porch, drawn to Zander with a force that would have terrified her if she'd had any other day. But she'd had *this* day, a before-and-after day, and he'd made it possible. He'd given her just what she needed.

She saw it all reflected in Zander, who watched her fiercely as his long strides ate up the ground between them. A wild energy flashed in his eyes that sent goose bumps up Penny's arms.

Without a word, he wrapped an arm around her waist and tugged her roughly into his body. She braced her palms against his chest as his mouth landed hard on hers, taking everything she could give. When she gasped, he slid his tongue between her lips hungrily, groaning into her mouth as his wide hands wrapped around her ribs.

Zander's mouth trailed along her jaw. "I want to know how it went with your mom and grandma. I want to know everything. I want to know how else I can help, but *fuck*, Penny, right now I need—"

The end of his sentence was muffled as his teeth dragged the strap of her tank top off her shoulder.

Penny fisted one hand in Zander's hair. "If you want to know how else to help," she gasped, "this is really helping."

His mouth closed on hers again as Zander walked her backward, his hands sliding up and down her back and over her ass. Soon she was pressed against a tree, bark rough on her back.

He loomed over her, one hand pinning her wrists overhead as the other cupped a breast, pushing it up from below so she almost spilled out of her bra.

"Fuck," he growled. "When my hands are on you I can't think a single sane thought. I just want to *take*." Proving it, he bent his head to the rise of her breast, sucking hard enough to leave a mark.

Penny wanted his marks all over her. Wanted Zander to take and take until she couldn't think or worry about anything except his hands on her.

Zander kissed her deeply again, then pulled back and nodded to where his hand encircled her wrists. "This okay?"

Penny nodded, breathing hard. "It's good. So good." She steadied her gaze on his, letting herself sink into the deep warmth of his gaze. "I need this. Need you."

A swallow moved down his throat like a boulder. "Say that again."

"I need you, Zander."

His eyes closed briefly, but he opened them again to stare at her darkly. "I need to get you inside and on a bed, now." His hands went to her ass as he hoisted her up to his waist. "Hold on, Penny."

She wrapped her arms and legs around him as Zander stomped through the trees to her cabin, holding her tightly. His mouth worked magic on her neck as he got the door open and laid her on the bed.

He kneeled over her, breathing hard. As his eyes raked over her body, Zander tugged off his shirt and popped open the straining button of his jeans, then cupped the long ridge of his erection.

Penny released a long whimper as she watched him, unable to tear her eyes away as he dragged down his zipper.

"You like watching me, baby?"

His voice was rough like the bark of the tree. She wanted to rub her whole body against it.

Zander curled his fingers around himself over his boxers as he leaned over Penny, sliding one hand up her bare thigh. His fingers moved easily under the bottom hem of her shorts, brushing over her soaked underwear before maneuvering the fabric aside.

"Fuck my life, Penny." Zander sank a finger into her as she moaned. "You get wet for me so fast. You need me this badly?"

He released himself to tug down on her tank top and bra, exposing her breasts and nipples. He swore again as his mouth descended on her, using his tongue and teeth, the thrilling ridge of his erection grinding where she was aching for him, making her moan.

"Please, Zander." Penny rolled her hips up, trying to reach for his pants.

"Say it again. Beg for it. Tell me what you need."

"You, I need *you*. Please get inside me."

There was the creak of the nightstand and the tear of the condom packet. Then Zander was back on his knees, tugging Penny's pants and underwear off and tossing them on the floor. He shoved his jeans below his ass and began rolling on the condom.

"Wish we didn't need that," Penny heard herself saying. "Wish I could feel you. Just you."

Zander squeezed the base of his cock. "Shit, Penny. You'd want that?"

She wanted to be as close to Zander as possible, like he was the solution to this empty ringing, the roots that would hold her to the ground. Her teeth bruised her bottom lip as she nodded. "Yes."

His jaw clenched. "We can't. You told me that the first time.

I'm not crossing your boundaries in the heat of the moment, as much as I fucking want to."

"I know. I know, I just wish—"

She wished for so many things. For a miraculous solution to her money problems, for a different set of choices these past years, and for this connection with Zander to not be temporary.

His mouth came back to hers, kissing her deeply as he seated himself inside her in one thrust, filling her perfectly.

"Imagine I'm bare. Just my cock sliding into you. Nothing between us. Just you and me, Penny. Just you and me."

Zander worked her ruthlessly, opening her up with an elbow hooked around her knee and grunting with every thrust. Penny's hands scraped at his back as she tried to get closer, pull him deeper.

When he pulled out of her abruptly, Penny cried out. But then his hands went to her hips, flipping her over and tugging her up to him.

"Don't stop," she gasped.

He slid back inside her easily, the angle from behind letting him hit a spot deep inside her.

Zander sucked roughly on her neck as a hand snaked across her stomach and between her legs. "Love being inside you, Penny. Feels like coming home."

He didn't ease her into her orgasm but took her directly to the brink. His fingers thrummed against her as he fucked her hard, until Penny was trembling and moaning and coming undone beneath him.

Zander followed fast, fusing himself to her and crying out her name like a prayer.

He dropped kisses across her shoulders before rolling to the side as Penny let herself sink into the mattress, blissfully boneless.

A few seconds later Zander sank back into the bed and rubbed small circles on her back. "Penny." His hand paused, his breath caught, then he continued. "I don't want this to end when I go back to Boston."

She rolled to face him. "What?"

Zander cupped her face with one hand and held her gaze. "That's what I came to tell you. I want to figure this out. I want to try, I want to be with you. Whatever that looks like."

Her heart threatened to beat out of her chest, but her head was spinning. "Where is this coming from?"

His thumb stroked just under her eye. "You know where it's coming from, baby. We always said this was real, and I know you feel it, too."

"I do. Of course I do, but—" Penny shook her head. "We said real, but temporary. That's what we agreed. That's what makes sense."

Zander's eyes closed for a moment, then opened with clarity and determination. "When you were with your family, I finally went into my papou's room."

"Zander." She stroked a hand down his arm. "How did that feel?"

"Pretty fucked-up, to be honest. It left me with a lot of questions, and I went to talk to your grandma, to ask her about him."

"Gosh." Penny couldn't help a small laugh. "It's been kind of a big day."

His fingers still held her face gently. "We ended up talking about regret. How I regret not coming back to see him, and how there's nothing I can do to change that."

Penny scooted closer. "Oh, sweetheart."

The slip of the name, one she'd never used with him, sparked a smile on Zander's face. "Your grandma said all we can do sometimes is prevent more regrets from forming." His gaze held her tightly. "And I realized that if I walk away from this like we planned, if I don't *try*, I'll always regret it. I don't want to live with that."

It was romantic, and sweet, and honest, and everything Penny had wanted to hear. The confirmation that she wasn't the only one dreading their separation, not the only one thinking dangerously about a future she couldn't have. But it didn't change the facts.

"What would that even look like?" she asked.

He gave a small shrug. "I don't know. I do know it's a five-hour drive, and I'll make it as often as I can. I know I'd fucking love to have you in my little apartment in Boston anytime. I know it would be worth it, Penny. This is special. This isn't something people get a lot of chances at."

"I know." She pulled at the comforter, drawing it over them together. This was what she wanted—the two of them tucked together, Zander at her side. But Penny didn't live by wants. She lived by seasons and market prices and nectar flow, by the demands of the real world. "What would the endgame be?" she asked. "My soul is in this place, and your whole life is in Boston."

His free hand raked through his hair as he frowned. "I don't know. I can't promise you it will be easy, and I can't see into the future. It's probably a terrible idea, but we're good at those, right? All I know is that if I didn't tell you how much I've come to fucking—" His eyes closed as he let out a breath. "How much you mean to me, how much I want to keep you in my life, I would regret it every day."

People did long-distance as a stopgap, but there was no future in which he and Penny lived in the same place. And she had so much to do here, waiting to see if the Honey Festival would be the Hail Mary she needed, figuring out what other options might keep her mom and grandma in their home if it didn't. She wouldn't be doing it alone, but he could never be the partner here that she dreamed about.

"Zander, I don't see how—"

"Don't answer now," he interrupted, perhaps seeing the conflicted resolve in her expression. "It's been a hell of a day, especially for you. I wouldn't have even brought it up, but I just . . ." He sighed. "Let's get through the next few days, make it through the festival, and go from there."

Penny swallowed hard, knowing they were just kicking the can down the road. But then Zander brushed his fingers over her lips, her cheeks, along the fall of her eyelashes, and kicking that can didn't seem so bad.

"Please, Penny," he whispered. "Give me this. Think about it."

If it was in her power, Penny would give Zander Bouras the whole world, so she gave him this much.

"Okay," she whispered back. "I'll think about it."

# CHAPTER 31

Zander slid the veggie lasagna onto the counter and collapsed into a kitchen chair with a sigh, grabbing for his sweating bottle of beer. He didn't drink much anymore—he'd gotten most of his partying out when he and Mal were young rebels—but today he was making an exception. After a few busy days of preparation, it was finally Honey Festival eve.

But before he could climb into bed and prepare for his 6 a.m. alarm, Mal and Quinn were coming over for a mysterious family meeting, and Zander was on edge.

Mal didn't call family meetings just for the hell of it, and she'd been short on details. Just a text that said, *Hey can we do a fam meeting tomorrow? I know it's awful timing with the fest but we need to talk. We'll come at 6, can u cook?*

Never in the history of time had "we need to talk" been about anything good, but when he'd called Quinn to pull something more out of her, she'd been tight-lipped. Which meant now he was in his kitchen alone with a lasagna, waiting for his ex-wife and his best friend to show up and tell him what was going on.

Penny was on her own to rest that evening. They'd been together almost nonstop prepping for the festival—supervising the tent setup downtown, moving in equipment, and putting out last-minute fires with vendors. When he was free at night, they were together. But they hadn't talked more about what might happen in just another two weeks, when Zander was set to return to Boston.

But while he tried to stay optimistic about keeping their relationship going, to trust that she wouldn't be able to let this go either, something about Penny had him on edge. It wasn't anything big, just lingering touches and looks verging on sadness. As though with every interaction, she was saying goodbye.

He was eager to help her game plan with the loan stuff, but only at Penny's request. A request that didn't seem to be coming. So as the Becker women waited to see how the festival went before sorting out next steps, Zander waited to see if Penny wanted him to be part of her life when those steps came around.

At six fifteen, Mallory swept in through the kitchen side door. "So sorry we're late!"

"I timed the food for your lateness."

Mal huffed. "That's rude. I'm not always late."

Zander and Quinn exchanged a look.

"You know—" Mallory pointed at each of them in turn. "You two can be very annoying."

Quinn consoled Mallory with a rub on the back. "You knew that from the start, babe."

Zander put out a stack of plates and pulled a salad he'd prepped earlier from the fridge. One more trip to the oven revealed foil-wrapped garlic bread.

"Whoa, Zander," Mallory cooed. "You made us a feast."

He shot Mal a sideways look. "Maybe I was working off some nerves after my co-parent said, 'We need to talk,' without giving me any context."

"I'm sorry." Mallory reached for a plate. "I didn't want to freak you out. It's nothing bad. We just wanted—to—"

"Talk. Yes, you said that. Tell me what's going on."

He dished up lasagna as Quinn and Mallory took their seats. Quinn scooted her chair close to Mal so their knees were touching, then squeezed her hand.

"First," Quinn spoke through a shaky voice, her bottom lip trembling.

"Wait." Zander's lungs emptied. "What the fuck is going on? Why do you look so nervous? Are you okay? Are you sick?"

"Zander." Quinn sighed with a smirk. "I'm fine. I'm better than fine. Mal and I—" She looked to Mallory, who was basically glowing. "We're getting married."

The spatula still in Zander's hand clattered to the table. "What?"

"We're. Getting. Married," Quinn repeated slowly. "You know, wife and wife, till death do us part and all that."

He blinked at her, a wire in his brain tripping over and over. "You don't believe in marriage. You think it's a useless institution that normalizes heteronormative values."

Quinn's face started going red. "Well, then I fell in love with your ex-wife and changed my fucking mind, Z."

"Plus," Mallory joined in, her voice cautious, "there are advantages, obviously. Legal protections and stuff. And Quinn can get on my insurance from work. But those are just perks. Mostly we just want to marry each other."

Zander stood slowly, looking between them both as something in him fizzed, bubbling up like the champagne he'd shared with Penny. "You just want to marry each other."

"Yes," Quinn said firmly. "I swear to god, Zander, if you throw some sort of fit about this I will fucking—"

But Quinn shut up when Zander hauled her out of her chair and yanked her into his arms. She squealed as he lifted her off her feet, whooping.

Quinn wiped at her tears as Zander plopped her back into her seat. "Oh my god!" She smacked his arm. "I thought you were mad, you fucking asshole!"

"I'll only be mad if I'm not your best man. Or maybe—" He looked to Mallory, who watched with glee. "Maybe I should be *your* best man. I think you two will have to fight over *me* this time."

When Mallory laughed wetly and threw herself at him, Zander pulled her close. "I'm so happy for you, Mal." He said it quietly, only for her. Because he'd loved her so much in his way, and because she'd helped him save himself all those years ago. "You deserve this." He kissed her forehead. "Just remember that I married you first."

Still laughing, she pulled herself from his arms to join Quinn for a kiss that Zander astutely did not watch.

"Jesus," he said once they'd all sat down again. "That was quite a family meeting."

"Actually"—Mallory's eyes darted toward Quinn—"that was just the first item. The other item is that, um, well . . ."

"I got it, babe." Quinn patted her hand. "Zander, we want to move back to Sullivan's Glen."

There were confusing upside moments, and then there were moments like *this*.

"Sorry." Zander shook his head. "It sounded like you just said you wanted to move to Sullivan's Glen."

Mallory leaned toward Quinn. "I told you this wouldn't go well."

"Just give him a minute," Quinn assured her.

"Hi." Zander waved from across the table. "Hi. I'm right here. Remember me, Mal? I'm the guy you asked to get you out of here? The guy you begged to run away with you to leave this place behind."

"That was seventeen years ago, Zander. We were kids. It's different now, for both of us. You know that."

Of course it was different. His memories of this place were jagged and angry; until this summer Sullivan's Glen had been frozen in his mind as the jail he'd had to live in, a sentence he'd had to endure.

And now? It was just a place, another town in another valley. Once he let his memories be just that—memories—the town had no power over him.

Or did it? Because now Sullivan's Glen was the place where his kid watched a baby bee emerge, where Zander went door-to-door downtown to talk to shop owners about the Honey Festival, where Candace Robinson told him she loved him, and Cynthia Becker let him cry on her shoulder.

And it was home to Penny Becker, whose imprint was everywhere. On every bee, in each flower, all over his stupid heart.

Oh, for fuck's sake. He liked it here.

"Mallory." He clung to some form of reality that made sense, that didn't ask him to uproot himself to come back to the place he'd been on the run from for almost two decades. "We live in Boston. Our whole lives are there."

"Are they?" she questioned. "Quinn and I work remotely, so we don't have work communities. You move from project to project, so you're always working with different people, and now you know chefs and investors and stuff all over the country. Our apartments are crappy and small, and we don't have any support systems there."

He winced. "It hasn't been so bad, has it? We've had a good life."

"Of course we have, Zander, and I am the luckiest woman in the world. But have you ever thought how it could be to live close to family? To have big dinners and holidays? To have backup when we needed it?"

"No," he shot back defensively. "I've never thought about it, because I don't have a family to live close to."

"You *do*," Mallory said fiercely. "You know you do. My parents have wanted for years to be there for you if you'd only let them."

Zander let his face fall into his hands. "This is a big bomb you're dropping. Have you talked to Winter about this?"

"No." Mal shook her head vehemently. "I wouldn't do that without you, you know that. But I think he'd be open to it. It's a good transition time for him, and he's made some friends. He's getting along well with my parents, and he has so much more access to nature. I think it's worth talking to him about it, feeling him out."

"Do you remember how pissed he was about coming here?"

"Guess what, genius?" Quinn jumped in now, slapping the table. "You were pissed, too. I recall having to drag your grumpy ass out of bed those first days. And now? Z, you're the happiest I've ever seen you." Her voice cracked. "You're the kind of happy I've always wanted for you. Can't you fucking see that?"

He swallowed, shutting his eyes like it might cut off the onslaught of feelings and questions. Because he *was* the happiest he'd been in a long time, and it was terrifying. Asking Penny to do long-distance without a real plan for the future was one thing. But this? This was going all in on those dreams he'd only let himself glimpse. And there would always be a voice in his head telling him it couldn't last, that he wasn't worth it.

"Look around," Quinn continued. "You've made this place a home. A beautiful, happy home. The kind you always deserved."

He followed her gaze around the room: freshly painted cabinets and brightened walls, the counter where remnants from cooking still sat on his cutting board.

This kitchen didn't lie. Neither did his room, or Winter's.

All along, he'd told himself he was making it comfortable for his kid, helping make his summer a little better. But maybe there'd been something in it for him, too.

Maybe his papou had left him this place for more than just selling.

He collapsed backward in his chair, sighing out a long breath. "This is a fucking lot, you guys."

Mal stood and moved to him. "I know. And we would *never* do this without you, Z. When we split, we promised to stay in the same place until Winter was grown, and I'll never break that promise to you. If you're not into this idea, it's dead in the water. And that's okay."

"But think about it," Quinn added. "Think about what you want, and what you deserve. And maybe what Penny deserves, too."

"Don't." He shook his head. "Don't bring her into this."

Quinn cocked an eyebrow. "Why not? She's a part of it."

She was the biggest part of it, and that was the problem. "Because what if I say yes, Quinn? What if I agree to uprooting all our lives and moving to this small fucking town in upstate New York and then Penny doesn't want me? What the hell will I do then?"

Just sit alone and grumpy in an old house, hopelessly in love with the town's beekeeper?

Quinn drew in a long breath and let it out slowly. "Zander, I can't convince you that you're worthy of love. I've tried, and you've continued to be a huge pain in my ass about it. I can't promise you what Penny will do, or assure you that everything will work out. All I can tell you is that you have to believe that your happiness is worth taking the risk."

Zander shook his head. "Mal, you've ruined her, you know that? Quinn used to be all 'Fuck everybody, we're better alone.' Those were the good ol' days."

"No." Quinn laughed. "Those were the sad old days. Simpler maybe, but sad. What do you say? You'll think about it?"

He looked around the kitchen again, then let his mind wander outside, where the *For Sale* sign still leaned against the porch. Obviously, some part of himself was already decided. Had maybe decided weeks ago and was waiting for the rest of him to catch up.

He nodded. "Let's talk to Winter."

Mallory's eyes bugged. "Seriously?"

"Seriously. Who am I to argue with the romantic notions of the newly engaged?"

"We could talk to him tonight," Quinn offered.

Mallory's bright fingernails rattled on the table as she sat back down. "Holy shit. Yeah, okay. Wow. Okay."

*Wow. Okay*, was right. Something seismic was shifting for all of them, just as the dings and buzzes of phone notifications lit up around the table.

"Maybe Winter needs something," Mallory mumbled as she pulled out her phone. But as soon as she swiped it open, her eyes went wide. "Holy shit."

Zander's heart plummeted. "Mal, *what*?"

"My mom said there was some kind of water main leak

downtown. No one realized, but it made everything wet under the road."

Quinn was staring at her phone, too. "RJ's texting, too, he said—"

"RJ?" Mallory interrupted. "Since when do you text RJ?"

Quinn blushed. "We've kind of been talking about starting up a queer hockey team. I haven't told you yet because I've never done sports, so I'm a little anxious."

"Babe! That's so cool! You'll look so hot in hockey gear—"

Zander cleared his throat loudly. "Can we focus, please? What did RJ have to say?"

"Oh yeah." Quinn glanced back at her phone. "There's a sinkhole downtown. Like, a big one."

"A sinkhole?"

"Yeah. He said half of Main Street is *gone*."

Zander rubbed his face. "What the—"

But then his phone on the table buzzed, Penny's name on the screen.

"Penny," he answered. "What's going on?"

"Zander." Her voice wobbled. "Zander, we're *fucked*. The Honey Festival is canceled."

# CHAPTER 32

"Holy fucking shit."

Zander took the words right out of Penny's mouth.

Side by side just past the caution tape, Penny and Zander stared at the sunken main street of Sullivan's Glen. Workers in bright orange vests milled around, putting up more tape and orange cones.

Penny took in a long, slow breath. She'd been doing a lot of calming breathing in the past twelve hours, since she'd gotten a call about an emergency downtown. Also crying, shaking her fists in the air, pacing her kitchen, and sitting on the ground between her beehives.

But as Penny assessed the damage of downtown Sullivan's Glen, where swatches of pavement protruded at jagged angles from a literal hole in the ground, she knew it could have been so much worse. Miraculously, there'd been a lull in traffic when the road had collapsed, so no one had been hurt. The only casualties were a few parked cars.

And the annual Sullivan's Glen Honey Festival.

Vendor tents slated for this portion of Main Street were jumbled in the chaos, some tipped over sideways into the sinkhole. Down the street, emergency crews disassembled the others. Penny had tried to help, but they'd quickly ushered her back to her side of the caution tape.

It was Sally from city hall who'd given Penny the bad news: while only one block of Main Street was sunk into the ground, the county engineers had concerns about the entire downtown. An extensive water leak, combined with record rainfall that spring, had turned everything under the asphalt to mud, and they were unsure how widely the danger spread. Until a full safety analysis could take place, the entire area would be kept clear.

"The area" included everywhere the festival was to take place.

"Okay." Penny nodded. "Okay. How can I fix this?"

Zander stared at her. "Excuse me?"

"There must be something I can do. Maybe I can help clean up some of the tents, see if any of them are salvageable for the deposit we put down. Do you think they'll let me help?"

"No, I don't." Zander held her arm, like Penny might jump over the caution tape. Which, in all fairness, she had considered. "I think that's a very bad idea."

"I could go over to the basketball courts, where you had the food stuff set up. Are the crates of ingredients still there? Because if we get them now before it gets too hot, I might be able to—"

"Penny. That whole area is closed—we've been over this. It's not safe."

"Oh my god, Zander. It's not like the ground is just going to collapse under me."

"That's literally what just happened. We're only standing here right now because they knew you wouldn't leave without seeing the carnage."

"Fine." She whipped out her phone. "I'll start calling the

vendors, make sure everyone knows. I'll tell them to sit tight while I figure out another weekend."

Zander grabbed her phone before she could pull up the spreadsheet. "Your mom is calling the vendors, remember? And this area is going to be blocked off for weeks, and all the weekends in August are already permitted for something else."

"Like that stupid garlic festival," Penny grumbled. "There has to be another time we can do this."

"Penny, there's not. We've double- and triple-checked."

"So what? We just accept that this isn't happening? I've been planning this for months, Zander. You've poured yourself into this for most of the summer, and now you're ready to just give up?"

"I'm not—" He shook his head and entwined their fingers. "I'm not giving up. But we need to face reality. This isn't something you can fix."

"If I work hard enough—"

"You'll make yourself sick and miserable." Zander pulled out his phone. "Hold on, okay? Stay right here, I'll be right back. *Do not move*, Becker."

He stepped away, phone to his ear.

When she'd called him the night before, half crazed and rambling about sinkholes, he'd come to her place immediately and held her as she sobbed into his chest. It was more than she deserved, because for all the ways her heart wanted to go along with Zander's plan to continue their relationship, she knew it couldn't work. He was a romantic, but she was a realist—she had responsibilities to worry about and no choice but to look at things rationally. Penny's first priority was Becker Farms, and she couldn't do that with her heart and mind hundreds of miles away.

She tried again to call her mom but was sent right to voicemail.

She was desperate now for some of her silver linings, because from where Penny stood, this was really bad: her deposits and investments in the festival were lost, and there was no telling how much would be covered by the bare minimum event insurance she'd purchased. The crates of honey she'd been banking on selling today would stay in the warehouse, as would the flyers telling the thousands of people who'd come to the festival about the Becker Farms apple harvest in the fall.

And all the festival vendors were out the day of sales they were expecting, and everything they'd set up the night before had been swallowed by the earth.

She and her mom and Mimi had agreed to wait to talk about the loan until after the festival, and now they couldn't delay. Penny could no longer cling to the hope that the Honey Festival would save Becker Farms any more than she could believe she'd have a partner to help her work through it when the dust settled.

"Sorry." Zander jogged back. "It was Winter. I mean Mallory. Winter wanted more screen time. It's a whole thing."

"Is he disappointed?" she asked. "He was excited about helping with the kids' area. He's been talking about the bubbles all week."

"Um, yeah." Zander squeezed the back of his neck. "Totally. Hence the screen time."

"Have you heard from RJ? I keep texting, asking about what he needs today. I know he had a ton of pies baked—do you know if they'll freeze okay? Should we go get them?"

"RJ's pies are fine," Zander answered. "He's just—well, I don't know where he is. Probably freezing pies. But I'm sure he'll let you know if he needs anything. Right now, he would probably tell you to relax and take care of yourself."

"Relax and take care of myself? Is that a joke? There has to be something I can do."

"There isn't!" Zander blew out a long breath as his face softened. He closed the space between them and held her face in his hands. "Listen. This sucks. I don't want to sugarcoat it. But it's not your problem to solve."

"Maybe it is, though."

She had to do something to put herself to use. That was the answer to the horrible, achy sadness she felt in her core. If this were the bees' problem, they'd be hurrying to clean it up and put everything to rights. She envied their simple, biologic directives.

"Penny, look at me." Zander's dark eyes were so kind, so caring. They made her think of fertile soil, ready to help things grow. "There's nothing more to do right now, okay?"

"I know," she admitted, feeling like an empty balloon. "I've been concentrating this whole time on paying off the loan, putting all this pressure on the event, and now I'm back at square one."

"Baby. I'm so, so sorry."

She looked back at the sunken ground and broken tents, thought of the wasted food and all the sales that wouldn't be. All the plans she'd—no, *they* had made, together—Zander at her side all summer, a co-planner in far more than name alone.

"It's so sad," she said. "We did this together, you and me. You were a big pain, and you made yourself a co-planner, and at first I was so mad, but really doing this with you was the best . . ." And she didn't want to cry again, because she was so tired of crying this week, but it was no use. "It was one of the best things I've ever done. It was something I've always wanted, to have someone truly at my side. And I was so excited to see it happen, and see the result of all of it together before you leave. And I'm just really sad that we won't get that."

"Penny." He said her name like it hurt, but also like it soothed the hurt. Like it was *everything*. "I feel that way, too. Doing this with you has been incredible. I didn't even know work could feel like this until this summer." He dropped a short kiss on her lips and drew in a deep breath. Finally, he said, "Let's go get breakfast."

"Get breakfast?" She gaped. "That's what you want to do right now?"

"Yeah." He released her face to check his phone, typing something quickly before stuffing it back in his pocket. "I think food will help. I really want to go to breakfast. RJ mentioned a diner he loves over in Greendale."

"Greendale is thirty miles away."

"They're supposed to have really good pancakes."

"Really good—?" Penny's jaw dropped. Behind them, Sullivan's Glen was in shambles, and Zander wanted pancakes. "Are you well?"

Zander smiled. "The festival went to hell. But I'm here with you, and we're going to get pancakes. So yeah, I'm well."

She shook her head as he pulled her toward the car, all the workers looking relieved that she might finally leave them in peace. "You're being super strange right now."

He kissed her before opening her car door. The kind of deep, languid kiss that felt like floating. Then he shot her one of his Zander Bouras troublemaking grins. "Don't mind me, Becker. I'm just trusting in the universe."


Two plates of pancakes and a trip to the Greendale Public Library later, Zander was finally taking Penny home. Apparently, sightseeing was Zander's coping mechanism. He'd also wanted to stop at a nature refuge for a "leisurely and very long stroll," but Penny just wanted to get home and pull the covers over her head. After a lengthy argument during which Zander managed to list fifteen reasons that a stroll would be just what she needed, he finally acquiesced and took them home.

The pancakes had been good, at least. Though Zander kept getting calls from Mallory— she was needing a lot of co-parenting advice today. And Penny enjoyed the peaceful drive with the windows down. But as they got closer to town, her melancholy took root again. She really would have loved to see the thing she and Zander made together, and she wouldn't get another chance.

Traffic slowed as they approached the turnoff to the lane that the Bouras and Becker properties shared. "What are all these cars doing here?"

Zander tapped on his steering wheel. "Not sure."

Most of the cars were pulling into the lane. So many that the line backed into the road.

"Where are all these people going?"

"Um, weird." More tapping on the steering wheel. "Don't know."

They finally turned in, and cars were parked along the side of the drive all the way to where the lane split. As Zander pulled through slowly, Penny gaped at the array of people and trucks and tents, like a circus had come to town and set up in Zander's yard.

If Zander thought the whole thing was weird, he didn't say so. He just pulled up near his house and put the car in park. Penny leapt out, only to have someone barrel into her from behind.

"Ooh, sorry, Penny!"

She spun to see a burly guy carrying large black bags under each arm.

"Patrick?" He was the goalie on RJ's hockey team. "What are you doing?"

"Putting the tents where RJ told me they should go?" He was breathing hard. "I better go, though. He said if we slack off, we don't get pizza."

"RJ?" Penny looked around the people moving around outside like busy little ants. "Where is RJ?"

Usually RJ was easy to spot in a crowd, but a surprising number of the people around her were as big as he was, most of them carrying things. Finally, she spotted her friend near a tree, smiling big and pointing somewhere as he talked to another one of his teammates. When RJ glanced over and saw her staring, his eyes widened before he bound toward her.

As RJ approached, two extremely familiar voices floated toward Penny from the path that led to her bee yard.

"I told you, Mother, I already talked to Macey and she said her truck is out of commission."

"Christ on a cracker, she's a dirty liar! I saw her driving the truck yesterday. She's just too lazy to get out of bed so early." Her mother and Mimi appeared on the trail, Mimi's finger pointed in the air. "I promise you, if we send one of the hunks over there to borrow her truck, she'll give up the keys in an instant, and we can start doing the rounds and getting everybody's shit over here."

Just past them, Janice from Neat Knit was laying out skeins of yarn on a plastic table, and nearby them, Ronaldo from the chamber of commerce chatted animatedly with Sally from city hall.

"Fine, but you need to ask one of the hunks to do it."

"Oh, Ruthie, I'd be more than happy to."

"Pen!" RJ slid in front of her, breathing hard. "You're here!" He gave a distinctly unfriendly look to Zander. "Zander, I thought you guys were going to be out all morning."

"Dude." Zander groaned. "I swear to god I tried."

RJ shook his head. "You had one job."

"You try bossing Penny around! I just barely got her to agree to the pancakes."

"You guys?" Penny interrupted. "What is going on?"

"Penny!" Penny was engulfed in her mother's arms. "Good morning, sweetheart. Did you already have breakfast in Greendale?" She shot a look to Zander. "It's still so early."

Zander mumbled something indecipherable and ran a hand over his face.

"RJ, honey," Mimi butted in. "I need you to direct me to your best hunk, and *stat*."

He wiggled his eyebrows. "We all know that's me, but if you're looking for someone else—"

"Excuse me!" Penny hollered. Everyone snapped their attention to her. "But what the hell is going on?"

RJ bounced on his toes, his smile big enough to swallow her up. "Isn't it obvious, Penny? We're saving the Honey Festival!"

# CHAPTER 33

"And that is a day in the life of a honeybee. Any questions?"

Penny blew a strand of hair out of her face, her forearms aching from the strain of holding up the frame of bees through her presentation. It was her second one of the day, with a stint at the table selling honey in between, and she was exhausted.

But she wouldn't trade it for anything. She was exactly where she was meant to be.

A few hands shot up in the assembled crowd, about fifteen people whom Winter had rallied from around the festival, promising them that they didn't want to miss this *really cool* demonstration. Their seats were placed across the bee yard from the hive she'd opened, and she'd been projecting through the netting of her suit for the last twenty minutes.

The demonstrations had been Winter's idea. "How cool is this?" He'd beamed, tumbling from the back seat of Mallory's car. "Everyone is gonna come *here*! Penny, now that the festival is here, you can show everyone the bees!"

She'd just blinked, shaken her head, and lowered herself to a seat in the grass before finally speaking. "I have no idea what's going on."

Because everyone had something to do, Zander brought her up to speed. He sat beside her, telling her how her mom had suggested relocating the festival to their properties.

"She called the vendors, and a lot of them were on board, so we got to work. My job was to distract you this morning to keep you away a little longer."

"The Greendale thing."

"Yeah." He'd laughed. "The Greendale thing. I kind of failed."

"In your defense, I didn't make it easy on you. Why the big secret?"

He'd only raised his brows.

"Let me guess—because I would have taken over and tried to do all the work myself?"

"Because it's not always your job to save the day. Because everyone wanted to do this for you, Penny."

Then they'd walked around, watching the festival take shape.

There were three rows of tables where festival vendors were putting the finishing touches on their sales displays; a pavilion for community organizations under one big tent; and a kids' station under another, complete with books, a therapy dog for kids to read to, and Hula-Hoops and bubbles just for kicks. Janine Gregory had parked her coffee and lemonade truck in Zander's driveway, and Zander's kitchen was already filling up with all the salvageable supplies intended for the culinary tent.

Mallory's parents organized people to put up signs downtown, directing them to the new location, and once they finished the manual labor portion of their day, guys from the hockey team would shuttle people to the festival from a nearby lot.

It was chaotic and bright, messy and joyous. Not unlike the festivals she'd attended as a girl, when it was still her grandmother's small passion project, not much more than a glorified block party. It had a cozy feeling, the vibe as relaxed as the sway of flowers in the August breeze.

"Not everyone could come," Zander had told her gently, walking her to the bee yard where they'd set up more tables to showcase the Becker Farms products. Back on a blanket in the kids' area, Winter was making signs to advertise Penny's beehive demos. "And there's no telling how many people will actually see the signs downtown or hear that the festival wasn't canceled after all."

Penny knew what he was saying: this wasn't the Honey Festival she needed to save the farm. It wasn't even close.

But god, it was beautiful.

And if it couldn't last, if she couldn't find a way to avoid default, at least she got to have this day.

Especially as she took it all in with Zander's fingers entwined with hers. Whenever she glanced his way, he was watching her, a peaceful smile on his face. She'd promised to talk more about their relationship after the festival, and every second that ticked down squeezed her lungs a little tighter. Penny knew what she *wanted* to do, and she knew what she *should* do, and she had no idea how to square the two.

But that moment wasn't here quite yet. First, she had some questions to answer.

She tugged at the canvas sleeve of her bee suit as she surveyed the raised hands. One was bouncing up and down in the back of the crowd as a small girl peeked through elbows, eyes glued to the frame of bees in Penny's hands. She'd had this posture through the whole demo, eyes wide at Penny's every movement.

It wasn't a stretch to see a younger version of herself in the girl's eagerness.

Penny nodded to her, smiling through the netting of her hood. "Let's start in the back."

The girl's eyes went even wider as she fiddled with her ponytail. "The queen bee is in charge, right?"

"Actually, no," Penny answered. "No one in the colony is in charge. They all just sort of know their role."

The girl frowned. "The queen isn't the most important, then?"

Penny laughed. "No. She's just doing her job like everybody else. Her job is to lay eggs. And it's the job of a lot of the other bees to make sure she can do that. They keep her clean and bring her food, not because she's telling them to, but because it's part of keeping the colony alive."

The girl's little nose scrunched. "Do they *like* doing all of that?"

Penny paused, shuffling her feet as she considered the question. "That's a hard question to answer. It's their role in the colony, but I don't know if you could say they *like* it. I guess we'll never know."

Penny slowly slid the frame back into the hive, then replaced the lid. "A lot of the time when we talk about the lives of bees, it's tempting to compare ourselves to them." She stayed focused on the girl. "And in some ways, bees have some stuff to teach us, right? About working together and about cooperation."

She paced away from the hive. "But in a colony, when a bee isn't useful in the hive, it's kicked out. If a queen isn't laying eggs anymore, they make a new queen and get rid of the old one. They're not trying to be cruel to each other, but for the colony to survive, each bee has to have its function. That's why they each exist."

Penny looked back to the girl, then let her gaze drift across the crowd. She saw familiar faces and new ones, and there, in the back, leaning against a beech tree, her mother, looking as beautiful as she ever had.

For most of her life, Penny had treated her bees as her role models. They had perfect systems, miraculous organization, and a work ethic that put other creatures to shame.

But her own life was much messier. It was fly-by toast with her mom and Mimi, warm greetings at the farmer's market, and spa nights with RJ. It was a perfectly organized event sinking into the ground, only to be resurrected by the sheer love and grit of the people around her.

And the beautiful woman standing under the tree, the one who Penny looked just like, who'd helped create a life for her family not by sheer will and sole determination, but by letting people help her. By trusting the universe.

Penny blinked back the heat building behind her eyes as she tore her gaze from her mother.

"Luckily, we get more leeway as people, right? We get to rest and have fun. We get to dip our toes in a cold lake, and we get to sleep in on Sundays. We get to take care of our most vulnerable, give our elders a break, and spoil our children. We get to rely on each other."

She looked across the bee yard, where a now-familiar path cut through the grass.

"We get to fall in love."

She brought a shaky hand to her face, only to have it blocked by the netting. Penny was breathing hard. No, she wasn't breathing at all. She had to get out of there. For one of the first times in her life, the bee yard was the last place she wanted to be.

"We're going to have to end it there for now. Sorry to cut things a little short. Make sure to visit all the vendors while you're here. Thanks for coming!"

She speed walked past confused onlookers, brushed shoulders with her smiling mother, and sprinted down the trail Zander had started down that very first day. The one she was counting on to lead her to him now.

# CHAPTER 34

"I can tell you one thing."

Mimi stood at Zander's side on the front porch, surveying the festival spread before them. Her eyes gleamed as she watched people milling from tent to tent. Behind them, through the open doors of the house, Zander could hear RJ finishing up his third demo of the day, walking people through his crust construction. It wasn't the culinary tent Zander had imagined, but somehow having people gathered around his kitchen table, sampling honey as RJ cooked for them, was better than anything Zander could have dreamed up.

"Your grandfather," Mimi continued, smiling out at the festival, "would have hated this."

Zander waited for the sting that came with any mention of his papou but found himself smiling instead. Because Mimi was absolutely right.

"Can you imagine?" he said. "All these people tramping around? Parking on his grass? Making a mess of his kitchen?"

Mimi howled a laugh. "I reckon he would have run 'em all off with a broom in his hand."

Zander raised a fist in the air, bellowing: "Go do something useful with yourselves!"

Beside him, Penny's grandmother sighed and shook her head. "My first winter here, I swear I thought I'd made the worst mistake of my life. I looked around and thought everything was dead and I was just about doomed. Then spring finally came inching along. Sprouts started coming up in the garden and the greenhouse. Leaves began poking out in the orchard. Everywhere you looked, it was that new green of springtime, bright and chipper."

She patted Zander's back and turned to him with a smile. "I know it's the last thing you expected, but you're like the new green around here, Zander. For this house and I think for Penny, too. For her sake, I hope she realizes that and doesn't let you walk out of her life."

"Thank you, Mimi." He swallowed hard, catching a look back at the house, then at the festival below. "I hope so, too."

Zander's heart stalled as Quinn approached. She'd been busy all morning helping out and blowing bubbles, and Mallory had been managing hockey players while RJ cooked, so he hadn't been able to talk to either of them about their conversation with Winter. When Zander left to find Penny the night before, he'd given them the okay to float the idea of a move to Sullivan's Glen, trusting them to handle it delicately enough to gauge Winter's feelings about it without pressuring him to give any specific answer. He knew Mal would have waited for Zander to get past the chaos of the canceled and reinstated Honey Festival, but now that the seed of this move had been planted, he was eager to see if it might really come to something.

He also wanted to talk to Penny about it. But they'd been so damn busy.

Quinn approached with a smile, wiping her dark bangs off her forehead. "Hey, loser! Look at this damn thing we pulled off!" She exchanged cheek kisses with Mimi, faux-whispering in her ear, "Even though Zander couldn't do his one job."

"Okay, you know what?" Zander harrumphed. "I challenge anyone in this county to tell Penny Becker what to do. Seriously, keeping her out all morning was an impossible task."

Mimi laughed. "You have my sympathies, honey. I would never have dared volunteer for that job." She patted his back again, then headed down the porch with a glint in her eye. "I do believe it's time to boss around some more hockey players."

Zander waited until they had a sliver of privacy. "How'd it go with Winter last night?"

Quinn's eyebrows rose along with her smile. "Someone is invested in this outcome now, is he?"

"I'm not invested, I just—" He sighed. He was definitely invested. "I don't want to be invested if Winter's against it."

Quinn squeezed his shoulder. "I get it. I don't mean to fuck with you. Not *too* much, anyway. So we started by asking Winter what he thought about leaving Boston. He asked what we meant, and we said, 'You know, would you be interested in living anywhere else? Maybe with some more space?'"

"And what did he say?"

"He said, 'What, like here?'"

The little candle of hope Zander had been nursing since the day before sparked to life. "No shit."

"No shit. So Mal said, 'Would you want that?' and he shrugged and said, 'That'd be cool, I guess.'"

"*That'd be cool, I guess*?" Zander repeated in disbelief. "That's enthusiastic for him lately."

"Yeah, it is." Quinn looked at Zander seriously. "He said he likes the kids he met here, and that spending time with Mal's parents isn't as boring as he thought it would be and is sometimes fun. And he likes the trees and space. He also said he likes getting to hang out with Penny."

Quinn watched him as it settled between them. "Zander, this could actually be a thing that could happen."

"And you would want that?" With everything happening at once, Zander and Quinn hadn't been able to talk about any of this one-on-one. He couldn't deny that his heart was now 100 percent on board with this, but only if Quinn's was, too. "You would seriously move here? Because you know if you don't want to, Mallory would never—"

"I know. She wouldn't pressure me at all. Believe me, Z, she and I had this conversation about a thousand times before we came to you." Quinn shrugged and looked around, her shoulders visibly relaxing as she scanned the festival and the trees beyond. "Maybe it's a pre-midlife crisis. Like cis dudes get sports cars and I get the urge to move to a small town and learn how to play hockey and spend evenings playing board games with my loving but uptight in-laws. Whatever it is, I like it here. I think it could be home."

Zander tsked and shook his head, his body warm all over. "I'm going to have to hug you now, and it's going to be big and smushy and you won't be able to get away."

She winced. "But you hugged me yesterday!"

"That was an engagement hug. This is a—" He wrapped her up and pulled her to his chest. "This is a thank-you hug. Thank you for being the pain in my ass I've always needed."

Quinn squeezed him back, then allowed him a few more seconds before pulling away. "You'll talk to Penny?"

"I'll talk to Penny."

"And you'll let yourself believe she could want you, long-term?"

He nodded. "I'll do my best."

"I'm so sorry to interrupt." A voice appeared from Zander's side. "I asked who was in charge, and someone pointed me your way."

Zander did a double take, looking around. A tall, thin white man in a floral button-down was standing close, holding hands with a shorter man with darker skin and a crisp polo.

"They told you I was in charge?"

"Um, Z." Quinn nudged him. "You kind of are."

He rubbed a hand through his hair. "I mean, I guess. My, uh, partner and I."

He meant partner as in the festival, but using that word to describe Penny was . . . really something.

"Oh, super." The man smiled big. "I'll cut to the chase. What are your rental rates, and do you have availability in October? And yes, *this* October. Our wedding venue a county over had an unfortunate fire incident and now we're scrambling to find a new location. We're planning a small ceremony, but right now we're facing having to do it in our apartment in the city because nothing else is available."

"Rental rate?" Zander shook his head. "I'm not following."

"For your event space." The man swept an arm in front of them. "It's beautiful here, and we just love the cottagecore vibe. Amir and I think it would be absolutely perfect."

Zander followed the man's gaze to the transformed lawn, covered in tables and tents.

"Oh," he stuttered. "Um, well, it's not really—"

"Tell you what," Quinn interrupted with a charming smile. "Can you leave your contact information so Zander can look at the schedule? Then he can send you some quotes."

"That'd be great." The man pulled out a smooth leather wallet, then a business card that declared him *Dennis McFadden, financial analyst*. "I understand this is very late notice, so of course we'd pay a premium if you can pull it off. We'd also be looking for a caterer, someone who could arrange an intimate but elegant meal for our guests. And a wedding cake. Something delicious."

Zander blinked, giving a quick glance back to his kitchen. "I think I could find you someone for that."

"Amazing." Dennis beamed. "I look forward to hearing from you."

"Yeah." Zander rubbed the back of his neck. "Great. Okay."

As the men walked away, Quinn slapped his arm. "Oh. My! God! Destiny much? The universe is at work here, Zander!"

"Wow." Zander chuckled, his body full of shaky nerves. "That was interesting timing for sure. I don't know about the universe stuff—"

But then he caught sight of something across the field, coming from the trail to Penny's place. Someone dressed in white from head to toe. Someone moving fast.

Zander Bouras didn't believe in the power of the universe. If anything, he'd felt a victim of the randomness of it all, the pain of being a pinball bounced around by forces outside his control. But now, watching a fully suited Penny Becker stride through the grass, whipping off her gloves and dropping them to the ground, he considered the powers of *his* universe. The powers of transformation and hard work, of fighting to give himself a chance even in the years when he seemed to be the only one to do so. Of forgiveness for the people who'd tried to raise him through their own wounds. And for himself, who'd wasted precious years of his life hating everything because he didn't see another way.

And he considered love. The kind that built families and

communities, that bound them together through service and laughter and grief and honesty.

And goddammit, he deserved it all. Starting with the ray of sunshine coming his way. Her face was obscured by the suit netting, but it didn't matter. He felt those blue eyes trained on him, warming him to his bones.

Quinn cleared her throat. "Oh damn, it's happening. I'm going to go ahead and walk away now."

He nodded, eyes never leaving Penny. "I think that's a good idea."

"I love you, buddy."

"I love you, too. Now please fucking *go*."

Quinn laughed as she left, and then the world around him went fuzzy as Penny reached him.

Her chest lifted with heavy breaths, but she was smiling. "Hi."

"Hey. Everything okay?"

"Yes. *Yes*. I wanted to talk to you. It's important. I want to say something."

Her fingers searched for the zipper of her hood, but her hands were shaking.

"Here." He swallowed hard. "Let me help."

Zander eased the zipper along the teeth to detach the hood, then lifted it to gaze at her flushed face and freckles.

"You wanted to say something?"

She blinked at him, just looking. "Yeah," she said finally. "Yes. I do. I was over with the bees, talking about their roles and the work they do, but also about how humans are different because we're not bees and we can go to lakes and take care of each other and—"

"Penny." He cupped her sweet face. "Slow down. Take a breath."

"It's just . . ." Her eyes gleamed with welling tears. "I want to tell you yes. Yes, I'll figure out a way to try this, even with the distance. Because life is special and we aren't bees and I think we—no, I *know*—we both deserve something beautiful and happy and joyful. And we should give ourselves the chance."

Everything around them slowed, and it was only Penny Becker and the sky that matched her eyes. Zander let his forehead fall against hers. "You're sure?"

She nodded against him. "Yes. I know it won't always be easy. But you were right. I can't look back and wonder what could have happened."

Penny stepped back and took Zander's hands in hers. "I promise to try," she told him. "I don't know what's going to happen to the farm, but I understand life will keep moving. I know the people in my life are the most important things. And Zander, you're one of those people now."

Zander didn't bother blinking away his tears. But even as he wanted to pull Penny to him, an old voice still whispered inside him, telling him he didn't deserve another great love in his life. That this happiness would burn up and vanish when he held it too tightly.

Then Penny smiled up at him, and he told that voice to fuck off.

Penny's gaze flicked to the house behind him. "I'm going to miss having you next door. But I'll do my best to be a good neighbor to whoever moves in."

"About that." Zander let out a long breath. "What if you didn't get a new neighbor?"

Her brows pulled together. "What do you mean?"

"I mean, what if I stayed in the house?"

"Zander." She shook her head. "You can't do that. You can't

move away from Winter. I know you wouldn't want that. I would never want you to do that for me."

"I know that. And you're right, I couldn't leave Winter."

"So what are you even talking about?"

"Mallory and Quinn came to see me last night," he told her. "They're interested in moving back here. It would mean all of us leaving Boston."

Penny looked stunned. "You're not serious."

He stroked his thumb across her knuckles. "I am. They made a good argument for being closer to Mal's family, having more space for all of us. We haven't officially popped the question to Winter, but Mallory floated the idea, and he was positive."

"But what about you? This is the last place you'd want to be."

"Maybe it was," he said. "When it was a symbol and not a real place. But since Mal and Quinn brought up the idea, I can't stop thinking about it. Really making this house a home for Winter, slowing down my life, exploring what family can look like, for all of us." He squeezed her hands. "For you and me, if you'd want that."

She was quiet for a moment, just blinking at him. Then she smiled, her freckled cheeks rising on her beautiful face. "That sounds pretty great."

His body melted with relief. "You think so?"

"I really do."

Penny threw herself at him, winding her arms around his waist and gripping his T-shirt. Zander surrounded her in her embrace, laying kisses on her golden hair.

When he couldn't wait any longer, he moved a hand to her chin and tipped her face to his. The kiss was slow and light, the sparkling of sunshine on a lake.

After a moment, Penny pulled away and held one warm palm to his cheek. "I love you, too."

Zander's stomach swooped. "But I haven't—"

"I know you haven't said it. But you've shown it. Over and over." She nibbled her bottom lip. "I'm not wrong, am I?"

"No." A full laugh burst from his belly. "No, you're not wrong. I love you. Maybe since that first day I saw you in this hot bee suit."

"Oh my god, this suit is *not* hot." Penny giggled brightly. It was a sound he'd never grow tired of, especially knowing how much of herself Penny held back from other people, how hard it was for her to trust and show her vulnerability. He'd always treat her love like the gift it was.

"It absolutely is." He trailed a finger up her arm. "I'll prove it to you tonight. Wear it over to my place with nothing underneath."

Her scandalized gasp was absolutely adorable.

Before Zander could goad her further, RJ popped out from the house, his apron covered in flour. "Pen!" He looked rapidly between the two of them. "Oh, shit. Something is happening here, is it?"

Penny nodded. "Um, yeah."

"Okay." RJ smiled at them both. "I am super happy about this, whatever it is. But also, Natasha just called and said one of the Brads is down by the street complaining about the traffic. And someone inside whose brother's wife works for some home goods chain in Toronto is wondering about bulk pricing for candles, and I don't have a clue. I really don't want to bother you guys, but—"

"RJ." Penny laughed, laying a hand on her friend's substantial forearm. "It's fine. We'll go handle it."

"Okay, cool." He looked knowingly at Zander. "I can't wait to hear every detail about what's happening here."

Penny smiled and shooed RJ. "Go make your pies, we've got it."

As he whirled back inside, Zander handed the suit hood back to Penny. "Sounds like we have some work to do. You want to handle the Brad while I talk to the people inside?"

"I can do bo—" She paused, narrowed her eyes at him, and smiled. "Yeah, that'd be great."

He leaned down to brush a kiss on her cheek. "I'll catch you later, Penny Becker."

"I'm looking forward to it." She pressed a gentle kiss to his lips. "And Zander?"

He gave himself another moment to lose himself in the blue of her eyes, as vibrant and promising as the sky behind her. "Yeah?"

She spread her arms as wide as her smile. "Welcome home."

# EPILOGUE

**TWO YEARS LATER**

For Penny Becker, nothing beat standing in gauzy late spring sunlight with bees in her hands.

Except maybe drinking tea on the porch with Mimi, or planting peppermint with her mom, or lazing in bed with Zander, tracing her fingers over his latest tattoo—a group of honeybees crawling across a comb.

But this was pretty great, too. The morning was crisp, wildflowers spraying color across the field outside the house she'd moved into the year before, the house with the yellow kitchen and the fairy lights still strung up in their bedroom.

After getting the official green light from Winter and deciding on the move from Boston to Sullivan's Glen, Zander'd returned to Boston to pack up his apartment and help Mallory and Quinn with theirs. From there, it was remarkably fast—they all were back in town by September, in time for Winter to start middle school in Sullivan's Glen as Zander prepared to host a wedding on the property in October.

A bee landed gently on Penny's forearm as she remembered that fall, and the bumps they encountered blending their lives together. She and Zander had their first blowout fight when he insisted on using the event deposit to pay toward the Becker Farms loan. Penny would hear nothing of it, ranting at him in the garden about how he couldn't just sweep in and solve her problems for her. He argued back that this was what partners did, and that she should let him decide what to do with his own damn money.

The fight had ended quite gloriously in her bed.

Once their tensions were worked out, Zander offered up a proposal: his payment toward the loan would be an investment, not a bailout.

Excited by the planning for the wedding, he'd put together an LLC and begun proper zoning and permit processes, building a business that would last beyond this one event. Winter was given naming rights, so Becker Farms' neighbor was now known as Honeybee Haven.

"And what is Honeybee Haven," Zander had asked her, stroking a hand across her hip, "without the honeybees next door? Like it or not, Becker, my future is tied in with yours now, and I need Becker Farms almost as much as you do."

Eventually, with her mom and Mimi on board, she'd agreed, and entered a partnership—a business one, on paper, vetted by local contacts who knew about these things—between Becker Farms and Honeybee Haven. With a substantial payment toward the loan, she was then able to refinance to a more manageable payback timeline.

And the wedding had been stunning—a chuppah set up in the grass with the changing leaves behind them, with tables and a dance floor under tents nearby. RJ practiced cakes for a full month before, delighting everyone in town with free samples. Quinn and Mallory's wedding—a small affair with a sundae bar and a punk band—followed the next spring, and Honeybee Haven had been booked ever since.

The personal partnership between Penny and Zander was just as fruitful, but slower moving. Their relationship was real and deep and the most thrilling thing Penny had ever known— but all of that made it scary, too. They both moved tentatively at first, letting themselves believe it was real, and that it would last. Though Penny had long dreamed of having a partner, actually having one took practice and trust. Likewise, Zander was prone to doubts that Penny would continue to want him there, like she might look up one day and find him lacking.

But they did it every day: trying and talking and listening, staying up for hours to learn about each other, being late to start their days because they couldn't stand to get out of bed. And every day, it all worked, just like the beautiful balance of a beehive.

She'd moved in with him after a year, and had walked into their bedroom that day to find it brimming with bouquets, flowers in every corner.

"It's only half as bright as you make me feel," he'd told her.

Now, Penny held the frame in the sun, scanning it for any abnormalities. Winter had done the hive inspection the day before, and she trusted his work completely. But he'd told her he'd seen something weird on one of the frames, something she should look at more closely. Whatever it was, this frame was clear. She slid it back in the hive and pulled out another.

"Penny Becker." A familiar voice brushed her skin in the breeze, alerting all her senses. "My sweet farm girl, always working. I thought you were taking the morning off before our meeting?"

A new prospective client was coming over to see Honeybee

Haven and talk about their wedding. Whenever possible, Zander liked to have Penny in on the first meeting to, as he put it, check the vibe.

She peeked at Zander over her shoulder, which was a mistake. He was so distracting in his tight T-shirt and dark beard that she almost dropped the frame. "I'm just checking this out. Winter said he noticed something he didn't recognize."

"Don't let me stop you."

She rolled her eyes but kept up her inspection. Sometimes Zander liked to do this—lean against a tree and watch her work. He never said a thing, but he said enough other times—dirty, tempting things—that she always knew what he was thinking.

Penny turned the frame in her hands, and something in the corner glinted in the sun. She pulled the frame closer, squinting at the unexpected object embedded in the honey.

"What in the—"

Lowering the frame to the top of the hive, Penny reached for the curious item. It was a ring—a golden band with a small amber stone the color of honey. The bees hustled around it, inspecting the foreign object with interest.

She set the frame down and pulled the ring from the comb, stretching honey out in long golden threads.

"Zander, this is so weird." She lifted the ring into the sunshine, turning it around in her sticky fingers. "Look at this. How do you think it—"

At first she thought he'd left, because his usual spot against the tree was bare. But then her gaze drifted down . . . down to where Zander, in his pink T-shirt and surrounded by wildflowers, kneeled in the bee yard where he'd interrupted her work—no, interrupted her whole life—two years before.

"Oh my god."

Zander cleared his throat. "Penny."

"Oh my *god*." Penny covered her mouth, the ring shaking in her other hand.

His wicked mouth grinned. "I guess you found the ring."

"I guess I—" She shook her head. "Yeah. I guess I did."

Zander's eyes welled. "If you don't want to marry me, I get it. Marriage can be important, but it's not necessary. I could live my whole life with you without it, if that's what you want. I don't want you to feel any pressure." He choked out a laugh. "I mean, I know I'm doing the whole down-on-one-knee thing, so it feels like pressure."

Penny moved toward him. "Zander—"

"It's just." He ran a hand through his hair as a tear poured over his lid and tracked down his cheek. "Penny, I love you so much. I love living with you and working with you. I love how you've become part of my family with Winter and how I've become part of your family with your mom and Mimi. You're one of the smartest, most passionate people I've ever known, and you always keep me on my toes and make me excited every day. I'm safe with you, and I can grow with you, and I want everyone to know. I want to stand on that hill with you and have everyone I've ever known watching while I pledge myself to you."

She lowered down, kneeling in front of Zander. "If you would—"

"But maybe this is too much." He sniffed and shook his head. "It's too good, right? Like everything we have. I shouldn't want more. If you don't want to take this step, I'll totally understand and we can just pretend this never—"

"Zander!" she squealed right in his face, watching his eyes go wide. "Will you shut up for a minute?"

"Oh." He blanched. "Yeah, sorry. I'm a little nervous."

She arched her brows. "I noticed."

Penny took his hands, holding the sticky ring between them. Everything he'd said, she felt, too. The overwhelming love and joy, the safety to be who she was, even as she kept exploring that for herself.

Behind him, the new green leaves of budding elms rattled, and she thought back to that story he'd told her. About that first time he'd walked over from his grandfather's house, when he was just a lonely kid strolling through the woods and he'd seen her family there: the Becker women, laughing together. *You had everything I wanted*, he'd told her of that day.

Since hearing that story, she'd thought a lot about what might have happened if she'd seen him there, if she'd invited him into her life. If she'd said to him what he'd needed to hear: You're welcome here. This is home.

It was a silly fantasy, and one she didn't really want to come true, because the years between brought him Mallory and Winter, and made him the man she loved now.

But she could extend the invitation now, and make sure he knew that he was wanted here, forever.

Penny leaned forward, brushing her lips over his wet cheeks, then at the side of his mouth, and finally over his lips. Zander cupped her face, and as they fell into a kiss as bright as the flowers around them, Penny slid the ring onto her finger.

When she pulled away, Zander still looked nervous, his teeth worrying his bottom lip. But Penny only smiled and held his hands.

"Zander Bouras." She saw the instant he noticed the ring, couldn't believe her luck that the elation on his face was because of her. Penny was ready to welcome this man home every day of their lives. "Will you please marry me?"

# ACKNOWLEDGMENTS

First, to the readers of *Birding with Benefits*, whose enthusiasm for the book truly gave flight to dreams I'd never dared dream: Thank you for reading, for listening, for checking out the book at your library, for passing it on to friends, for recommending it to your book club. Thank you for sending me your excitements via email, for creating beautiful posts online, and most of all for telling me how the book inspired you to look for birds everywhere you go. Each time there is birdsong in the background of *Honey Bee Mine*, please know I put it there thinking of you.

Before writing *Honey Bee Mine*, I went forth with a different book, one that didn't make it to publication. And though my readers won't have a chance to learn all the great snail facts I acquired in my research (at least not yet), I give thanks to the inspiring folks who helped me during that time: Jeff Sorenson, the actual snail guy of Arizona, as well as Sami Hammer and Melissa Van Kleeck-Hann. Thank you all so much for your time and conversation, and for the work you do protecting species in Arizona and elsewhere.

I had the great pleasure of doing hands-on beekeeping research for *Honey Bee Mine*, and for that I want to thank Noel

Patterson and Monica King, two incredible local beekeepers who inspired much of the beekeeping in the story.

The events in *Honey Bee Mine* take place in the Finger Lakes region of New York state, homeland to the Haudenosaunee Confederacy, made up of the Mohawk, Oneida, Onondaga, Cayuga, and Seneca people. You can learn more about the Haudenosaunee Confederacy, including their incredible history, current activities, and land claims in New York, at www.haudenosauneeconfed eracy.com.

Please know if you crossed my path—virtually or in real life—anytime in 2024 or 2025, you are part of these pages. You might have made me laugh on a day I was feeling stressed, served me a decaf Americano when I was close to deadline, or treated me kindly when I couldn't meet for coffee or a walk because I had to write. Your energy, support, love, and creativity were my fuel, so thank you.

To Amy Giuffrida, my intrepid and incredible agent: I wouldn't want to be on this ride with anyone else. Thank you for your advocacy, your faith, and your ability to smile and nod at me when I spiral.

To Abby Zidle: You picked me up from the slush pile and changed my life. I could not have started my journey in publishing in better, wiser, or more compassionate hands. Thank you for your faith in me, your guidance, your laughs in the comments, your honesty, and your keen editorial voice, which pushes me to be a better writer.

To Ali Chesnick: You stepped into big shoes with grace, poise, and remarkable good cheer. I am proud to work with you and can't wait to see what we'll do together. Thank you for your sharp eyes and beautiful spirit, and for returning emails faster than anyone else in publishing.

To the writers who read early versions of this manuscript and helped me fall in love with Penny and Zander: Laya Brusi, Rachel Griffiths, Jess Hardy, Livy Hart, Jessica Joyce, Jenny Lane, Erin Langston, and Karsyn Zetah. You are all incredible writers, fantastic readers, and wonderful friends. I started writing this book with a half-broken spirit, and you all made me whole again. Thank you, thank you, thank you.

For my friends all over the place who cheer me on, I am nothing without you. Kate, Colleen, Connie, Ellie, Jeremy, Becca, Katy, Lila, Mike, the whole cool crew at TFS (go solar!), my Lady Hawks from STG, all the inspiring folks at TASC, and so many more! Making you all proud and excited is the coolest thing I've ever done.

To the bookish communities and individuals who fill my cup over and over: Why Choose & Smutfest, plus special pals Amy Buchanan, Bonnie Callahan, Lauren Layne, Maggie North, and the dozens of writers who make my life better but whose names I can't fit here! Special shout-outs to Jen Deluca, my friend, mentor, and confidante; and Jessica Pryde, my library colleague and general partner in romance crime. My life is richer with both of you in it.

To everyone at the Pima County Public Library: You're the best! Special thanks to the crew at Woods who cheered me through the release of *Birding with Benefits*, and my family at MID who cheered me through the writing of *Honey Bee Mine*. I am proud to work with you all.

It's been an enormous blessing to land at Gallery Books. Big thanks to the team of people who support my books and my career, including Jen Bergstrom, Carrie Feron, Eliza Hanson, Fallon McKnight, Sydney Morris, and Caroline Pallotta. I bow down to copyeditor superheroes Nancy Tonik and Polly Watson. I didn't know copyedits could be fun, but Polly makes it possible. Huge kudos to cover designer Sarah Hogan and interior designer Hope Herr-Cardillo. I also want to thank former Gallerinas who had a huge hand in the success of my debut: Michelle Lecumberry and Julia McGarry.

I have deep gratitude for queer and trans folks living their beautiful truths, especially in our terrifying times. While this book focuses on an M/F pair, I strive to fill all my books with examples of queer joy, and am constantly learning from queer and trans authors, peers, and coconspirators. Special thanks to Jon Reyes, who read a book about a certain snail scientist I had to put aside but whose conversations about queer love and communication infuse these pages. A huge thank-you also to sensitivity reader Mey Rude for her careful and compassionate read of our alt trans girl Quinn and her knuckle tattoos. Thank you, Mey!

One of the best things about this experience has been making my family proud. Enormous thanks to my dad, who has supported every one of my creative endeavors across a lifetime, and everyone who has been here through the years loving me and my kids: Peggy, Jen, JJ, Matthew, Charn, Taras, Lev, Mary, Bob, Ray, Iris, Courtney, and our little ray of sunshine Zinnia. Family is a hard, complicated, and beautiful thing (if you've read this book, you know what I mean), and I'm glad you're all part of mine. And as always, I give unending gratitude to the spirit of my mom, Libby, who made me a romance reader and is cheering me along every step of the way.

Carter, Hazel, and Emery: When it comes to being your mom, I am a writer with no words. Seeing you grow up is simply the coolest, most amazing thing I could ever imagine doing. Thank you for your cheerleading as I write and for your excitement at every turn. I don't care how many books I publish: you will always be my absolute favorite creations.

To Rob: Giving you that pizza twenty-five years ago was the best decision of my life. I pity everyone in the world who doesn't get you as a partner, but they'll just have to deal because I found you first. I love you, and I'm sorry I never tighten the caps back on bottles tightly enough before I put them back in the fridge.

Because these are acknowledgments, I'll end by acknowledging that the world feels like a particularly scary and sad place right now. I hope this book brings joy and respite to people doing the work to show up for their families, neighbors, and communities. I am indebted to the generations of BIPOC activists who have taught me what it means to stand for justice, and am grateful for everyone who continues to rally, resist, and create. We can do this.